THE   ON
THE   OCK

FRANCIS KING
THE MAN ON THE ROCK

First published in 1957 by Longman
This edition published 1986 by GMP Publishers Ltd,
P O Box 247, London N15 6RW

© Francis King 1957

British Library Cataloguing in Publication Data

King, Francis, 1923-
  The man on the rock.
  I. Title
  823'.914/F/ PR6061.I45

  ISBN 0-85449-022-1

Printed by the Guernsey Press,
PO Box 57, Braye Road, Vale, Guernsey, C.I.

To
JOHN CROFT

CONTENTS

I

TUESDAY

K IKI has gone out and I am watching her from my bed as she waddles across Prince of Wales Drive, a brief-case in one hand and in the other the bag from Mykonos into which she has stuffed the things she is going to take to the Laundromat during her lunch-hour. Now I feel sorry for having made her cry, even though the sight of her swollen body balanced on those absurd high-heeled shoes also renews my exasperation against her. She is going to be late, and when she returns home this evening, she will be tearful and discouraged:

"A horrible day!"

"Well, you know that he has this mania for punctuality." (Yes, that's the kind of thing that I bring out. I suppose that a loving husband would at once rush to console her: "Oh, you poor darling! Tell me all about it.") "Time's money. You've heard him say that often enough. Though in our case—we seem to have unlimited time, but damn little of the other stuff!"

"I did such a stupid thing. I thought that next month was October, not September. And now I've sent two people off to Athens to see a Festival that will be invisible." At that she would be half crying and half laughing. "What will he say when he finds out?"

Kiki is always making mistakes of that sort; I'm not

1

exaggerating in imagining that example. Three nights ago she gave me two Quadronox tablets instead of two Veganin. How I slept, and slept, and slept! She became quite hysterical trying to wake me for breakfast, and that morning she was more than an hour late at the travel-agency where she works. I can't think why old Pavlakis doesn't sack her. Except that his father was once a tenant on the family-estate in Thessaly, and I dare say that he gets a kick out of ordering her about; I know that I should if she'd once seen me pattering barefoot up her village street.

There's that girl pushing the perambulator with the twins in it: at least Kiki, who speaks to everyone in the block, says that they're twins. " Oh, wouldn't it be awful if Avgerinos turned out to be twins! " But she doesn't really find the idea awful at all. " Well, if that little weed of a chartered accountant can produce two, it doesn't seem impossible." " Oh, do you really think so? " She pretends to be horrified. " Don't be silly. Doctors nowa-days can always tell those things in advance," I say.

Avgerinos, I should explain, is a Greek name (because we are Greeks) which means 'Dawn'. Kiki has decided that this is what we are going to call our boy; it's a boy, she's already decided that. The name is to remind us of a dawn after a College Ball—not that I should have thought either of us needed reminding. It was then we decided to get married; or, rather, Kiki decided, because I had decided long before. 'Brightest and best of the sons of the morning . . .' Kiki, who was reading English at the time, tends to quote things like that; it's odd, because Irvine, my American friend, has the same habit.

That girl with the pram certainly has a sexy way of pushing. The driver of the coal-van outside the paper-mills has got down to help her with it, as she waggles her tail up the slope into Battersea Park. I bet he wouldn't

2

do the same for Mrs. Mumfitt, who lives next door; in spite of her weak heart, weak bladder and varicose veins. She's stopped to talk to him now, stroking her blonde hair. I wonder if it's real; I wish Kiki were blonde. Oh, damn! Now that car has parked there, and I can't see them at all.

Silly oaf! Look at that grin on his black face as he climbs into the cabin. Must be at least fifty.

Well, I suppose I'd better drink some of this orange juice that Kiki has put here beside me. If I don't finish it by the time she gets back, there's always a scene. "How do you think you'll ever get better if you don't do what Dr. Arthurs told you?" "To hell with Dr. Arthurs!" (Lying in bed like this makes me bad-tempered.) Kiki blinks her eyelashes rapidly up and down, as she always does when she's upset or annoyed: "I go to all this trouble to squeeze all these oranges, and then you drink about half a glass all through the day. Apart from the waste." Ugh! I've never cared for oranges, even though we had three or four acres of orange-trees on our farm at home; and since I was told to drink all this orange-juice, I care for them even less. Now a glass of 'retsina' —that I could swallow at one gulp even at this hour.

This cystitis makes me feel wretched: or do I feel wretched merely because Kiki goes out to work every morning, and I have to lie here alone for the next eight or nine hours? We Greeks would no more think of seeking solitude than we would think of seeking pain. Irvine used to grumble because, when he went for a rest to one of the islands, he could never go out for a walk alone without someone rushing off after him to offer him his company. That he chose to be by himself was something he could not explain: since even prisoners, monks or those suffering from infectious diseases are rarely condemned to solitude in Greece.

3

I never read books now; when I do read I prefer, like most Greeks, to read the daily papers. But I've got through all the back numbers of *Kathimerini* and *Vima* and *Thesavros* that my friend Christo brought me the Sunday before last, and in any case I am tired of reading about Cyprus. English stupidity, Greek megalomania and American interference: well, I've had enough of all three, thank you. If only we hadn't had to give the wireless back! But that was the second instalment we'd missed, and they wouldn't wait any longer. So here I am, with my thoughts, and this disagreeable sensation which I have from my cystitis. I feel somehow soiled, degraded, disgusted with myself: but whether that is a symptom of my illness or my solitude I cannot, as I have said already, decide.

I had the same feeling with that dose I got in Salonica. It was just before I met Irvine; I was only sixteen, though after all I'd been through everyone said I looked at least twenty. I caught it in that park which in those days lay thrown down like a crumpled, dusty pocket-handkerchief, between tram-lines that hissed and clanged perpetually with those mustard-coloured coffins on wheels which (so the Greek story went, though I don't believe it) had been bought second-hand from Hong Kong. They've changed all that now: there's the new Institute of Macedonian Studies where there used to be a row of tin shacks which the owners called garages, the cobbles have been smoothed over with asphalt, and there are Italian trolley-buses whizzing along in the place of those Hong Kong coffins. In the park they have a refreshment kiosk, and they've tipped gravel into the holes where, on a rainy night, one could step in mud up to one's ankles. But the women are still there and the occasional tourists; the peasants, in the uniforms of soldiers, hoping to earn ten drachmas off the tourists to

4

spend on the women; and the tattered urchins spying on the tourists, the soldiers and the women in between selling pea-nuts, shining shoes or scavenging for fag-ends.

Those women are too old, too ugly or too diseased to work in the houses. In any other European country, Irvine used to say, they would have made some attempt, however futile and pathetic, at elegance and youth. Few of them bother to paint their faces, which are pinched, tired and earthen from hunger, work and exposure; not one dyes her hair. Often they wear brown or black woollen stockings rucked about their angular knees, peasant blouses and peasant-kerchiefs, and peasant-pigtails which, in the rain, give off that smell of damp sheep huddled together, which I know so well from my childhood. They are teased and bullied by the soldiers, and answer them back in shrill, strident voices, interspersing obscenities with screams of "Let me go! " and the cackling that a hen makes when it's pulled off its eggs. When they have trouble with a policeman they must, as they put it, 'settle with the tax-collector' either behind one of the clumps of bushes or in the disused Jewish cemetery where they also take their paying clients.

The one who gave me my little present was an exception to this rule: I don't suppose she could have been more than seventeen. She came from Chalkidike, I remember she told me that. I dare say she had been sent as a child into domestic service and, after a few years of drudgery and bullying, had decided to run away. Perhaps the son of the house had seduced her. It makes me sick when I read in our papers about our 'enslaved brothers' in Cyprus and I think of a little slut like that working from six in the morning until twelve o'clock at night for three or four pounds a month.

How clearly I see her now! After more than ten years. She was wearing a soldier's tunic, heaven knows where she'd got it, over a cotton frock in that terrible winter cold. Her hands, when I touched them, were swollen and raw with chilblains, and she had a smile that was like the grimace a cat makes when it's about to scratch you: you expected her to hiss. I was astonished by the fullness and beauty of her uptilted breasts (Kiki never had breasts like that), because the rest of her body was so emaciated that one could feel every bone. If you've been hungry as I so often have, you don't care for the feel of bones. Round her neck she had a bootlace with a cross dangling on the end of it; she told me that she'd had to sell the chain. She made love as they all make love in that park, as though she were scrubbing a floor. But what else can you expect for half a crown? Then, after I'd given her the ten-drachma note I'd got off a German sailor I'd led to one of the houses, she had the cheek to ask for more. "Go to the devil!" I shouted at her, and I gave her a push so that she almost sat down on one of the bushes behind which we had hidden. Then I told her to do one or two things to herself which it would obviously be impossible for her to do, and made off laughing, while she screamed behind me.

Well, she got her revenge! Fortunately in Greece you don't have to see a doctor in order to get your penicillin, and as I managed to find a job the following day, on a road-gang, I had the money to pay for three shots. "You'll need another to be sure," the spectacled, stooping chemist said, handling me as if I were a cow. "The hell I will! And how do you think I shall pay for it?" For, by then, the road-job had ended, as the foreman's nephew had arrived from his village looking for work, and mine was the work he was given.

Now I'm beginning to wonder. Do you suppose this 'cystitis' might be that old dose flaring up again? Should I mention it to the doctor? There you are, you see.

6

Those are the sort of morbid thoughts that come into your mind when you're alone, with nothing else to occupy you. I wish I didn't feel so depressed. I wish I could stop thinking of that skinny little skivvy—she gave it to me, didn't she? I wish I could stop thinking of all those nasty, ill-tempered things I said to poor Kiki, about her father, and the dirt in the flat, and the way she couldn't even make a cup of tea or boil an egg properly. God, I felt awful when she rushed off into the lavatory and I heard her being sick. I thought that after the first few months they began to feel better, but she just seems to feel worse and worse and worse. There are times when I hate myself, and the best thing then is to go out to pick up a girl, to play backgammon or cards at a café, or to dance in a tavern. Little chance of doing any of those things, except the first, in this god-awful country— even if I didn't have this plague.

I must get Kiki to move that ikon. If I lie on my side, as I'm doing now, I have to stare at it, and I'm tired of doing that. I'd rather have one of those pictures from *Esquire*; a blonde bursting out of her brassière, or lolling in a bath of foam. Funny how I've always liked blondes and I have to go and marry a brunette. I managed that badly. Married to the only daughter of one of the richest Greeks in London, and I can't even afford to pay the never-never on a wireless, let alone a telly.

We could sell that ikon, I suppose; I dare say it's valuable—must be, considering where I got it. Irvine was angrier with me then than I'd ever seen him before. We were touring Mount Athos in the yacht which he called a 'bargain' because, instead of paying five hundred dollars a month, he had got it through me for two hundred: which, none the less, allowed me a commission of twenty, though of course he didn't know about that. "I can see that life in Greece is going to be much cheaper for me, now that I've got you," he declared. How little did he guess then how much more expensive it was going to be! He was delighted, repeating over and over again: "Three hundred dollars! Think of that! Three hundred dollars! That's what you've saved." Like many people generous to the point of folly with those who appeal either to their love or their pity, he could also be incredibly mean. When he invited his friends in to drinks, he would often decide to give them Martinis, only to change his mind: "No, let them drink 'ouzo'! After all, if they come to Greece, they must get used to the Greek way of life, mustn't they?" His small change he kept in a little purse, and little purses on men are, I've always thought, an ominous sign. In restaurants while eager to press on me more food than I could possibly devour, he would calculate to the last farthing how much our share of the meal cost when we were with others. His tips were minute, unless the waiter was either handsome or full of complaints about the long hours he worked, the ill-temper of his wife, the health of his children or the soreness of his feet. Then he would shake the coins out of that horrid little purse of stained leather until they avalanched on to the clean tablecloth and even on to the floor.

We arrived at one of the Russian monasteries at dusk, and Irvine, who was standing at the prow of the yacht, a beige woollen muffler flapping its end around him as he held his little pink hands clasped over his little paunch, cried out: "Spiro, Spiro, look!" "O.K.," I said. "O.K. I can see." I was lying in a deck-chair, half asleep and half awake, and furious that, instead of going to Rhodes or Cos or even Loutraki, we had come to this benighted peninsula with not a woman in sight and hardly a man who could be called a man. "It's like a fairy-tale," Irvine went on excitedly, in that voice of his which often

8

made other Americans snigger and nudge each other: not educated Americans, of course, but people like accountants, storekeepers or the foremen of excavations. "Some fairy!" I muttered to myself. "Now, Irvine, you lazy boy! Open your eyes and look." Thank God, I thought, that neither of the crew knew English. But that voice! You can recognize that kind of voice in any language, can't you?

We were entertained by the guest-master, who was called Father Zosimos, and leaned on a stick when he wasn't trying to lean on my shoulder or that of one of our crew—because (so he said) of his rheumatism. Irvine's grandfather had been a diplomat in the Czarist Foreign Service, and Father Zosimos had also served in the Czarist Foreign Service before the Revolution: so we were given the best of everything, which wasn't saying much. "What a charming old fellow," Irvine said when we were alone in our cell. "Charming," I answered. "I could see the fleas hopping about in his beard." Irvine giggled at that: "Spiro, Spiro, you naughty boy! *Che cattiva lingua!*" "Look, how about leaving out the French?" I suggested, though I knew it was Italian. "You're educated, I'm not. Try to talk to me in English only and, if possible, in words of one syllable." Irvine loved that. He loved poverty, simplicity and ignorance, since he himself was rich, complex and over-educated. And I knew that, and used to play him up.

He began to shake some pills out of a bottle, and then looked round for a glass. "I must take my entero-vioform," he said anxiously. "I feel *uneasy* in my little intestine. Do you think that fish was off? It had a bitter taste to me." Irvine was always fussing about his health, and sighing that I was so healthy. He picked up a carafe which was full of cobwebs and peered down into it.

9

"I'll get you some water," I said, taking the carafe from him.

"Do you think it's safe?"

"Of course. Mount Athos is full of springs. The best water in Greece." Now I felt sorry for him, as he stood there, perplexed and worried, while the single candle bounced the shadow of his paunch, little intestine and all, against the ceiling as though it were a balloon. I was thinking, as I have so often thought: 'He's a good man.' But it's a pity that the good are so often ridiculous.

That night Irvine hardly slept at all, and when he slept, he talked. I had heard people talk Greek in their sleep before, and English, and even French, but it was the first time I had heard anyone talk all three of these languages at once. At intervals, still in his sleep, he would rub his hands briskly together as though he were cold. All this, I needn't tell you, got on my nerves, and eventually I shouted out: "Irvine! Stop it! Stop it! Irvine! Do you hear?" Then he woke up, and, sitting up in bed, looked all around him.

'Oh, oh, oh!" he moaned. Then he jumped out of the bed, brushing his hands over his silk pyjamas as if he were trying to put out flames.

"What's the matter?" I asked.

"Bugs! The bed is crawling with them."

I laughed: I was used to bugs, fleas and even lice after my months with the rebels in the mountains.

Irvine knelt down and began scrabbling in a rucksack from which he produced a D.D.T. bomb, which he began frantically squirting, as though it were a fire-extinguisher, at first over himself, then over the bed, and then indiscriminately about the room. Coughing, I protested:

"You'll make the room impossible to sleep in."

"It's impossible already. I shan't sleep a wink." He

lit the candle, placed himself gingerly on the only chair in the room and then, rocking himself backwards and forwards as if with stomach-cramps, began to peer at a pocket Bible which he always carried with him.

"You'll be cold," I said. "Put on my raincoat."

"Oh, do you think so?" he said, delighted at this attention. "Well, perhaps I'd better."

When I next awoke the candle was still burning, embedded in a mound of wax that was the same soiled, streakily grey colour as poor Irvine's unshaven face. The dawn was beginning to break. Irvine had put aside his Bible, and one leg crossed unnaturally high over the other, was leaning forward and gazing at me, while a cigarette burnt itself away between his pink fingers, a caterpillar-like ash curling downwards from its tip.

"Haven't you slept at all?" I asked.

Irvine shook his head. "I was thinking of that ikon. You know, the one of Saint Spyridon. That's your patron saint, isn't it? You looked so like him while you were asleep. I used to think that your head was wholly Classical, but it's not, it's not, you know. Asleep like that, you looked Byzantine, positively Byzantine."

We Greeks are vain, as any foreigner can guess from the frequency with which we comb our hair or clean our nails in public. When you walk down a main street in Athens, you will see a number of men, some handsome, but many plain or even ugly, staring into the windows of shops. Do not imagine that they are looking at what is displayed inside those windows. They are looking at something which pleases them far more: the reflection of themselves. I am Greek, and I am also vain. When Irvine said such things to me I felt neither embarrassed, as an Englishman would, nor angry, as an American would: being a Greek, I merely felt delighted.

"I wish I could draw you," Irvine went on. "As you are now, sitting up in that bed, with your pyjama-jacket open, your hair over your eyes, and your arms outstretched—yes, like that!—as you begin to yawn." He sighed: "I wish I could have that ikon."

"Well, why not?" I asked, yawning again.

"Why not?"

"Everything has its price. Do you want me to get it for you?"

"No, no, certainly not," he repudiated the idea. "Certainly not. It's unthinkable. No, no!" With his small hands he made a gesture of pushing an invisible object from him.

Mischievously I then and there decided that before we left the monastery Irvine should have his ikon.

Irvine had begun to dress, scratching as he did so at the weals which were coming up all over his plump, pink body. We had slept in the Czarist suite.

"Royal bugs," I said. "The last blood they sucked was probably Romanoff."

"Well, yes . . . yes, that might be so." Irvine smiled, as if I had applied some ointment to his itching skin. It always amused me to play on his snobbery.

All the previous evening, while he supervised our meal, Father Zosimos had talked continuously of the poverty of the monastery: Irvine, he knew, was an American, and in Greece the word American is synonomous with being both rich and a sucker. Once Phanoroméni had been the vastest and wealthiest of all the monasteries on the Holy Mountain, at a time when the Russians had hoped to use the peninsula as the staircase for their descent on the Eastern Mediterranean. Father Zosimos stroked his beard, shifted uneasily on his skinny haunches, and sighed as he talked of those days in a mixture of French and English. Now the monks were all old, for no new recruits came to them from their fatherland; the Greeks regarded them with suspicion, and would like to see them off the Holy Mountain; their revenues had diminished, they lacked the strength to work what little land was left to them. Irvine had nodded at this doleful saga, from time to time interjecting "Terrible! Why, that's terrible!" I knew that, unless I was careful, Father Zosimos was going to squeeze a large donation out of him. . . .

After breakfast, when Irvine had left Father Zosimos and me alone together, I straddled my legs as wide apart as I could, put my hands deep in my pockets, and said: "So things are pretty bad here, Father?"

"Very bad, my son, very bad." Father Zosimos joined his hands over the stick he had before them, and then put his forehead on to his hands. "Is your friend a Catholic?"

"No. A Protestant."

"And the yacht? Is that his?"

"We hired it in Salonica."

"A beautiful yacht. An expensive yacht. We had such a yacht to sail on the Black Sea, when I was a boy." He sighed. "Why didn't he sleep on his yacht?"

I shrugged my shoulders. Why indeed? "I suppose he thought it would be more interesting to sleep in this monastery. He didn't sleep alone," I added.

Father Zosimos looked startled.

"Bugs," I said.

"Bugs! Impossible! In our monastery!"

"Bugs," I repeated. Then I pursued: "So things are bad, eh?"

"Bad, bad, bad."

"If you need money, why don't you sell some of this junk you have around you?" I looked about me contemptuously.

"Sell! Sell what?"

"You say that often you have nothing to eat but a handful of olives and a crust of bread."

"Often only a crust of bread."

"A man like you has been used to better things."

"Ah, if I would tell you about those dinners——" Father Zosimos broke off. "The Lord giveth, the Lord taketh away," he said piously, but with a sob in his voice.

"My friend likes one of your ikons. That one, over there."

"Ah, Saint Spyridon," Father Zosimos said, gazing first at the ikon and then at the tiles between his legs.

"He would like to buy it," I said softly.

"Buy it! But that's impossible, impossible." Father Zosimos tossed his head restlessly up and down and from side to side, as a horse does when tormented by flies. "Does he—does he think it—er—valuable?" he suddenly asked, scratching his chin with one of his grimy, palsied hands.

"Oh, I don't know about that!" Luxuriously I, in turn, scratched myself with the fingers in my trouser-pocket. Then I smiled: "He likes it," I said.

"Well, it's impossible. We couldn't sell it. Quite impossible."

"A pity," I said.

Now I was beginning to feel sorry for the old boy, as I always feel sorry for people when I wheedle or hector them into doing what they don't want to do.

"A pity," I repeated.

"How much does he think that it's worth?" Father Zosimos asked after a pause, looking at me slyly, with his head tilted on one side while, with the thumb of his left hand he made a gouging movement inside his right nostril. "Eh?"

"Oh, I don't know. Twenty dollars."

14

"Twenty dollars! Twenty dollars, that ikon! It's fourteenth century. We had a professor from Oxford here last year and he said that it was very, very valuable. Twenty dollars!" he snorted, still digging away at his nose.

"Well, twenty-five."

Eventually I got him to agree that thirty dollars was the true value of the ikon, and by then he was as restless and uncomfortable as a man who has taken a dose of salts: shifting himself from one of his sharp buttocks to the other, and massaging his belly with his hand while he cast furtive glances in turn at me, at the ikon, and at the door.

Suddenly he said: "The difficulty is the law."

"Ah, that's always the difficulty—isn't it? But one gets round such things. Who'd notice if the ikon went? You say the prior is blind. And most of the other monks look half-blind too. Anyway, you have that monk who paints ikons, the one you showed us yesterday. Who's likely to notice the difference?"

We discussed the subject for at least another half-hour, during which I persuaded Father Zosimos to take one of my English cigarettes. "For the lavatory," I winked, because I knew that the monks were forbidden to smoke. But it began to get on my nerves when he kept holding the cigarette under his vast, battered nose and sniffing at it, as though it were a bottle of smelling-salts, while his head and his eyes rolled simultaneously from side to side, so that soon I jumped to my feet.

"Anyway, think about it," I cried out impatiently. "Thirty dollars. That's what he'll pay. Thirty dollars."

"Thirty dollars," Father Zosimos ruminated, still drooling over the unlit cigarette.

"Take it, or leave it."

All that day we saw no more of him, and I decided

that I had failed. Well, he wasn't a Greek, I consoled myself; he was a Russian. With Russians one couldn't be sure. A Russian might murder for thirty dollars, and yet refuse to sell an ikon for the same sum. I was in a bad mood, and went to sleep in one of the courtyards, throwing myself down on a patch of grass which had overgrown the stones, in the middle of a lecture which Irvine was giving on Byzantine monastic architecture. "We must find that pretty little fountain. Robert Byron mentions it," he was saying. "Count me out." "Now, come along, you lazy boy! You're not the one who missed his sleep last night. Come! Get up! " "Count me out." Irvine looked down at me hopelessly, one hand clutching his *Guide Bleu* against his bosom, while the other held his open exposure meter pointing down at me as though it were a revolver which, in his exasperation, he would willingly fire into my face. I shut my eyes, I yawned. "Count me out," I murmured again.

In those days I could always tell what Irvine would be feeling, and I knew exactly what he was feeling then. He was upset, that was his first emotion, because he was not merely eager to "educate" me, but had also persuaded himself that I myself was eager for whatever education he had to offer. "Spiro's naturally so intelligent, he has such good taste. It's a tragedy that the Civil War interrupted his education." I'd overheard him talk like this to his friends. "Now we're making up for lost time. . . . And, really, no teacher could ask for a better pupil." Secondly he was exasperated, because he had not yet got used to the truth (as he did later) that he might buy my time, but he could not buy either my obedience or my love. Thirdly, he was proud of me. I say this without vanity: as I lay there in the sunlight, in the open-necked shirt and the dark-blue corduroy trousers which he himself had given me, my arms pillowing my head and my eyes shut, he was congratulating himself on having acquired such an attractive companion. He knew he had been lucky.

"Nasty boy!" he said at last, wandering away disconsolately.

We boarded the yacht at dusk, and though a number of the monks descended like a flock of elderly tattered vultures in order to pick Irvine clean (he seemed to be handing out dollar-bills all round) there was no sign of Zosimos. It was only as we put off and our engine began to cough and spit a vile blue smoke that, suddenly, I caught a glimpse of the old boy hopping and lurching down the steps to the quay, his stick brandished in one hand while the other grasped a brown-paper parcel. "Stop! Whoa!" I shouted to our captain. "Wait! Stop!" And as the yacht chugged round, I leapt for the shore.

"I've got it, I've got it!" Father Zosimos panted breathlessly, thrusting the parcel at me. "The Good Lord forgive me, and all sinners at the Day of Judgment! Take it, my son, take it!"

"Why, Father!" I cried. "How kind this is of you! What generosity! Thank you, thank you!" I leapt forward and kissed him first on the left cheek-bone, on the expanse of grey skin between his rheumy eye and his beard, and then on the right cheek-bone. Meanwhile I was conscious of a reptilian hissing:

"The dollars! The dollars!"

"Yes, indeed, Father. I'll tell my friend. Thank you," I shouted, so that Irvine could hear. "Thank you very much. Now I must run. Good-bye, Father. Good-bye! Good-bye!" At that I raced away from him, still hearing that anguished "The dollars! The dollars!" and leapt on to the yacht. "Get going!" I cried out gleefully to the crew. "Full steam ahead."

17

"Well, there it is," I said to Irvine, tearing off the paper and handing the ikon to him. "It's yours."

"The ikon!" Irvine was stupefied.

"I knew I could get it for you. At a price," I added.

Irvine goggled, choked, and at last managed to say:

"But it's—it's . . . that kind of sale is strictly forbidden." Like most people who are unnaturally law-abiding, Irvine derived an intense, if guilty, pleasure from any breach of the law committed by others than himself.

"Now don't you worry about that. That's their headache. Come on—take it!" I commanded. "Come on."

Irvine held the ikon in both his hands, and stared down with the uncertain, wistful expression of a savage gazing for the first time at his own reflection in a mirror. Then, after many seconds, he glanced up. "How much?" he asked fearfully.

"Nothing."

"Nothing?"

"It's a present," I said. "A present from me to you."

"Oh, Spiro! But you must have had to pay a fortune."

"That's my business," I said. "Isn't it? When you're given a present, you don't ask how much it cost."

"But I can't accept this from you."

"Why not? You're always giving me presents. Why shouldn't I give you a present for a change? I've been wanting to do it for a long time—ever since I got paid for that two-weeks job at that Gallery. But I didn't know what to get you. You seem to have everything."

Irvine was overjoyed: after all, he wasn't to know that the fifteen odd pounds I had got for sitting all day at a desk trying not to look at some daubs painted by a friend of his, had long, long ago been spent on that slut Lydia— or was it Titsa in those days? I knew that when he got

18

back to Athens and showed the ikon off, he would say: "Spiro gave it to me. Can you believe it? Wasn't that sweet of him? Wasn't that touching? And then people say that the Greeks are just out for what they can get from us!"

"Dear Spiro . . ." he said, putting an arm round me and squeezing my shoulder. "I shall never forget this."

This gratitude made me feel uneasy, and it was in a cross, impatient voice that I answered him: "Oh, it's nothing. Nothing at all. Greece is full of ikons." Then I pushed his arm away.

"Not ikons like this. I shall treasure it always."

"You've a hundred more valuable things at home."

"For me this has a greater value than the lot."

That evening I drank too much, and after Irvine had gone below feeling, as he put it, "a little weary" (Irvine always preferred that word to 'tired'), I began to boast about the ikon to old Panayiotis and his nephew Boulis, while we played cards on deck in the light of a paraffin lamp. They both roared with laughter, Panayiotis slapping the leathery soles of his bare feet, as he rocked back and forth on his haunches, showing gums into which the rotten teeth appeared to have been struck haphazard like the charred ends of matches. "Sh!" I quietened them both. "Not so loud! Not so loud!"

I might have known that Panayiotis would tell Irvine, because only two days before I had caught him out trying to cheat us on the petrol bills. "You needn't have blabbed," he reproved me on that occasion. "And let my friend be robbed?" "He's a rich man. You know that we are poor." "I know that you're a bastard."

I was asleep when Irvine came into my cabin and threw the ikon at me, bruising my forehead. His little chin was trembling, and his albino eye-lashes were blinking up and down: "You disgusting little thief!" he

19

shrilled at me: in his rages his accent always became unmistakably American. "Liar . . . liar . . . deceit . . . trusted you . . . fool that I am . . ." The disconnected phrases came out with the same acrid plop-plop-plop as the smoke from the engine of our boat.

I rubbed my forehead, too stunned both by the blow and by his discovery of the truth to attempt to protest. At last I managed to stammer out my apologies and then, slowly recovering my wind, to explain: "I know I shouldn't have done it. But I did it for you. You can't imagine how I feel, having to accept your generosity day in, day out, and knowing that there's nothing I can do in return. You wanted the bloody thing, didn't you? Didn't you? I didn't want it. I had seven dollars on me, but of course it was useless to offer him that. And he kept putting the price up and up, so that I got mad at him. Well, I know I did wrong, of course I did wrong. But it was for you, Irvine—for you! Not for myself."

Suddenly I began to cry: it's easy for Greeks to cry, and there's no shame in doing so. But in England or America for a man to cry is something terrible, and to have to watch him do so is like having to watch someone cut his own throat. "Don't, don't!" Irvine shouted out. "Oh, Spiro, don't!" It was then that I learned the trick; after that, as a last resort, I knew that I always had a way of getting the better of him. "Spiro, don't!"

"Leave me alone! Don't touch me!" I buried my face in the pillow and went on with my sobbing. And, really, I was not being insincere. No one likes to be caught out in a lie; to be woken up by having a worm-eaten ikon flung at his head; and then to think that perhaps he's cooked his goose and the good times are over. "Oh, I hate myself, I hate myself! But you made me do it! You made me do it!"

Soon Irvine was talking to me in what I came to call his 'nanny' voice.

"Now, now, that's enough of that," he said, seating himself on the bunk. "Quite enough. Stop it, Spiro! Stop it at once! There's no harm done. But the ikon must be returned. As soon as we reach Salonica, you must find a way of returning it. Is that understood? Spiro, is that understood?"

"Ye-e-es!" I wailed.

"Very well. Then we can forget all about it. Now pull yourself together! Spiro, pull yourself together! I said, we can forget all about it."

In his innocence he never guessed that I should forget all about it to such an extent that the ikon would remain in my possession.

There it is now: it's odd and, in my present mood, somehow depressing to think of it hanging first in some Byzantine church, and then being carried into the depths of Russia, who knows how far, and then working its way to Phanaroméni, and last of all to Battersea, to take its place between one of Kiki's water-colours, of the bandstand in Kensington Gardens, and a photograph of herself, her mother and father, and that asparagus-like milk-sop of a brother of hers.

I must look again at that letter which came from Irvine this morning. I was so cross that he sent us only twenty dollars that I crumpled it up and threw it under the bed. I dare say it was the disappointment that made me be so beastly to Kiki. God! The dirt under there! Nothing stays clean in this place for more than an hour or two. Look at my hands. And in Athens I could go for three days without washing them and no one would know.

How I hate Irvine's writing! There's something so affected about it. I won't say that it hasn't any character,

21

because Irvine himself is affected. But when I used to see his pen moving over the paper, as slowly and carefully as if he were lettering a poster, I always had to resist the impulse to go near him and pretend accidentally to jog his arm. Well, in the end, I did jog his arm, and managed to blot his copy-book. . . .

Twenty dollars. . . . That's generous, from a man whom one's ruined: even if he refuses to believe that you're the one who has ruined him, whatever you say.

DEAREST SPIRO,

I have been worrying about you and your Kiki ever since I received your letter last Thursday. I am sorry that everything has gone so badly for you both, that the apartment—or should I say 'flat'?—is so drab and uncomfortable, and that you yourself are sick with such a disagreeable complaint. I remember that I myself had the same trouble when I was in Beirut, and I suspected that I had drunk some polluted water. Fortunately dear Homer Mannheim—you remember him, don't you? we all went to Sunium together that Christmas Day when you insisted on bathing, and we feared you would die of pneumonia—well, Homer had a wonderful German, or Swiss, drug with him and within twenty-four hours I was as bright as a daisy. Needless to say, with my terrible memory, I can no longer recall the name—Sanosomething, I think. Anyway, do ask for it at your drugstore . . .

There's a lot more of that: Irvine collects illnesses and medicines as he once used to collect pictures. He gave up the picture-collecting because it was too expensive; but I'm sure the bottles and doctors are far more expensive than an occasional Tsarouchis, Ghikas or Braque. Let's go on to the next paragraph. Ah, that's more like it . . .

. . . you know, my dear, that you are the only person for whom I care in a world for which I seem to care less and less and less, and that I would do anything in my power to help you. But you also know that so far from being a rich man I have now become a poor one. Lucy is once again out of hospital, and though she is well enough to potter about the house, I do not know how long we can hope this recovery will last. It is in the nature of her illness that there should be recurring cycles and since I could never endure that she should be placed in a public institution (that, as you know, was a promise I made to our mother) I can visualize no end to the expense of having to maintain her. For the present she seems to be happy, and her devotion to me, and dependence on me, both touch me unbearably . . .

There's a lot more about that lunatic sister of his: since he writes later that 'during her worst spells she seems to lose all contact with reality', I've never been able to understand why he feels he has to pay for her to go to a private home. As if she would know the difference! But that's typical of his sentimentality. In Greece, he'd give five shillings to a 'blind' beggar-girl in the streets who everyone knew could see a wink well enough as soon as her day's work was ended, but would haggle for threepence with a plumber, who had to support a wife and six children, over the cost of repairing a tap.

. . . I cannot tell you how much I miss both Greece and you. Will I ever get back there? Will I ever see you again? You are young, and you cannot be expected to understand what it is like to feel that all the best things are no longer ahead but behind one. The happy years are over—before one even realized how happy they were! I live in this horrible little mid-western town, from which I once thought I had escaped for ever and ever. I go to my horrible little glass-fronted box, and scribble away at my 'foreign correspondence' for eight hours a day. Then I go home, and Lucy looks at the television or asks me what I have done, while I try to read. My eyes are getting worse. The doctors think that in five years I may be totally blind. Oh, if I could tell you of the despair I feel sometimes, and the longing for the sun and the wine and the laughter of Greece! This is not a country for old men . . .

I can't help smiling when I read that phrase about 'the sun and the wine and the laughter of Greece!' Irvine could always deceive himself! When he was in Athens he would wear sun-glasses even to look at the Acropolis by moonlight, he never ceased to grumble about the 'retsina', which he declared tasted exactly like pine-disinfectant—as if he had ever drunk disinfectant! —and, as for Greek laughter, there was nothing that irritated him more than what he called 'this oafish, idiotic sense of humour from which your fellow barbarians suffer'. Now, in retrospect, all that has acquired a glamour, I suppose. He's forgotten that in summer he used to get heat-bumps and mosquito bites which he would scratch till they festered; he's forgotten his complaints about the noise of the taverns, the dirt of the streets, and the impossibility of buying wrapped bread; I dare say that he's even forgotten our terrible quarrels together and the way that I betrayed him, imagining now that our relationship was one of a calm and mutual devotion.

God, but I can't help feeling sorry for him! I know how he dreaded to return to America, a country for which he felt what I used to feel for my father; how he used to talk of buying a house on Mykonos, or Hydra or Andros and bringing his sister over, as soon as his mother died; how he used to say that it was only by the Mediterranean that he felt he was truly himself. "But what do you find here?" I would often ask in exasperation. "You—among other things." "Well, you won't find me here much longer. I'm just waiting to spit the dust of this rubbish-bin of a town out of my mouth for ever! America, Canada, Australia—those are the places for me! Where there's work, and money, and things happening every minute." I used to say that purposely to annoy him. "No, no, no!" he would then cry out, making that gesture with both his little hands of pushing something physical away from him. "You don't know what you're saying. You don't understand the horror of living outside Europe." "I've learnt enough about the horror of living in Europe, thank you."

Many of Irvine's friends were the same kind of expatriates as himself. In one way or another they were all of them odd; they were all people who felt there was no place for them in the countries of their origin. They settled in Greece firstly because the Greeks are individualists, and respect, instead of depising, oddity; and secondly because they would delude themselves that their oddity was not something innate, which they carried with them wherever they travelled, but simply the natural result of being a foreigner. "I feel at home here," I would often hear such people say. But they did not mean that. What they meant was that in a foreign country they could persuade themselves that their homelessness was merely something physical, not spiritual.

I have rarely felt guilt in my life, but I feel it now whenever I think of Irvine. We modern Greeks differ in that from the ancient Greeks; they were so tormented by guilt, and for us guilt hardly exists. We only suffer shame: the shame of being found out, of being shown up, of losing caste and face. But truly I feel guilt, as I remember what he did for me and what I did to him in return. But for him, I suppose I'd be a pimp hanging about Constitution Square, the Zappeion Gardens or the docks; or a seller of hashish; or a thief. Who knows? I don't suppose I'd ever have settled down to an honest occupation, answering bells at one of the posh hotels, delivering letters, or slaving away to erect one of those concrete chest-of-drawers which they're sticking up all over Athens. But for me, Irvine would now be head of the Society in Greece, or manager of their New York Office, or Director of their Mission to Europe—something like that. Instead of which, he sweats as a correspondence clerk for the same wage which he got when he was a boy just down from College.

I can't go on reading his letter, it makes me too unhappy. I seem to hear him talking to me, here in this room, in those long, carefully balanced sentences full of words which I used to have to ask him to explain. There, in the shadows between the curtain and the bookcase, I even seem to see him, looking at me with those sad, devoted, reproachful, always forgiving eyes, while his small, pink hands are clasped in front of him, like a child's when it's saying its prayers. I never thought I cared for him, any more than I cared for Helen Bristow, and yet now I know that I cared for them both. Perhaps I can only care for people that I've treated abominably just as, during the occupation, the Germans, after having starved us and beaten us and shot us, seemed slowly to acquire an odd kind of tenderness for us too; just as, when I was a prisoner in the Civil War, I used to see men throwing a crust of bread or a handful of olives at some girl they had just raped, or even attempting to console her weeping.

Strangely, Irvine makes me feel more guilty than Helen Bristow: even though he only lost his job through me, whereas she went and killed herself. I suppose it's the feeling that, in her case, there was no need to get into that state. After all she had a husband who was dull certainly, but rich and good-looking and kind and not unintelligent. She had her house in Psychico, and her work at the Anglo-Hellenic League, and her bridge-parties and cocktail-parties and dinner-parties. Whereas Irvine had nothing but me. Sometimes he used to tell me that, and I used to say crossly, because even then it made me feel guilty: " Oh, don't be silly! You have all those friends of yours. And your books, and your pictures, and your music." To which he would reply: " Truly, my dear, I wouldn't care if I never saw any of those friends again. And as for this rubbish "—he waved his hand about the room—" I'd give it all for a day of your company." I knew that this wasn't hysteria, as in the case of Helen; I knew that it was a quiet and considered judgment, and that he meant every word of it.

It's odd that he and I never slept together; everyone in Athens was certain that we were lovers, and since he knew that, obviously the fear of what people would say could not have deterred him. I suppose it was that religious, Papist side of his character which I could never begin either to understand or share, and which always annoyed me for that reason. Once he explained to me that in the eyes of his Church to have a permanent physical relationship with someone of his own sex would be a far greater sin than to have a series of promiscuous relationships. I should have thought it would be the other way round; I remember that I was amazed. Sometimes he would touch me momentarily, or fondle me, running a hand up my cheek or through my thick, curly hair. But he did not care to be touched by me or, indeed, by anyone, in return. He was curiously prudish: even though we shared the same flat for nearly four years, he would never allow me to go into the bathroom to shave while he was having his bath, and on the beach, on the hottest days, he would never take off his shirt. He would be cross if I blasphemed, chiding: "Spiro, Spiro, Spiro! Please, my dear!" and he would blush if I made a remark that was in the least bit dirty.

If he had wanted to sleep with me, I suppose I should have consented: after all, when I was down and out in Salonica, I slept with men far less attractive, to whom I was under far less of an obligation. And I did it as a prisoner. That wouldn't shock a Greek. I remember how astonished Irvine once was, when two of his Greek friends were discussing a politician who had recently become a minister:

"Of course he's a pansy."

"Oh, no, no, no!"

"What do you mean? He lives with E, doesn't he? It was E who discovered him when he was a waiter."

"Yes, but I happen to know that it's E who's the passive partner."

Irvine could not understand this exchange; but really it is simple. In Greece, in any relationship, whether between two men, or between a man and a woman, there is one person who derives power and humiliates, and there is another person who loses power and is humiliated. Provided one is not the person who loses power and is humiliated, one will not be criticized.

Yes, I could have slept with Irvine if he had wanted it; I think I should have preferred to do so, for then I should not have felt myself under so much of an obligation to him. "But how *could* you?" an English friend once said, when I confessed this to him. "He must be at least fifty and, oh, he's so terribly unattractive." Once again I had to point out a difference between Greece and the West: "You all are interested, first in the person, and then in the sexual act. With us, it's the other way round." I laughed. "You know all about our shepherds and their favourite ewes."

I wonder if Irvine ever slept with anyone at all. He told me once that as a young man in America he used to have to 'date' girls and even make a kind of clumsy half-love to them, in order to keep his self-respect and the respect of his fellow-students. When he used to wander about the parks at night, was it merely for the excitement of the darkness, the danger and the proximity of all that vicious, furtive activity in the shadows around him, or did he himself, however guilty and clumsy, plunge into that muddy pool? I never dared to ask him; he never told me. Certainly he had had other friends, whether foreign or Greek, before me; and from time to time, after he had met me, he would attempt to make such friends again. But out of jealousy and some instinct of self-preservation, I would always make it my business to snap each of such links. On one occasion, when a letter came from an Italian sailor whom Irvine had met in Naples, I destroyed it at once. On another occasion when a student from Patras telephoned to the flat and Irvine was out, I said 'wrong number' twice, and then on the third occasion shouted down the telephone: "Whom do you want? Don't you know that this is the Russian Embassy? Have you any information for us?" That made him ring off quick enough. In the case of Dino, I behaved even more badly. But I don't want to think of that . . .

There's that wretched cat again, scratching about in the pot on the balcony which Kiki planted only yesterday. It's extraordinary how animals come to look like their owners: or is it that the owners come to look like their animals? I don't suppose the cat dyes its coat that extraordinary orange colour, whereas the hair of that awful Mumfitt woman is certainly not natural. God! It's begun to make a mess. What can I throw at it? My slipper. Hell. . . . Now I've chucked it into the street.

I'd like to cut up that cat with a pair of garden shears. I'm not sure that I wouldn't prefer to cut up Mrs. Mumfitt. Snip, snip. At those enormous breasts of hers. Probably there'd just be a couple of loud bangs, and a smell of rubber and bad air.

It's only eleven o'clock, and I seem to have been lying here for a life-time. I can't even telephone to anyone, because they've cut it off. At this moment Kiki's father is probably seated under a fur-rug in the Rolls, while the chauffeur drives him to the City. Her mother is still in bed, alternately eating her breakfast and screaming, in true Greek fashion, at the maid who is running her bath and putting out her clothes. Her brother is lying full length on the sofa, his shoes on the brocade, while he puffs at a cigarette and reads the *Daily Mirror*: he has a hang-over and has decided not to go to the crammer's, after a scene with Daddy. Soon he'll pick up the telephone to ask his starlet from Mitcham if he can take her to the film première. All that money and so little taste. . . . All that money and so little for us. . . .

It would serve them right if they lost it all, and Kiki and I became rich; if they had to grovel on the floor for a crust of bread and a drink of water from us; if the Communists came and made Daddy go back to the rocky half-acre from which his father started; if their hands bled from working, and their backs ached, and that little rotter got kicked in his flabby bottom. . . .

Oh, I must try to read; or sleep; or somehow make these hours pass. Otherwise I shall begin to worry again about how we're going to keep ourselves, about my residence-permit, about poor Kiki. I don't want to think about either the past or the future. But what is there in the present? Just lying here alone, with this disagreeable feeling, the sunlight on the curtain, that cat on the balcony, the people on the street.

Oh, there's the blonde with the pram! She's looking up, she heard my whistle!

Hell! She's talking to Mrs. Mumfitt.

". . . I gave him a teaspoonful of paraffin. The vet said it was the best thing. His eyes are ever so much brighter this morning, and his coat is coming up."

"Well, that's a load off your mind."

"Oh, yes, a real load off my mind."

"Yes, you must be relieved."

"Yes, oh, yes, a great relief. When I saw him this morning, so perky and bright, I said to my sister, I said to her, just look at Whiskey. Just look at him, I said. Oh, we were relieved! It was a load off our minds!"

Silly bitches. The same thing over and over again, just like one's memory. Over and over again. Over and over again. . . .

II

WEDNESDAY

I T'S odd to wake up from that dream and find that it's not night-time, with Kiki asleep beside me, but eleven o'clock in the morning, the sunlight on my face. I still feel like a terrified child, my heart is still thumping, and the sweat trickling down my face still seems to be blood. It's the dream of that night when the rebels found my elder brother and me hiding in the shed, behind a pile of seed potatoes. Poor Stelio! He was only two years older than I and I don't suppose they would have killed him if he hadn't sprung out at them with that sickle in his hand. I remember how he straddled me, in an effort to protect me, and how I crouched, gripping his muscular legs and screaming: "No! Stop! Stop! Stop! No!" both at him and at them. There were seven of them, and at the time I did not realize, in the darkness, that they were men from another village, but thought that they were from ours. One was grappling with Stelio for the sickle, while another groaned, doubled up over a hand from which, I discovered later, the tips of two fingers were lopped. Then a third who, like the rest, seemed momentarily stupefied either by pain, surprise or horror, struck Stelio in the mouth with the butt of his rifle. He reeled, and I felt his weight upon me, too heavy for me to support. Again someone struck, with a splintering sound, and I heard Stelio gulp, as thought he were about to retch. Then I felt the blood, dripping on to my face. . . .

That's the dream. That's what I was dreaming. That's how it happened.

My father was a priest, and my brother and I had quarrelled with him that evening, because when we thought he had gone out for some time we had put on the wireless to listen to the 'bouzouki' music which we both loved but which he had forbidden us to hear. For him, as for so many of the older people, this music, coming from Peiraeus and the ports of Asia Minor, was something ignoble and degrading, with associations of theft, drugs and unnatural vice. He came back earlier than we had expected, to find us both practising the beautiful 'hassapiko' or butcher's dance, our arms over each other's shoulders and our fingers clicking in time to the music. Our mother was watching us, stitching away at the same time at a piece of embroidery, her eyes grown small and hooded from the effort of peering either at us or down at her canvas. It was an autumn night, dry and serene and clear, with an almost full moon rising behind the mountains.

My brother and my father quarrelled, shouting bitter things at each other, while my mother worked on, her needle poised and one hand, rough and seamed from work in the fields and the kitchen, smoothing her stitches. She did not intervene because, like myself, she knew that it was useless.

Afterwards, when we were ordered to our room, Stelio threw himself down on to the bed which we had shared for as long as I could remember, and lay there, silent, in the thick woollen vest and underpants which Greek peasants wear even in summer. All that day we had been whitewashing the shed in which he was later killed,

33

and his vast hands, in the flickering light of our candle, seemed to be wearing white gloves against which his swelling forearms showed the brown of honey. Unlike me, he had not bothered to do more than dip them into a bucket of water: he was neither vain about his appearance nor fussy about cleanliness.

His sixteen-year-old face, which had long since ceased to be the face of a boy, was set in lines of stubborn petulance and exasperation. "I'll leave here. I'll go to sea. I'll go to Salonica. That'll teach him. He can't find anyone else to work for him as I do, and what do I get for it? I'm sick of this life I can tell you. We live here like beasts. What's the point of it all? What's the point of it? That's what I'd like to know. One might as well be dead."

Even now it frightens me to think of that irony.

I tried to soothe him: I told him to have patience, when he was eighteen he could go as a volunteer into the air-force, things weren't so bad. I sat on the bed beside his sprawled body, and took his hand in mine, amusing myself with chipping off the flakes of whitewash by rubbing my own carefully-tended nails against his square, roughly-cut ones, as I went on: "You must marry a girl with a large dowry. That's the solution. A girl with a property of her own."

Men say such things to each other in Greece, and they do not say them as a joke.

He grunted. "What girl would want to marry me? What have I to offer? Eh? What have I to offer?" he demanded again, as though he were angry with me.

To that I could say nothing. Although our father was a priest, we were poor, and we had almost ruined ourselves when we had to provide a dowry for my eldest sister. She had married a dentist in Edessa, a man of a hideous refinement who wore crumpled and greasy made-

34

up check bow-ties sent to him by a cousin in Detroit, and grew the nails of his little fingers to mandarin-like lengths as though in order to use them to excavate the teeth over which he pored all day. Two of our olive-groves had bought him a dentist's chair and an electric drill, both of them salmon-pink. He liked to see me, because I was then a student at the French Lycée in Salonica, but he was ashamed of poor Stelio. Once when we both visited him, he told Stelio to shave, and himself put a pan on to boil, got a towel from the press, and set out the soap and the razor. I noticed that he gave Stelio a blade that had already been used, and that the soap was of a kind normally used for washing clothes.

"It's all right for you," Stelio was saying. "You've got brains. You're cunning." The word 'cunning' in Greek implies admiration, not condemnation. "One day you'll be rich. You see. And then you'll forget all about us." He was half joking, half serious. "You'll be ashamed of us in the end. When your grand friends ask you about your family, you'll make up stories about us. You've always been good at stories, haven't you?"

Poor Stelio! If he could see me now, lying here thinking about him because I can afford to do nothing else, with that pile of bills on the end of my bed and the room cold because they've cut off the gas. He was wrong about me; either I was too cunning or not cunning enough. But at least about the stories he was right. When I first met Irvine, I told him that I was a Greek refugee from Roumania; there were a lot of them in Salonica in those days, and to hear them talk one would imagine that none of the Greeks there had ever owned less than a thousand acres. For a while it amused Irvine to think that I was descended from a family of Greek hospodars, though how he imagined that a name like Polymerides could be of the same antiquity and eminence as Ypsilantes or Capodistria remained a mystery to me. But, when he learned the truth, it amused him even more that I had come from a village of two hundred inhabitants on the foot-hills of Mount Vermion—"You would think he was an aristocrat, wouldn't you?" he would say to his friends. It pleased him that he had taught me to change my underclothes regularly, to wash my hands after going to the lavatory, to eat asparagus in my fingers instead of with a knife and fork, to eat an apple with a knife and fork instead of in my fingers. I was a work of art at which, for four years, he slaved: not realizing that the more I learned from him, the less I needed him. Would either Helen Bristow or Kiki have ever spared me more than a brief glance if I had not been dressed in the clothes he had ordered for me from Tsochas, washed myself with his Roger et Gallet soap, or perfumed myself with his Floris after-shave lotion?

I climbed into the bed beside Stelio, after having splashed some cold water over my face and my hands. In those days I never brushed my teeth: that was also something which I was taught to do by Irvine. We drew the sheep-skin rug up to our chins, and then Stelio put out a hand and snuffed the candle, its bitter fumes lingering in the still autumn air. Soon he was asleep, one arm thrown across me. I lay for a long time, thinking of what he had said to me: I'd got brains, I was cunning. I knew that was true, and the knowledge of it filled me with exaltation. I would be rich, I would buy poor Stelio a farm of his own, I would marry an American millionairess. Everything was possible; all the strings were in my fingers. I'd leave the village, and our father with his perpetual sermons on the wickedness of the modern world in general and our wickedness in particular. I'd never come back. But no: I'd come back, my Cadillac flinging the mud up on either side of the

rutted street so that it spattered the passers-by, I'd step
out with my beautiful wife, who would pull her fur-coat
about her and make a little face as the villagers gathered
around to greet me and stare; I'd shout out for wine for
all, and then I'd say: 'Let's have some music. Let's have
some "bouzouki".' I'd give my father something for
his Church, peeling off the thousand dollar notes from a
pile I drew from my pocket. I'd persuade my mother
to leave him and go with us to California or Florida.

These waking fantasies slowly became dreams, as the
large harvest moon rose red from behind the mountains
and I snuggled closer to Stelio. I doubt if I could sleep
now in such proximity to another man: certainly not to
someone as unwashed and unshaven, with the smell of
sheep and oil on his body. There are nights now when
even the nearness of Kiki makes it impossible for me to
sleep, and I have to get up and go into the sitting-room.

My memory of what follows is confused: memory is
merciful, and that is something which novelists, describ-
ing in exact detail their characters' recollections of
horrible or agonizing experiences, seldom understand.
When I was nine I had my tonsils taken out in Salonica,
under a local anæsthetic; but I can recall nothing of the
event except being strapped into a chair and then being
given a chipped enamel basin to hold—I can still feel
that rough gritty surface on my hands. Apparently I
struggled and screamed, and for weeks afterwards
suffered from nightmares. All that is gone. When
people who have been in road accidents are asked by the
police to say exactly what happened, they suffer the same
blankness.

Now, when I try to think back to that night, it is
difficult for me to impose any sequence on those events.
It's as if they had all exploded up into my face, so many
splinters of glass, so that I cannot say which of them was

first to pierce me. We woke to the rattle of carbines, shouting, the banging of doors and shutters, and then a single prolonged scream. Stelio leapt from the bed, over my crouching body, and I crept after him to the door. Our room was off the kitchen from which, in turn, a door led to the room in which my father and mother slept together. "What is it? What's happening?" "The rebels." As we crossed the kitchen, we heard my mother imploring: "By the Christian mothers that bore you . . . By the Virgin . . . By the Christ who died to save you . . ." What an appeal! It was because my father was the priest that they had come to the house. Outside the clamour of voices, barking of dogs, and rat-rat-rat and whistle of bullets had grown so loud that we barely heard the two shots in the room outside which we were standing. Then a strident voice shouted: "No, no! Don't waste another bullet! That'll do for the two dogs!"

Stelio grabbed my arm. "But we must go to them! We must help them!" I protested as we climbed out of our bedroom window and, seeing men in the street at the back of the house, crawled towards the shed.

"They're dead," he said. "They've killed them. Didn't you hear?"

After that I remember nothing until the blood trickled warm and salt into the corners of my mouth, and someone was kicking at me savagely: "Out! Get out! Go on, get out!" A rifle-butt crashed down on to my shoulder, and I stumbled and cried out with pain.

Perhaps it was only a few minutes later, perhaps an hour, when I stood with a number of the boys of my own age, many of them whimpering, under the plane-tree in the main square where we would often sit on summer evenings, throwing dice, bragging to each other, or whistling at the girls. The men of the village were being lined

38

up against the wall of the café opposite, they and their captors shouting at each other the same blasphemies which they shouted at their sheep or their goats. If anyone struggled, he was clubbed by the rifle-butt. There were men who came out naked, making absurd gestures of modesty in order to hide their shame. I saw old blind Panayiotis tapping his way with his stick, as though he imagined he was being shepherded along to the café to play on his clarinet for a feast-day dance. The village-idiot was there, a creature of my father's age, who wandered around talking gibberish in the piping voice of a child when he was not stealing, tormenting stray cats or dogs, or committing obscenities before a secret audience of village youths. A rebel suddenly thrust him aside, with such violence that one of his shoes came off and he himself landed on his bottom, sniggering and crowing. The women kept up a wail, like the lamentation they make at a funeral, but when one of them went forward to intercede with the man who seemed to be the ringleader—he was a lawyer from Castoria, I discovered later, and his name was Georgios—he struck her across the face with the back of his hand. She was pregnant.

After the shooting, the rebels began to collect stores of corn, olives and wine, and to load the donkeys and mules, while the women wept over the bodies or attempted to drag them into their houses. Again I was kicked: "Give us a hand here—unless you want to join that heap of stinking carrion." It was true that the dead stank; I had never realized before that blood had a smell.

Last of all they set fire to the village: but like everything else they did, this was done with a haphazard violence. Many of the houses did not catch, just as many of the bleeding bodies in the village square were not really dead. There were about forty strangers, and seven-

39

teen of us children: fourteen boys and three girls. We were told to march, and those of us who hesitated were cursed at and struck. Once again I was reminded of the way the peasants herded their animals.

We went up a path into the mountains, and the rebels gleefully broke open a carton of cigarettes which they had looted from the store and tossed the packets to each other. They were laughing and joking together, with the gaiety of peasants at a 'panagyri'—a religious feast—who have come out of church and can now give themselves over to a night of drinking, singing and dancing. At some time I had been allowed to pull on some clothes and a pair of shoes, but as we mounted higher and higher, so that the moon seemed to sway over our heads like an enormous orange lantern from which the pale ribbon of our pathway shimmered gently downwards, my whole body was shaken by shiver on shiver. Was I cold? Or was it shock? Many of the children were crying, and one, a fat boy called Phœbus (it would be hard to think of a more inappropriate name), kept collapsing on to the stones with a feeble wail, his hands clutched to his chest, until a kick, a blow or a shout made him stumble onwards. Even then I knew that he would not last for long.

Of the three girls, two kept up a ceaseless keening. They were sturdy and tough, but they were also plain, with flat faces, small eyes, and incipient moustaches, so that I could not guess on what principle they had been chosen by the rebels. Perhaps someone had been reminded of the girl he had left behind in the village he would never see again, of a mother, of a sister. The third girl, who was called Stella, was only fourteen, and she was the beauty of the village. She had, even at that early age, the withdrawn gravity which is so often found among women who are conscious of a more than exceptional beauty, and it did not desert her now. Her face was expressionless, as she walked ahead of me, and behind two boys, of eleven or twelve, whose arms were thrown over each other's shoulders. She had a scarf tied over her head—not a peasant-scarf, but one with the Acropolis printed on it, cheap dye on cheap rayon—a Mykonos skirt, a blouse and green cardigan, and, astonishingly, a brown leather handbag. I had always thought of her as frail, with her narrow wrists and small pink hands, so rare among the girls I had met, her slender thighs and her almost boyish torso, on which the breasts had only just begun to appear. But she never flagged; she never put a foot wrong; and unlike the other two girls, one of whom was wearing a pair of wooden slippers which incessantly clattered and slipped off, she had got into walking-shoes.

At last, high up in the mountains, in a region overgrown with scrub to which I had never penetrated before, we came to a cave where, it was obvious, the men had slept before. Georgos, who was one of those who had been riding on a mule, descended, and stretched himself, a hand pressed to the small of the back, in the gesture of a peasant who had tired himself out with hacking at olive-trees all day. On mule-back, seated sideways after the manner of Greeks, with his massive profile silhouetted against the moon, he had looked the kind of man who might lead a revolution to success. But dismounted, standing there on his thin, too-short, slightly bandy legs and poking his neck from side to side as a donkey does when one has taken off its halter, he seemed a pathetic figure. When he spoke to his men, his voice had the unnatural stridency of a schoolmaster who is afraid that he may not be able to keep a class in order. Normally his voice was not unmusical, but with the kind of soft refinement with which I was familiar from both my brother-in-law and many of my Greek teachers at the

41

Lycée. He had an enormous moustache up to which he would raise his girlish hands (his little-finger nails were also grown to prodigious lengths) as one touches the handle-bars of a bicycle from time to time when one is free-wheeling down a hill.

That night we were given nothing to eat, and we did not dare to go near to the fire which the men had built up. Instead we huddled together in a little group, like sheep being taken to market in the back of a truck, some of us shivering silently, some whimpering and snivelling and some whispering together, either in false bravado or in apprehension. "What will they do with us?" "Oh, I expect they'll eat us, when they run out of food!" I answered: at which Phœbus, who had been lying curled up, like an over-large fœtus, his thumb plugged into his mouth, let out a wail of anguish. "Don't be silly, I'm only joking." "We must escape," Lakis, a boastful and domineering youth whom I had always detested, announced, as he drew on a cigarette. He, alone, had a packet of cigarettes on him. "Give us a draw," another boy asked. "It's my last but one," Lakis said, inhaling the smoke and then blowing it out through his nostrils: but he held the cigarette momentarily to the boy's lips.

"What do they want us for?" The original question renewed itself.

"A ransom."

Lakis scoffed: "Some ransom! What ransom would they get for us? We're not rich capitalists."

"They might use us to get some of their comrades released."

"That's more like it. Cut off a toe or an ear, and post it to the Government in an envelope." My joke, which was not entirely a joke, produced yet another anguished wail from Phœbus.

42

A sombre youth called Memmus, whose head had been shaved either as a punishment at school, or because it was infested with nits, or even perhaps in a deliberate effort to accentuate the monastic ascetism of his long, bony face, said with solemn precision: "They'll take us over the border, that's what they'll do."

There was dismay, astonishment, scepticism.

"Well," he retorted, "don't you read the papers? That's what they do. To Serbia, or Roumania, or Bulgaria."

"Bulgaria would be worst," someone said inconsequentially.

"But why, why, why?" others demanded simultaneously.

The monk-like youth fixed his large, red-rimmed eyes on them: "It's obvious," he said. "They'll need soldiers when they return. Won't they?"

The men round the fire were becoming wilder and wilder. Flagons of wine, also looted from our village, had been travelling back and forth between them, the cave was full of the reek of burning mutton, and now someone had begun to play the mouth-organ while three or four voices bawled out a song. Some men lay outstretched, their arms behind their heads, some sat against the side of the cave, the firelight splashing up on to their unshaven faces, some lolled in each other's arms. Mingling with the song one could hear the sound of bones being crunched or cracked open, hiccoughing and belching, and cries of "To your health, Manolis! To your health, my lad! To your health, Aristides!" as they swigged from the flagons, throwing back their heads. From time to time a single figure, or a group, would stagger out into the darkness that was not really darkness, but only seemed to be so because of the enormous fire. Georgios, their leader, did not join in all this conviviality.

He lay on one side, so close to the flames that one wondered how he could bear their heat, his head supported on an elbow while he gnawed at a bone. But even this action he seemed to perform with a daintiness that was almost effeminate.

Suddenly one of the figures that had tottered in out of the darkness, a giant of a man whose blond hair fell over a forehead that was low and immensely wide, came towards our group. "Where's the girl? Where's that girl?" he demanded in a drunken growl.

"Save me! The Lord save me! Save me!" one of the two plump girls began to squawk, beating her arms up and down as though they were wings, and dashing, at the crouch, from one corner of the bottom of the cave to the other. Her companion had thrown herself on the earth, pressing her breasts, her face and her knees into it, as though she could thus become invisible.

"You—get up! Come on!" He pointed at the girl who was called Stella. She gazed back at him, neither insolently nor apprehensively, but with her usual air of cold withdrawal. "Come on!"

Suddenly the solemn monk-youth leapt up between them, his thumbs thrust into his canvas-belt in a pathetic attempt at defiance. "Leave her——" He did not complete the phrase, as he reeled against the slithery wall of the cave and then slumped to his knees, one hand raised to his mouth while the other shot up to ward off the second blow which never came. He began to spit, saying: "Look what you've done. . . . Look . . . my tooth . . ." as though he were still at school and, during a rag, someone had been too rough.

The blond giant caught the girl and dragged her to her feet. She made no sound, but her mouth was slightly parted, and her frightened eyes, glittering points in the white face, shot hither and thither. She made one effort to free herself, but he gripped her by the hair, tugging her head downwards and under an arm. His fellows, who had only now turned round to watch him, began to shout out jeering obscenities, and one or two even followed him out into the darkness, either to await their turn or to see what would happen.

We waited, united in a silent horror, excitement and shame. I felt my scalp tingle, my pulse race: I thought that, being so near to me, all the others must hear the extraordinary beating of my heart. After many minutes, Lakis got to his feet, and I followed him. "Where are you going?" someone demanded. "To piss," he retorted coolly. "Stay where you are." "Do you want the whole cave to stink?" I could not help admiring his courage. "Let them go out. Andrea or Niko will see that they don't get up to any tricks," Georgios said, flinging a bone on to the fire where it sizzled and spat. He picked at his teeth with one of those lance-like nails.

Lakis went to a bush and I to another: as we made water, we both peered around us. One of the guards sat on a rock, his sheep-skin coat thrown over his shoulders and his rifle gleaming between his out-thrust legs like a rod of silver. The other guard was pacing back and forth, muttering to himself: a dwarf of a man, with a pendulous belly and tiny feet, encased in pointed boots which came up to below the knee. Not a Macedonian, I discovered later, but a Cretan who had escaped while being taken to Germany for forced labour at the end of the occupation. Cradled in the hollow of a greyish-brown rock, that shot up, at a tilt, towards the moon like some enormous decayed molar, a dark shape was groaning rhythmically. At first we assumed that it was the giant and Stella, but when Lakis tiptoed over and peered into a darkness that had the illusory sheen of water, he came back to whisper: "It's the poor devil who lost the tips of

45

his fingers." Somewhere in the village the stumps had been bandaged, and gibbering and half-fainting he had been hauled up on a mule: he was a boy, probably no older than Stelio.

The guards were watching us, but as friends, not as enemies. The dwarf came over: "Who's the girl?" he asked in a squeaky voice.

"She's from our village."

He continued alternately to question us and to wish he were in the giant's shoes, with a rough, yet comradely, frankness that verged on the obscene. We might have been having a conversation under the dusty plane-trees in our village square, and the familiarity calmed me, no less than the quiet and coolness out there after the pandemonium, smell and stuffiness inside the cave. What was happening to Stella no longer seemed to be terrible; and I could even think of the lopped fingers of the groaning youth without any nausea.

Suddenly the giant loomed up from behind some bushes, fumbling at his buttons and then brushing his hair off his forehead with one of his vast, clumsy hands. The dwarf guard called out to him—"Well, how was it, Manolis?"—his voice shrilly see-sawing, in his excitement. Manolis said nothing, beyond cursing as he caught his foot and almost fell over, both arms flung outwards as though to grapple with some invisible opponent. He went into the cave, and we heard what sounded like the baying of hounds.

The dwarf went, gingerly, over to the bushes, and the other guard trailed behind us. I passed the dwarf, and he let me do so, to my surprise, so that had I then thought of it I could have had a sporting chance of making my escape. But at that moment I was impelled only by those mixed motives of pity, duty and morbid curiosity which draw people to an accident.

Stella was lying curled up, as Phœbus had lain in the cave, her knees almost touching her chin, so silent and still that I assumed, in horror, that she was dead. I ran to her, but when I put out a hand I was conscious of an eye looking at me fixedly, like a rabbit's when one takes it from the snare, through a dark, clotted fringe of hair. Suddenly she screamed, as though waking from a nightmare, and kicked with her legs. "Go away! Go away!" she began to sob, drumming with her hands on the earth, and the four of us retreated behind the bush. The dwarf said: "Poor girl!" The other said: "She'll learn." Lakis surprised me by putting in: "I could do with a slice of that myself," in a cool, impudently grown-up tone. It was what, with shame, I had been thinking myself; but I could never have said so. "Couldn't we all!" the taller guard laughed. "I had a woman in the village, but she must have been a grandmother. . . ." The obscenities passed back and forth, and I thought: Lies, lies, lies, the usual peasant lies. I felt superior, even to Lakis.

All at once the giant thrust between us, went to the bush, and threw a hunk of meat over it, at the girl, as one might to a dog. She was once again completely motionless and silent, and even when he growled at her "Eat! Go on! Eat!" she remained as she was. He stood a little apart from us, swaying on his heels, his hands in his pockets, while he stared up at the moon. From time to time he hissed between his teeth, as dancers do in Greece in order to keep away the evil spirits. We none of us said anything. Then, pulling his right hand out of his pocket, and once again using it as though it were a comb to brush his hair off his forehead, he slouched towards the bush. The dwarf caught his arm: "Leave her! She's had enough! She's had enough, Manolis!" but he let go when the giant turned round

47

with a curse that seemed to be only a magnified version of that previous hissing.

He disappeared and we waited: then the dwarf tip-toed to the bush, the other guard, Lakis, I. We heard the sound of clumsy endearments: "My pigeon . . . my little doll . . . my spinach-pie . . .": the last surely the most absurd of all. I peered through the bracken, going down on one knee, while a thorn grazed my elbow. He was kneeling beside her, and her body was thrown across his, her breasts on his lap and her forehead apparently touching the earth, though the dark hair that fell forward as a screen made it impossible to see. One arm was around his neck, and the whole posture gave one the illusion that she was trying to drag herself out of some quick-sand which kept sucking her downwards. Suddenly she jerked up, tossing her hair away from her face on which the tears glittered momentarily in the moonlight as though they were melting flakes of snow. She gave a strange, groaning cry. Then she clutched him to her, her left fist pressing into the small of his back, while she put her lips to the palm of the large, calloused hand that lay on his knee, open.

We drew away, we said nothing. I felt dazed, as I had felt during those terrible hours in the village; I felt a weary elation; I felt disgusted and shocked. Lakis and I returned to the cave, and though we sat side by side, for a long time neither of us spoke to the other. Someone whispered: "Well, what happened?" Lakis tossed his head upwards, as Greeks do when they wish to indicate no. One of the other girls squirmed against me, with a kind of voluptuous concern, her sturdy muscular body seeming to go soft and dissolve. "Is she all right?" I stared in front of me. "Is she all right?" she repeated.

"Oh, shut up!"

Eventually, one by one, we dropped off to sleep. Round the fire our captors had already begun to snore, except for the dwarf who, relieved by one of his fellows, was now sitting on his haunches, alternately gnawing at a bone, gulping wine and belching. He had drawn off his boots, and his stockings were steaming. The stench of so many unwashed bodies in that airless cavern must have been terrible; but in those days I was so used to the smells of dirt, manure and sheep, in which I had been brought up, that I was not concerned. My whole body was aching, as though after a night of ceaseless pleasure; and I had those sensations of lethargy and self-disgust which follow such occasions. I thought of my mother and father, of the village, of our house, of Stelio: but, in panic, I discovered that I could feel nothing at all—I might have been thinking of the characters and places in a book I had been reading. Then I forced myself to visualize that terrible scene which, since then, I have so often tried to force myself not to visualize: the growing weight of Stelio's body on mine, that warm, sticky trickling. But even that left me unmoved.

I took off my jacket and made a pillow of it under my head. In one of its pockets I had a penknife and a box of matches, and by the next morning both these things were missing. I never discovered who took them, though I always suspected Lakis. For a long time I lay on my side, watching the dwarf. Like Georgios, he squatted so near the fire that one expected his bushy eyebrows to shrivel up, his wax-like blob of a nose to melt, and his fine, dry red hair to crackle into a blaze. He had taken out one of those strings of amber beads, a relic of Turkish days, with which Greeks play to amuse themselves. From time to time, there was a rustle and a dry click, as a bead was passed through his little hands, all the fingers of which were exactly the same length, except for the thumb, which seemed to grow out from the wrist.

During the days that followed we walked without ceasing, keeping to the mountain-tracks in order to avoid being seen. When I returned to Salonica and was interrogated by a long-nosed young Englishman who had recently come out to Greece, supposedly as a member of the British Consulate Staff, but in fact as an expert in Slavonic languages, I remember he asked me: " Well, were they kind to you?"

"Oh, yes," I said, "very kind."

He did not like that answer. "Didn't they ill-treat you?"

"Oh, yes. They ill-treated us."

He shrugged his shoulders, put down a pencil that was as sharp as his blue nose, and turned to his Greek colleague to say something in English: I suppose 'This man is a half-wit'. How was he to know, coming fresh from the School of Slavonic Studies, that in Greece to be kind and to be brutal are not incompatible. How often one sees someone kick out at a mongrel and then stoop down to fondle it; cuff a child over the side of the head and at once smother it in kisses. To me there had been nothing strange in Manolis' tenderness to Stella after he had raped her; there was nothing strange in the weeks that followed, in being alternately cursed at like an animal and addressed like a human being, starved and fed, commanded and coaxed, struck and caressed. Helen often used to say that the Greek character was explicable only in terms of mediæval humours.

There was much cruelty, but none of it was systematic; few things are systematic in Greece, cruelty least of all. As a punishment, one of the boys would be tied to a tree, where he was supposed to remain, upright, without drink or food, while we all slept. But after an hour someone would release him, and as like as not, he would be given one of the cigarettes which the rest of us so much coveted. Phœbus, who had succumbed to a violent dysentery would at one moment be cursed, jeered at and clouted for being a disgusting pig; but at the next moment, half-fainting, he would be lifted on to a mule. In short, we were treated as the peasants have always treated their animals and each other.

Soon we captives had divided ourselves into three separate groups. First, there were those who had, from whatever motive, entirely thrown in their lot with their captors: Lakis, for example, who had been appointed our overseer and was treated by the rebels as one of themselves; a stupid, jolly tough called Aris who, having apparently forgotten about his butchered father and brothers, was in love with the romantic notion of himself as a bandit, toppling over the society to which he felt he had so few obligations; and Stella, who had adroitly transferred herself from Manolis, a magnificent specimen but without power, to the puny Georgos who was able to keep her for his use alone, and so saved her from the others. Secondly, there were those, like myself, whom detestation of the rebels kept from any active collaboration, but whom prudence likewise kept from any active defiance. Thirdly, there were three youths, of whom the monk-like boy was one, who showed an admirable if unwise refusal ever to compromise. These last made it clear from the beginning that they were going to escape; one managed to slip away one night, in a mist, and a second, after being starved and beaten and tied up in a sack for his first attempt, eventually got away when only two men were on guard over us, the others having set off on a foray to a village. After that the monk alone was left of them. His face and body were always covered in swellings and bruises, which showed the violent colours of putrescence, vivid mauves and purples and arsenic greens, on his grey skin. Where the tooth had been knocked out there was a gap over which the lacerated lip stuck out like a grimy frill. He had become pitifully thin, as had Phœbus: the one because he was so often given no food as a punishment, and the other because any food he ate was at once painfully evacuated.

One by one the collaborators began to join in the raids on isolated farm-houses or on villages that were no more than a rash of hovels in a crease of the hills. Lakis was the first, and he returned, flaunting a wrist-watch, a pistol which must have first been used in the War of Independence, and a vivid American batik-shirt, no doubt a present from some relative in the States. Aris was the second. He had gone on this raid, but had taken no part in it, and had returned, his freckled peasant face drawn, yellow and covered in small blisters of sweat over the nose and forehead, as though he had just vomited. But like a dog which has looked on while another dog has worried sheep, he could not now resist the craving to take part in a destruction which none the less filled him with disgust and self-loathing. Soon he was obviously enjoying it as much as, if not more than, any of the others.

Inevitably, from time to time, someone was wounded or killed. A village was better guarded than had been expected; or a detachment of soldiers happened to be in the vicinity; or the inhabitants had drilled and organized themselves and were heavily armed. If the expedition had been a success, it meant that we had bread to eat, perhaps even a bone to gnaw, or a cigarette at which to draw before it was passed on to someone else. If the expedition had been a failure, there would be a sullen brutality in the behaviour of our captors which would continue until their fortunes changed.

My town-shoes soon wore through, and I had to bind

my feet in rags to protect them from the jagged stones up and down which we had to scramble. Others who were wearing peasant-shoes of sturdy leather soled with rubber from old tyres (ironically, in the past I had always disdained such foot-wear) were more fortunate than I. Our clothes became ragged, and showed stains of meat, grease and earth. All of us were infested with lice, and as I think back now the recollection of stripping in the weak autumn sunlight and then scouring my clothes and my body, fills me with horror. At the time this seemed the least of my tribulations: a Greek peasant is no more surprised to see lice on his person than a maggot in one of his apples. Where thorns had scratched me, I, like many of the others, found that, instead of healing, the places came up into inflamed ridges which itched and throbbed alternately. Painful cracks appeared at the corners of my mouth, and my eyes, which perpetually watered, would be stuck together when I awoke in the morning. I had dreams such as I have never experienced since: sometimes of horror, but more often of luxury and splendour, of immense banquets, houses that were palaces, long beaches stretching away glittering and empty under the sun, express trains, liners, aeroplanes. Even during the day, as we trudged up and down the mountain slopes, my mind would become dazed with such fantasies which acquired all the hard brilliance of hallucinations.

Phœbus became worse and worse. He was strapped on to a mule, and as he jolted along, whimpered, muttered and cried out occasionally "Mummy! Mummy! Mummy!" He had attached himself to me— God knows why, since he filled me with revulsion. "Spiro! Spiro!" he would call, if I ever fell behind in order to rest, to chat or to relieve myself. "Don't leave me! Stay with me! Stay with me!" He was too weak to ride the animal; too weak to climb off it when his illness demanded; too weak to talk except in those agonized cries that had little more than the force of a whisper, or to weep more than a few, burning tears that rolled slowly down his cheeks. That night he lay in my arms, nestling under my chin with one thumb plugged into his mouth: the stench was unbearable, and yet I was, for the first time, consumed by pity for him. He was so plain and so stupid: so obviously the mother's darling. I tried to think of the life he would have led: respectable, narrow, censorious, useless. No doubt surrounded to the end of his days by women, who would bully and cosset him and shield him from disasters like this. I stroked his forehead, and found it burning.

Now he was delirious, muttering about some clothes which his mother had told him to wear or not to wear; about a lesson during which he had been accused of cribbing; about a visit of his grandmother, some oranges, a torch. All at once he gripped me, the saliva trickling out of his mouth on to my hand: "Spiro, am I—am I going to die? Am I? Am I?"

"No, of course not. No. No."

But when I awoke the next morning he was stiff on my lap, one finger curled into the lapel of my coat so that I had difficulty in removing it.

Everyone shrank away, and pretended not to see, as we made preparations for the day's march before us. I, too, went on with the loading of the donkey which was my charge, as though nothing had happened. But my hands were shaking, and my mouth was as dry as when, out of hunger, I gobbled the unripe blackberries that we often found along our path. I had found to my horror that one of my sleeves was saturated with some kind of nameless discharge, and could not decide whether to abandon the coat, giving way to my squeamishness, or to continue to wear it as a protection against the growing cold. One by one, with rough shouts and slappings, the donkeys and mules were persuaded to totter up the mountainside under their swaying loads. An old man, who had been one of Phœbus' chief tormentors, stepped across the piled circle of ash where our fire had been, and looked down at the little body, fingering his droopy grey moustache.

"What are you going to do about this?"

I went on with doing up a strap, as though he had not addressed me.

"Well?" he demanded. "You're not going to leave the poor bastard out like this, are you, for the animals and birds to get at? Aren't you going to give him a Christian burial?" He was a man filthier than all the others, on whom the dirt seemed to be crusted, and he never spoke without repeated obscenities and blasphemies, though he rarely spoke at all. Even his own comrades disliked him, and called him 'The Boar'— because of the two yellow tusks on either side of his mouth, his small, pale-blue eyes, and his pink prick-ears. "Go on, dig a bloody hole for him, if you've any sense of bloody decency. Go on!" He shouted to another boy, Makis, who had become my best friend: "And you!"

There was no spade, but with a flint Makis began to scratch away at the earth, sitting down on the ground, his legs crossed, while the old man stood over him. I found an iron stake, and gouged and tore at the soil with that. We did not dig deep, but even that exertion, in our state of fatigue and semi-starvation, saturated our clothes with sweat. "More, more! Go on, you bastards!" the old man grunted at us. At last he was satisfied. "All right, put it in! Put the poor bastard in the bloody hole!"

It was like lifting some construction of wire and plaster: one expected that, at a jolt, the body would break up and crumble.

Suddenly the old man went down on his knees, pulling off the frayed black cap which sat, like a charred muffin, square on his head, and shouted at us: "Kneel! Kneel! Have you no respect for the dead?"

We knelt, and with us the two plump girls, one of whom now feared she was pregnant, the dwarf, and Manolis. The old man began to rattle off the last prayer for the dead, mispronouncing certain words and omitting others, so that the effect would have been comic in any less ghastly context, and from time to time clearing his throat and spitting a blob of phlegm sideways and away from the grave.

"Everlasting memory," we murmured. "The earth be light . . . Everlasting . . . memory . . . earth . . . light . . ." The words, like drops of water, now fell singly, now ran together in a heavy trickle. The old man rose with a groan, dusting his knees:

"Cover him up!" he commanded. "Cover up the poor bastard!" With our feet and hands we began to scrape the earth back; then the old man trod it down, and that, more than anything else, filled me with horror. I wanted to cry out, and one of the two girls did in fact cry out, biting on the back of her plump right hand, which, once so clean, was now as grubby and scored as a gypsy's.

All that day I could eat nothing, and I did not wish to speak. Our captors were excited because we were now nearing the Yugoslavian border, and were supposed, at a village some ten miles distant, to pick up the guide who was to lead us across. They joked and bawled out songs, and spoke of the life which awaited them. In their ignorance they imagined that they were entering a Land of Promise: no work, unlimited food and drink, women, soft beds, sleep. Georgios tried to check these fantasies, for he knew of the reality that awaited them; but he had no effect. It was as it used to be when I tried to stop Stelio in his grandiose plans for my future, or when I myself was carried away and then had to remind myself, 'Things are not like that, things do not get better, things will always be the same, you will always be poor.'

When we at last bivouacked for the night, I went and lay far away from the others, and strangely no one told me to come closer. Once again I could have escaped, had I been in the mood to do so. I covered myself with some sacks, smelling of the raw meat which had been carried in them, and then with the rug that I placed under the wooden crupper of the donkey of which I had the charge. But still I shivered. Twenty yards away the guard alternately coughed and yawned. I had never felt so conscious before of the loss of my home and my family; of the squalor, uncertainty and discomfort in which I was living; of my hopelessness, and loneliness, and grief. How would this journey end? Would we ever cross the border? And, if we did, what would become of us? Like Georgios I had no illusions that what lay beyond it was much better than what lay this side of it: probably things were the same, or worse, or much worse.

Makis came towards the spot where I was sleeping, bare-footed, but wearing his trousers and shirt, as we all did at night, as a protection from the cold. He went to a bush and stood in its shadow to relieve himself. Then he wandered over to me.

"I can't sleep."

"Nor I."

"Poor Phœbus. Well, at least we buried him."

"I expect that some animal will dig him up again," I answered brutally.

"Oh, no!" He was a shepherd-boy, with a flat, triangular face on which the down had just begun to show, sturdy legs, and hands on which the nails were bitten close. He squatted on the ground beside me, as the shepherds do for hours, balancing on their haunches, while they watch their sheep. "How do you think this will end?" he asked.

"Who knows?"

"Do you want to go over there?"

"Of course not."

"Do you think it will be better there? That's what they say. They say that——"

"Rubbish."

"I'm frightened. What's to become of us?"

Suddenly he slipped under the sacks and the blanket. "I'm cold," he said; and his teeth chattered, his mouth to my ear. I felt his body against mine, his hands clutching at me. It was as if he were drowning.

We clung to each other, face to face, knee pressed rigidly to knee, while gradually the warmth returned to our filthy, shuddering, aching bodies, in slow, surging wave on wave.

When we arrived at the village where we were supposed to pick up the guide, we found that it had been burnt to the ground and that there were only a few women and children left. From the hill-side this village looked exactly as our own village had looked when we had cast hurried, backward glances at it while goaded on by our captors; and the tales we heard from the impassive-faced or wildly sobbing women were of the same useless acts of savagery and violence. But in this case, not the Communists, but the Nationalists were the perpetrators. It amused me to hear our captors burst out into outraged blasphemies: "The swine! The swine! May the Lord shrivel the guts of the godless bastards!" Everywhere there was a nauseating stench of burning.

Many of the women begged the rebels to take their children with them, lamenting: "What life can we offer them here? How will they eat?" The older and stronger children were picked out to accompany us: some of them gravely solemn, as though they had not yet woken from the daze into which the previous day's violence had stunned them; some of them eager, boastful and over-excited; a few of them snivelling, the backs of their hands pressed to their snotty noses, or their snotty noses pressed to their mothers' bellies. Many of these families spoke Greek haltingly or not at all, being composed, not of Slavs (we are always told in Greek schools that there are no Slavs in Greek Macedonia), but of what the Greeks have decided among themselves to call Slavophones.

With these puny, ragged additions to our party, we continued to trudge towards the border. There was an atmosphere of nervousness and suppressed excitement which seemed to envelop us all like a thundery cloud: occasionally detonating in the bawling of a song, a quarrel about something as trivial as whether to skirt to the left or the right of a boulder, and rowdy practical jokes—the dwarf, when he was squatting to relieve himself behind a bush, was pelted with stones and bits of rotten stick. Georgios looked sullen and morose, and spent the journey in whispered confabulations with Lakis and two members of the gang in whom he used to confide. At the village we had heard rumours of a strongly guarded frontier, and of patrols that were on watch even in the most inaccessible and precipitous regions. Makis and I had decided that it was now, or never, that we must escape.

Lakis pointed down. "That's the stream of which they told us. We must be near, mustn't we?"

"Not so much noise! Quiet, quiet!" Georgios admonished us, as he had been doing for the last few hours. We went on, in silence now, except for the crackle of a twig, the sudden grind and scuffle as a foot dislodged a cataract of scree, a cough, a whimper from one of the children, a whispered "Where are we? Where are we?"

Suddenly a rifle crackled from the hill-side which rose up on our left, and at once we dived into the under-growth, pushing our way through bushes which tore at the rags in which we were covered, at our faces and bare arms. Every so often, someone would trip with a mut-tered blasphemy. A voice was hallooing as the shepherds halloo to each other, from hill-top to hill-top. Then a whistle blew, piercing through the damp autumn air. "Run! Run!" Georgios cried. We had at last broken out of the undergrowth on to a plateau, and below us we could see figures in uniform. "Run!" he shrieked. "Run, damn you all!" Suddenly, upwards from below, there was a rat-tat-tat, and little, faraway umbrellas opened up, grey against the dun soil. The blond giant leapt as though he were breasting the tape in a race, and then fell, with a prolonged wail, his hands to his groin. I threw myself down, and Makis threw himself down beside me, our faces pressed to the soil which seemed to breathe a bitter, sulphurous stench up into our nostrils. When, gingerly, I raised my head, I saw that Georgios had pulled off his shirt and had tied it to the shepherd's staff which he always carried with him. Brandishing this before him, he screamed: "On! On! On!" The rest of the party hesitated, and then surged forward. Again there was a rat-tat-tat. The earth seemed to shake as though an enormous electric-drill had been plunged into its side, and the air shook with it. People were fall-ing, but it was impossible to tell whether for protection or because they were wounded or killed. Georgios shrieked at them again, waved an arm, and stumbled on. Lakis was only a step behind him, Aris was on his left. Lakis suddenly broke away, ducking behind a rock, from the base of which a splinter shot up into the air, as one sometimes sees a cicada jump in summer. Georgios continued, then faltered, dropped his banner, and returned, arms outspread in panic, his mouth a black hole. Aris did not stop. Suddenly Georgios screamed, and doubled over, screaming again and again and again and clutching his stomach, like a woman in childbirth. Something scarlet was dangling from his mouth. He spun round and round, kicking the stones so that they clattered about him, and then the screaming ended. Aris was still running, on and on, and though we never knew for certain, we supposed that he, alone of them all, reached the other side.

Most of the gang had died with their leader, and of us from the village only seven remained. Among those killed were the monk-youth and one of the plump girls —the one who had thought she was pregnant. It was only after long interrogation that Makis, Stella, Lakis, I and the other survivors succeeded in persuading the Greek soldiers who found us that we were the victims, not the allies, of the rebels. Ironically Lakis had been the first whose story was believed, and Stella the second. After having been cursed, kicked and shoved as brutally as in those first days of our captivity, we were now spoiled, cosseted, and stuffed with food. I devoured a whole tin of American bully-beef, washed down with ouzo, and at once had to go off into the bushes to vomit. Then I lay down on the ground, my face clammy and my shirt drenched in an icy sweat. Suddenly I began to cry. It was an involuntary action, like the vomiting, and one no less painful, as sob after sob shook my whole frame. Near at hand, as I lay with my face in the cool grass, I could hear Stella talking to a handsome young lieutenant from Kolonaki, the Mayfair of Athens:

". . . I can't tell you what we suffered. Of course for us girls it was worst of all. Often it seemed as if only God was between us and—the most terrible things. It was a miracle."

The lieutenant had a pink and white face and a little auburn moustache which he stroked as he listened to her, making sympathetic "Tchk—Tchk" noises between his small teeth. . . .

. . . That's someone at the door. Oh, it's Kiki! It must be Kiki. But why has she come back so soon?

"Darling! "

"Yes." She comes into the room.

"Back so early? Why? What's the matter? What is it? "

"You might at least say that you're pleased to see me."

"Well, of course I'm pleased to see you."

She waddles over to the bed, and puts her lips first to my forehead, then to my cheek, and then to my mouth. She grunts contentedly, slipping over on to the bed while the basket she's been carrying in one hand falls to the floor. Once she broke four eggs like that. It's odd that she should be more passionate now than she ever was before she expected the baby, and that I should find her so much more exciting. . . . I slip a hand into her blouse, and a button flies off. "Take care, take care," she tries to say: but she can't say it properly, because my nose is squashing her nose flat.

Suddenly she pulls herself off me: "Have you got a temperature? " she asks.

"No, I don't think so."

"But you're wringing wet."

"I had a dream."

She knows about my dreams. "Poor darling! " she exclaims, putting out a hand to brush the hair away from my forehead. "It must be wretched for you to be here alone all day—with nothing to do but have nightmares."

"No more wretched than for you to have to work for that bastard."

"Oh, he's not bad, really he isn't. He's invited us to a party—if you're well enough."

I know those Pavlakis parties: too much food, too many people in that Bayswater flat which smells as if someone had just been ironing nappies in it; Pavlakis bragging to his English guests about his Alexander Certificate, his work as a Liaison Officer in Cairo during the war, or the growth of his business, and then going over to one of his Greek guests to shake his head solemnly and mutter about Enosis and British bad faith; Mrs. Pavlakis recounting the story of how they've had to sack their maid because she helps herself to the marmalade without asking; the two daughters, as white, cold and uninteresting as blancmange; the cocky son, whose nails look as if they were in mourning for one of the motor-cycles he's always smashing up. . . . God!

"Thanks, dear. That's a party I shall miss."

"It's their silver wedding. That's how I got away. He's asked me to go to Harrods to buy something for his wife. So I jumped on the 39 bus, and decided to come home to get your lunch."

"What did you buy her?"

"Oh, that brooch—do you remember, that brooch we saw together. The opal brooch. She's also an October birthday. You must remember it. We hadn't any money, and I was so afraid that you were going to steal it for me!" That, of course, had been a joke; but I really think that I got her worried, as I began to elaborate a plan for her to go in and talk to the assistant while I pocketed the brooch. Kiki is never sure what I may not do next—with good reason.

Now I'm furious. "Well, why should that old cow have it? No, this is too much. The brooch was meant for you. It was for you, Kiki! I wanted it for you!"

My indignation delights her and she heaves herself right on to the bed, slipping her little feet out of court-shoes that are none the less too small for her—Greek toes always have a crumpled look, as if they needed pressing. She laughs into my ear: "Silly! How do you suppose we can pay forty-five pounds for a brooch, when we haven't even got the money for the gas?"

"We'll get it," I say.

"I wish I knew how."

"Anyway she won't like it, she won't appreciate it. Neither will he. She'd rather have a string of cultured pearls which she can pretend are the real thing. Like that picture he will insist is by El Greco—or his gold-plated watch. Appearances, appearances—nothing else matters to us Greeks. Old Pavlakis would carry round an empty camera-case for show. And so would your father," I add viciously. "If it weren't that he can afford to buy a dozen Leicas."

"I telephoned to Mummy this morning," she says.

"Oh, yes?"

I don't dislike Mummy nearly so much as Daddy: but for him, I could soon flatter and coax the old cow into doing what I wanted. She was attracted by me from the first, I know that, and since she could not have me for herself, she unconsciously decided, as mothers so often unconsciously decide, that her daughter would have me instead. But having made the present, she at once regretted parting with it; and then she began to try to persuade herself that really the present was trash and unworthy of a girl like Kiki. She's a silly and shallow woman, but not at all unkindly.

"She's promised to send us something, but Daddy mustn't know. She's not even supposed to speak to me. It's hard for her, terribly hard, poor thing—having to account for every penny."

"Two or three less cakes at Fortnum's every day, and she could save something for us." Like most middle-aged Greek women, Kiki's mother has taken, not to drink, but to what she calls 'pastries'.

Kiki sighs and looks unhappy. "I thought Daddy would have come round long ago. Particularly with the baby coming."

"He will, don't you worry." But I have begun to doubt this.

"I'm so sick of his telling me that I've made my bed and now I must lie on it."

"If we don't pay the instalment soon, you may have to lie on the floor."

There's a knock at the door, followed by a ring, and the sound of someone whistling 'When Irish Eyes Are Smiling' drearily flat. Kiki begins hurriedly to do up her blouse and pat at her hair with her tiny, podgy hands. Then she gasps, half on the bed and half off it: "Oh, Lord! It must be the milkman. What are we going to do? He'll have to be paid."

"Sh!" I clap a hand over her mouth. "Don't move, don't make a sound," I whisper. "He may think we're out. You left a note for him?"

Kiki nods, because she can't talk with my hand still there. Now we can hear Mrs. Mumfitt's voice: ". . . Well, she's out, I know, but he ought to be in. She said he was poorly, that's what she said, when I saw her at the bus-stop, poorly, she said. You can take that as you please . . ." The old bitch gives that laugh of hers which sounds as if ice-cubes were being rattled in a cocktail-shaker: she keeps it for the milkman and old

Colonel Chaloner and any of naughty pussy's 'pranks'—as she refers to peeing on the stairs and things of that kind.

We can't hear what the milkman answers, because like an expensive car he only makes a noise when something is wrong with him—then he groans and grunts: "Ooh! Ooh! This sciatica of mine—it's no joke I tell you," until everyone in the block knows about it.

As soon as we hear Mrs. Mumfitt's door being shut and 'When Irish Eyes Are Smiling' being whistled beneath the window, I give Kiki a push, and in her stockinged feet she tiptoes into the hall. When she comes back, she holds up a milk-bottle.

"That's very odd," she says.

"What's odd?"

"Only one. And I distinctly wrote 'Three, please'. Look!" She holds out a scrap of paper scribbled over with her childish writing. "What can it mean?"

"A mistake."

"Perhaps he knew we were here."

"Perhaps."

"And he wanted to show us that we couldn't have any more milk until we had paid our bill."

"Then why did he leave the bottle."

"Oh, don't you see! He's a nice man, he's always been friendly to us, and so he didn't want to cut us off *completely*. Not at first, at least." She goes on like this for a long time, analysing the milkman's feelings, until I check her irritably: "Look, darling, I'm really not as interested in the milkman as you or Mrs. Mumfitt. And if you're to cook us some lunch before going back to the office, you ought to get started."

She goes into the kitchen, and for a time I hear her singing to herself in that high, clear, slightly shrill voice of hers which is so like a boy's. It's a Greek song—'The

Girl Wants the Sea '. And lying here, I think of Vouliag-meni, the two bays separated from each other by a peeled wand of a beach which, suddenly, at the tip, blossoms into a peninsula, covered with stunted pine-trees under which, at night, one could lie with some girl. . . . Then the bays would be like two clashing half-moons, with the taverns along the coast-road beyond glittering in an arc of stars. One would smell resin, and dust, and salt, and human flesh. One's head would be dizzy from wine and a long day of swimming and physical excitement. . . .

Suddenly the song stops and " Oh, damn! " I hear her exclaim.

" What's the matter? "

" Nothing, nothing."

But already I smell burning.

III

THURSDAY

TO-DAY I feel better, and though both Kiki and Dr. Arthurs have told me that I must on no account go out, here I am, sitting in the deserted Pleasure Gardens. There's a young man opposite my bench digging a bed of chrysanthemums: a displaced person of some kind or other, to judge from that flat face with the high cheek-bones, pale blue eyes and sharp nose. He glances over at me from time to time, and then pulls the corners of his mouth down in a brief grimace, as if he were annoyed by my scrutiny. I have on Irvine's camelhair overcoat from Brooks Brothers, which I suppose will be the next thing I shall have to pawn; I dare say that when he sees me draw my gold cigarette-case and lighter out of its pocket, he decides to himself that I'm a rich dago of some kind. It would surprise him, certainly, if I called out and said: "Look, I once used to do a job like that in a public park. Only I didn't have a green trolley on rubber-wheels, which might have been stolen from the London Clinic, and I didn't have those fancy blue overalls. There was a wheelbarrow, and you had to be careful how you pushed it, otherwise the wheel fell off. It was lucky that it was summer, because I could work barefooted, in nothing but a pair of old army shorts, and that saved my clothes. There was no rucksack which I hung from a tree, with a thermos poking its nose out of it: just a bottle of tepid wine, from which I used to swig when our foreman was looking at a girl instead of at us. . . ."

It was difficult to make anything grow in that park in Salonica. Whatever we planted was either shrivelled up by the sun during the day or trampled down by the couples during the night. The rains dissolved the paths, and we would then tip cinders, carried in buckets on our aching shoulders from a nearby factory, into the cracks and holes. There was shade under the drooping tin-foil foliage of the eucalyptus-trees, but it was a shade sullen with midges, heat and smells of rottenness. In the centre of the park there was a bust of King Otto, around which clustered a number of photographers whose grubby white coats made them look like male-nurses in a provincial Greek hospital. They carried with them wooden boxes on tripods, dragging them about in their developer-stained hands as though they were cumbrous shooting-sticks, while they either bickered and gossiped among themselves or solicited the passers-by. Soldiers lay out asleep on the benches or under the trees; children squatted in the dust and played fretful, lethargic games which involved flicking stones or bits of wood into the air; an old woman knitted what looked like a giant's stocking.

Such was the scene when I first saw Irvine. He came towards us under the trees, taking those small, high, teetering steps which always made it appear as if he were making his way over an invisible ploughed field. He was wearing a seersucker suit, the coat of which rode above his plump rump and the trousers of which revealed a pair of short Greek cotton socks from which hung ravelled ends of rubber. The knot of a knitted silk tie was somewhere under a pointed ear, the tip of which was crusted with dry shaving-cream. Irvine, who was so fastidious about the way in which I dressed, cared nothing about his own appearance. In his hands he had a book which he kept opening and glancing at, as if hurriedly to read a sentence, before he pranced on. Suddenly he saw me, as I wheeled the lurching wheelbarrow diagonally towards him. He stopped; blinked his fair eyelashes; shut the book and quickly made off.

At once my fellow-workers began to jeer and point. "Amerikano! Amerikano!" they shrilled and whooped, falsetto, not because they knew his nationality, but because every foreigner was an American to them now that the Germans had gone. "Stay a moment! What's the hurry? Here—come back! Senta, Signorina! Signorina!"—this last from a youth who had worked as a stoker on an Italian boat. But there was no malice in all this uproar; and had Irvine turned round and retraced his steps, he would at once have been offered a swig of wine or a hot, dry fag.

However, he did not turn round, although he must have heard us. For a time we then discussed him—there is little new to discuss when you spend your whole day hacking at a stretch of baked mud which looks exactly like the stretch of baked mud at which you were hacking the day before—with that mixture of admiration, contempt, affection and envy that Greeks feel for foreigners. His clothes were not impressive, and it is clothes in Greece that usually determine class. But, on the other hand, as a skinny negroid youth piped out, he was doing nothing at half-past eleven in the morning; and, as someone else remarked, he was plump—"I bet he'll have a good dinner to-day!" Soon, the discussion deserted this particular American for Americans in general: with boastful anecdotes of encountering millionaires from Texas or women cabaret-stars from Neâ Yorkê; of meetings in the bedrooms of the Ritz, the Mediterranean or the Astoria Hotel; of tearful good-byes, letters unwritten because of laziness or unposted because of carelessness, addresses lost, dollars recklessly squandered. Everyone spoke of the uncle or cousin " over there " who was urging him to go across; but one had a sick mother, one had still not done his military service, one had worked for the Germans (but really as a spy), one was suspected of Communist sympathies (merely because he had refused to work for the Germans), one was not sure if he would really like America. Did we believe each other? As much, I suppose, as children when they play at Mothers and Fathers. If one is materially poor, it is necessary to be imaginatively rich, if life is to be supportable.

The next day, at exactly the same time, the same figure approached. It halted as before, and looked absently, first upwards at the trees, then down at a hole into which I had just been tipping cinders, and then, as though searching for an acquaintance, in turn at each of us. When the blue eyes met mine, the albino lashes flickered up and down, until with a ballet-like twirl, the whole body spun round in slow motion and folded up on to a bench. Some glasses, heavily horn-rimmed, were taken out of a case, polished on a handkerchief, and eased up and down the bridge of the nose as though being tried, for the first time, at the optician's. The book was opened, one small leg was crossed characteristically high over the other, and the end of the handkerchief was placed between the teeth to be rhythmically sucked.

Comments, many of them falsetto and most of them obscene, were bandied back and forth between us; but when the stranger paid no attention at all, we at last gave up. Not, however, before the negroid youth had called " Johnny! Johnny! " and tapped on his wrist, until a gold pocket-watch was drawn out from inside the crumpled seersucker suit and dangled in the air, splinters of light shooting from it.

When we broke off at midday, the stranger had still not gone. Already I knew that, though he never looked up and pretended to ignore us, he was there because of me: we Greeks have an extraordinary intuition about such things. I sat with the others under the trees, and ate the bread, olives and sheep-cheese which I had brought with me in the morning. But I was careful not to drink as much wine as the others, because I did not wish to fall asleep. One by one, they stretched themselves out, the abandon of their postures lending to even the ugliest of them a certain monumental beauty—they might have been a group of those chipped and dust-defiled statues which litter the basements of Greek museums. Then I got up, sauntered over to the bench next to that where Irvine was seated, and took a cigarette out of the battered tin which I carried in my shorts. I put it to my mouth, and sucked on it unlit, as I scratched at my back. I was aware that the stranger, though his head was still bowed over his book and his handkerchief still dangled from his lips, was none the less casting surreptitious glances at me. I went over to him:

"Have you got a light?" I asked in Greek. But at the same time I held out my cigarette, because I did not suppose that he would understand me.

"Certainly." He brought out one of those cheap German cigarette-lighters, which look like a lipstick-case and usually work so much better than the expensive American or English lighters coveted by Greeks, and flicked away at the wheel unsuccessfully for many seconds. "You try," he said.

The flame came at once.

I held out my tin of cigarettes: "You may not care for these."

72

" No," he said, " I've got used to my Pall Malls. Would you like to try one? "

I smiled and showed him the cigarette I already had: "I can't smoke two at once," I said.

" No, of course not. But keep this one for later."

" Thank you."

" Why don't you sit down? "

He spoke a Greek far more correct than my own: the Greek of elderly professors, men of letters, and the spinsters who spend their lives between the French and the British Institutes in Athens. He was careful to use all the case-endings that are day by day withering and falling away like dead leaves from the tree of our language, however hard the conservative attempt to glue them back. But his accent was terrible.

" What are you reading? " I asked.

" An English poet called William Blake." I peered over his shoulders. " Do you know English? "

" A little," I said in English. " So-and-so "—which is an exact translation of our Greek phrase.

" So-so," he corrected me. He continued to talk to me in Greek.

He asked where I was from, and I told him the lie about being a refugee from Roumania; it was lucky that Roumanian was not one of the many languages that he spoke. " Yes, I could see at once that you were—were of a different class from the others. That's why I watched you." The absurd thing was that one of my fellow workers was, in fact, the youngest ne'er-do-well son of an old and aristocratic Zante family, all the other members of which were either in exile or in prison as collaborators. " How rough they all look! Couldn't you get a better job than this? "

" Can anyone get a job in Greece to-day—without pulling strings? "

"Yes, it's terrible," he agreed. "Really terrible. But for a boy of your—your class and education . . ." He sighed, and chewed away at his handkerchief.

"And you—what do you do?" I asked.

"Oh, I work for a relief organization."

"What kind of organization?"

"We try to help people like you to find jobs here in Greece or—more often—to emigrate."

"Can't you help me to emigrate?" Though I said it with a laugh, he pondered the question seriously, bending forward as he massaged his skin.

"There are so many of you refugees," he said at last. "We have a queue stretching almost from here to Athens. And what with everyone having to be screened first by your people and then by ours—oh, it's heart-breaking."

"But you're the boss, aren't you?"

"Yes, of my little organization. But that's such a tiny part of the whole. And then being financed by the Catholic Church—well, that makes it harder for us here —though of course easier in Italy."

"Do you live in Salonica?"

"No, in Athens."

"I bet you live in Kolonaki."

"Well, as a matter of fact, I do." He sounded surprised. "How do you know that?"

"Don't all the foreigners live there? Except those that go out to Psychiko and Kifissia."

"You seem to know Athens well."

"Oh, I've been there only once. . . . Have you got a car?"

"No."

"I thought every American had a car."

"Oh, we have an office car—two as a matter of fact. But you know, it's silly to say this, I've never learned to drive."

74

"What! "

"I expect you can drive, can't you? "

"Oh, yes," I lied. "Though I need some practice."

"I think I'd be too nervous. Apart from being so absent-minded. I'm terribly absent-minded. And impractical." This last was not true: though Irvine liked, for some reason, to pretend that it was.

"Are you married? "

"No."

"How old are you? "

"Forty-seven."

I continued to question him, after the Greek fashion, until he protested: "Goodness, how inquisitive you are! "

"Aren't all Greeks inquisitive? "

"Yes, I know. And really I like it. It's nice to have people interested in one—in England, where I lived before I came here, no one seemed to care. Also, as I'm inquisitive myself, it means that I don't have to be ashamed of putting my own questions. Which is what I'm going to do now. You don't mind, do you? "

But at that moment the foreman shouted at me: "Have you got a new job with the American, or do you still want to work with us? " I had been so engrossed in our conversation that I had not noticed that the others had already drifted, yawning and groaning, back to their baskets and shovels.

"I must go."

"Shall I see you again? "

"If you like—of course."

"Well, I do like. When? What time? "

"Just as you wish. You say."

But when he dithered, biting on the handkerchief and scratching away at his chin, I said quickly: "This evening. Eight o'clock. Outside the Astoria Cinema."

"Good, good."

He got up, gave me a brisk little nod, and hurriedly toddled off, the damp handkerchief trailing downwards from one of his plump, pink hands.

"When are you leaving for America?" the negroid youth asked.

I hitched up my shorts, then grabbed my pick and hurled it at the ground so that splinters of baked mud bounced off in all directions.

"Take care you don't spoil your hands—*sir*," someone called out.

"What's his room-number?"

"Give us an American cigarette."

All of it was predictable: the usual banter, delivered in the usual grudging, admiring, envious, affectionate tones. I began to brag:

"Well, anyway, he's going to try to get me a job. He's a big bug. Head of American Relief. Must have a packet. You don't handle big sums like that without salting away a little on your own account. He's invited me to dinner. I suppose we'll go to the Olympos or to Flocca. Unless we go out to Aretsou—that's what I'll suggest to him. I want to see those Turkish belly-dancers."

"Has he got a car?" someone queried.

"He doesn't *drive*," I replied. "People like that don't drive."

Irvine arrived, breathlessly trotting, more than ten minutes late. He had an unfurled umbrella over one arm, in the hand of which he was clutching a thick, untidy wad of newspapers. "Oh, please, please, forgive me," he panted. "I've kept you waiting. Haven't I? I was at a cocktail-party at the Consulate, and it was all I could do to tear myself away from one of the Fulbright professors. A specialist on marketing. I was hoping he would give me some advice—whenever I do my marketing in this country, I seem to get gypped." That last word was one which I was often to hear Irvine use. No one was more afraid, or more conscious, of being 'gypped'; no one was more feebly impotent to do anything about it.

He was looking me up and down, with a scrutiny the intensity of which might have indicated extremes of either approval or disapproval, I could not tell which. Then he said: "Well, what would you like to do?"

"Whatever you wish."

"Let's eat somewhere. I badly need something inside me to soak up those Martinis."

He was tipsy, although I did not then know the signs: the 'ballet-movements', as Helen Bristow used to call them, becoming at once slower and more exaggerated; the fluttering of the short albino lashes becoming increasingly rapid; the head poking forward and twisting around as though he were wearing a stiff collar two sizes too small for him.

"Good idea."

"Where do you suggest?"

"Oh, I don't know. How about the Olympos, or Flocca?"

"No, no, no!" He made that gesture of pushing away some invisible object from him.

"Or one of the places at Aretsou?"

He glanced down at my shoes, the only pair I then possessed apart from gym-shoes, the cracks in them filled with the tomato-ketchup which is used instead of polish in Greece. Then he eyed my worn cotton trousers, a present from his homeland, the turn-ups turned down in order to conceal at least my shins, if not my ankles. Finally his eyes rested on my blue-and-white check shirt,

77

as he said: "I should like to go somewhere that is not—er—too fashionable. Somewhere really Greek. Where there's real Greek food, and real Greek dancing."

Irvine detested real Greek food, of which he used to say: "If, as the culinary authorities assert, the basis of all French cooking is butter, of all Italian cooking oil, and of all English cooking water, then I can only suppose that the basis of all Greek cooking is pee-pee." He also detested all Greek popular music—"It sounds as if Wanda Landowska and 'Fats' Waller were banging simultaneously on a harpsichord," he remarked on one occasion. But at that first meeting, I was not to know all this. Otherwise I might have guessed that the truth really was that he was afraid of being seen by his colleagues in the company of someone as shabby and grubby as I.

He played with an occasional potato-chip and sipped, with a wry, pained expression, at his glass of 'retsina', while he furtively looked around the tavern to which I had taken him. He always liked to think such places were centres of criminality and vice—the men who, with that characteristic Greek inquisitiveness, stared at him fixedly for minutes on end, were obviously planning to assault him; the cigarettes at which they drew greedily until they were no more than a pinched fragment of scorched paper and tobacco between the middle-finger and thumb, were of course 'loaded'; and when a young girl of thirteen came in to whisper something to a man who was, in fact, her father, she was, he insisted, a child-prostitute.

"I'm sure that man is drugged," he said on this occasion, indicating with his eyes a middle-aged labourer who sat blinking sleepily through a haze of smoke.

"Nonsense! He's a brick-layer. I know him. He's probably tired out after a twelve-hour day."

Irvine no more cared to have his fantasies of crime and squalor demolished in this way than a Greek cares to be mocked out of his fantasies of riches and grandeur.

"I don't know what my lady-colleagues would say if they could see me in here!"

"Are any of them young?"

"One or two."

"And attractive?"

"You might find them so. Do girls interest you?"

"Of course. I'm mad about them. And luckily they seem to fall for me. Oh, I always have a great success with women."

Greek youths talk like that; it was only later that I learned that to say such things made a bad impression on foreigners.

"I half expected you to turn up in those shorts you were wearing this morning." The joke was too near to the truth to be a joke to me.

"I'm a poor boy," I said sulkily. "How do you expect me to dress well on eighteen drachmas a day?" I added. "Eighteen drachmas. How far do you suppose that goes? I bet you earn ten or twenty times that."

Irvine looked down at the blotched table-cloth, embarrassed, as all foreigners are embarrassed, when Greeks compare incomes. The figure was nearer thirty times, as I later discovered.

"Surely you can get a better job," he said at last, in an accusing voice, as if only my own laziness or stupidity were to blame.

"Tell me where."

"A boy of good family."

"Can't you do anything to help me?"

"I?" First his cheeks, then his forehead, and then the tips of his ears began to redden.

"Even if you can't help me to emigrate, don't you have

79

any friends to whom you could speak for me? What about the Electricity Company? That's British, isn't it?"

"Oh, my dear child, you don't understand; you Greeks never do. If I spoke to anyone in the Electricity Company, so far from it helping you to get a job, it would only make things worse."

"Don't they like you then?" I asked ingenuously.

"No, no, no! Don't you see that in other countries . . ."

He began to explain how much more honest, just and impartial the Americans and English were than the Greeks; but then, as now, the notion of refusing to give a helping hand to someone you know in case he should deprive someone you do not know of a job, seemed to me both repellent and immoral.

We argued, and, as we argued, everyone else in the small crowded tavern first listened and then joined in.

"Well," said Irvine at last, overpowered both by the wine and the clamour about us, "what I *may* be able to do is to get you into our office here. No, now don't get too excited," he raised a plump hand. "I *may*, I said. Our despatch clerk is leaving us, and it's just possible . . ."

"Oh, it would be marvellous! Please, oh, please! "

He patted my arm, both touched and worried by my eagerness. "I'll see what I can do. But it'll be a delicate business. *Very* delicate."

I got the job.

The staff consisted, for the most part, of pious, well-intentioned and hardworking English and American women, and Greek men who, like myself, took advantage of them. We borrowed money off them, and then forgot to repay it; we sold the petrol, the stationery, and even items of furniture; when a parcel arrived for distribution, we substituted worn-out clothes or shoes of our own for the clothes and shoes inside. The office station-wagon took us to the beach or to football matches. From time to time, one of us would be caught out, and then the rest would have to pretend to exclaim in horror at his crime. "And to think that when he asked for that loan for his mother's operation, he was really using it to—to keep that woman," Miss Oppenheim would exclaim. "Ten tins of skimmed milk stolen!" Mrs. Van Ivens would rush in to announce: "Not a trace of them, not a trace!" "But thirty-three gallons of petrol this week!" Lady Dora Swanling would boom out in her deep bass voice. "Something must be wrong." Something was always wrong; but Miss Oppenheim, Mrs. Van Ivens and Lady Dora continued to trust us. Theirs was a faith that would have moved mountains; it was sad that it could not move us.

Occasionally someone would join the staff who shared neither their pious ideals nor their ladylike inefficiency. But he or she—usually it was a man—would soon be forced to resign. There had been a tough and bibulous Australian who swore impartially at his colleagues and those who applied for relief, calling them 'bloody frauds'. He drew up a log-book for the car, checked the postage imprest, and insisted on being present whenever a case was unpacked. "He's a businessman," Miss Oppenheim moaned, "and I'm sure a very good one. But he's out of place in an organization like ours. He doesn't seem to have caught our spirit at all." "And that awful cynicism!" exclaimed Mrs. Van Ivens. "Treating everyone as if they were criminals, until they are proved the contrary." "Besides," put in Lady Dora, "that drinking is such a bad example to the junior staff." Soon the Australian moved on and up, to direct a less parochial and more efficient organization.

81

I myself was irritated by the inefficiency around me, but this did not have the effect of making me more efficient: inefficiency rarely does. I had to keep a despatch-book, but soon I ceased to enter the file-references, and if I had to wait for a signature when delivering a letter, I would slip it into the letter-box and forge the signature later. Occasionally we received old American magazines which I was supposed to re-pack for distribution among our refugee centres; and these I would use, with a malicious delight, crumpling up their glossy pages, in order to get the boiler to light each morning. I was spoiled by the women, to whom I would tell atrocious stories of my 'experiences' in Roumania, and disliked by the men. Mrs. Van Ivens, a widow from the Middle West, would listen for hours, her heavy face becoming more and more lugubrious, as I told her of the destruction of our family castle—sixteen Rubens, three Velasquez and a Veronese all consumed to ash; my two sisters, educated in Switzerland and France, driven off to who knew what horrors; my own hairbreadth escape, disguised as a stable-boy. . . . "Well, for heaven's sake! Did you hear that, Dora? Well, that's—that's terrible, just terrible." She would ask me where I now lived, and how I managed to look always 'so spick and span', and how I passed my evenings. I would reply modestly: "Oh, I get along. You know, I have a little room in Tomba—that's what you'd call 'the other side of the tracks'! But I get along." "Well, I think you're very plucky—very, *very* plucky indeed." She would get up, lethargic and melancholy, fingering her grey hair, and a few minutes later would return with a bar of soap, a packet of tea, or some tissues from the P.X.

But soon I began to be bored and restless, as I had been at the American Farm School to which I had been sent after my escape from the rebels. I needed something to occupy me; and though I had something to occupy me, it was not something that I wanted to do. My monthly wage was what one of our ladies earned in three days; and whereas our other Greek employees had their parents' homes in which to live, I had to pay out a quarter of this sum on rent. I began to forget the days when I had hung about the docks and the park in order to scrounge a meal or fifty cents off a foreigner; the shame of knowing that I was unshaven, my clothes in tatters, and my feet stinking; the cold and discomfort of sleeping in the empty shop of an acquaintance, with cockroaches or rats scuttling over the sodden saw-dust. . . . And forgetting all these things, I began to yearn for something better. Slouching past Flocca in the evening, I would peer in at the people guzzling ice-creams and cakes inside: flashing jewellery, flashing gold-teeth, and heavy bosoms sagging over mounds of whipped cream. Outside the American Consulate the Cadillacs gleamed nose-to-tail, and from the upper floors there came the sound of music and foreign voices—to hell with the dirty bastards! Miss Oppenheim, an emaciated, middle-aged woman, whose face seemed to have been fashioned from brown-paper, bumped into me, as she struggled with her umbrella: "More rain! Mercy me! . . . But, Spiro, look at this *cutest* little brooch I bought myself. Isn't it a treasure?" I myself had no umbrella and no mackintosh, and she was standing in such a way on the pavement that my right foot was resting in the gutter. Then I made my way home, stumbling up the rocky path which had now become a cataract, ate a yoghourt, some bread and a handful of wrinkled olives, and then climbed into bed because it was warmer there than in the unheated room. The light was too weak to read for any length of time, even were I a reader. Sometimes I repaired my clothes; more often I lay moodily thinking of the future.

My Greek colleagues were jealous of me, because I was the favourite. When they could do so, they made trouble for me. Then one of the ladies would say: "Well, Spiro, I would never have believed such a thing, no indeed. If it hadn't been for Mr. Pantelides telling me about it, well, it would never have entered my head." "You ask Pantelides what became of the five tins of floor-polish which arrived for us last week." "Now, Spiro, Spiro, Spiro!" They never wished to hear anything that might destroy their childlike faith in us or the world, preferring, like Irvine in later years, the comforts of being deceived. For every misdemeanour they would at once find an excuse, saying: "Well, of course, I know that with Christmas coming, you probably found yourself terribly short of money. But why—instead of doing such a thing —didn't you tell one of us? I'd have gladly lent you whatever you wanted, yes, gladly. You *must* regard us as your friends."

Oh, Miss Oppenheim, Mrs. Van Ivens and Lady Dora Swanling: people like you and Irvine and Kiki are the predestined victims of people like myself. You need us as much as we need you: sometimes I think that it is you who make us what we are. . . .

I was corresponding with Irvine, because I knew that if I hoped ever to leave Salonica, he was my only chance. In later years I found that he had kept all my letters, but I kept none of his: indeed, I hardly read them. He was a man wholly incapable of adapting himself to the company in which he found himself, and what he wrote to me he would have also written, not a word changed, to his mother, to his boss in America or to Mrs. Van Ivens, had he only felt impelled to write at such length. There were pages about the influence of Byzantine iconography on El Greco; closely-reasoned comparisons between Balzac and Dickens, Solomos and Coleridge, Scalkottas and Schonberg; descriptions of visits to Aghias Loukas, the open-air swimming-pool by the Temple of Zeus or the house of the new director of the British Police Mission. His love was always of that kind that feeds, not on understanding, but on ignorance, of the beloved; and even to-day he probably knows less of my true character than old Mrs. Bacon, for example, who comes in to 'do' for us. How else could he have imagined that what he wrote could interest an eighteen-year-old boy, working by day as a despatch-clerk and spending his evenings either wandering about the town or lying in bed with a pile of old, dog-eared copies of *Romance*, *True Confessions*, and *Screen Story*? Yet certainly there were times when, out of sheer boredom, I would read his letters to the end; and by some odd process of osmosis made something of them mine.

When I wrote back I complained of my loneliness (which was real) and of my desire to be with him (which was not). I said that I had no friends, and that was not strictly true: I even had a girl, a maid at the house of a tobacco-merchant. I described my room, with the half-conscious aim of creating an impression of pathos: the wooden crate over which I had tacked some old oil-cloth, given me by Miss Oppenheim, in order to make a table; the wads of the *New York Times* and the *New York Tribune* which I put between the only two blankets I possessed (there was a certain artistry in the way in which I wistfully added: 'I wonder why it is that American papers are so much warmer than Greek ones'); the problem of what to use for boiling water when I had accidentally destroyed my saucepan by leaving it too long on the primus, and the solution—an old baked-beans tin. . . . To such news, Irvine would write back: "Truly, it breaks my heart to think of your life up there. But be patient—be patient! I promise you that I never cease to think of your problem." In each letter there would be one or two twenty-drachma notes, and on this money I would take my girl to the cinema, writing afterwards to say that I had used it to buy myself some socks, an English grammar or a corkscrew. I did not think he would care to hear about Eva; but there I was wrong.

Eva caused me trouble. I had set myself the task of seducing her, not so much because I found her attractive, as because I needed some success up which my morale, like a vine blown down in a gale, could begin to climb. After I had left the gang in the park, I had been through a period of excited euphoria, similar to that when I had escaped from the Communists; but soon that had passed. I cannot bear the consciousness of standing still: even to move backwards sometimes appears preferable. I had two objects now: the first, and the more important, to get myself a better job; the second to overcome Eva's resistance. Her life, like mine, was of a terrible drabness. She worked from seven in the morning, when she took a cup of tea up to her mistress, until eleven o'clock at night, by which time she had finished the washing up from dinner. Then, exhausted, she would go into her room which would have been better suited for a kennel, and often still wearing the underclothes she had worn all day, would fall into a sleep which, she assured me, was always full of dreams of me. Her excitements were those of her mistress: the dress her mistress had bought, her mistress's winnings at bridge, the party her mistress had given. Her boredom can be indicated by one specific incident.

One evening, when everyone was out, Eva answered the telephone, and a foreign male voice asked for her mistress. "And who are you?" the caller asked, in atrocious Greek, when she replied that the whole family was out.

"The maid."

"Ah, the pretty girl who opens the door. Yes, I've noticed you. What's your name?"

"Eva."

"Yes, you're a very pretty girl, Eva. Have you got a boy-friend?"

"That's my business."

"Would you like me as a boy-friend?"

"I don't know who you are."

The conversation continued, with Eva threatening to put down the receiver and the caller paying extravagant compliments, until at last he ended: "Well, Eva, I shall call you again. I like the sound of your voice. A very pretty voice—as pretty as its owner."

All this was recounted first to her mistress, who was as excited as she, and no less full of guesses as to the man's identity, and then to me—no doubt embroidered and exaggerated, for Eva had the vivid imagination of all Greek peasants. Obviously she hoped that the stranger would call again; and when he did not do so, as much because of her disappointment as from the desire to play a malicious joke on her, I myself telephoned, putting on a foreign accent while we conversed. She giggled so much that it was hard to understand anything she said except cries of "Ooh, the cheek of it!" "What sauce!" and things of that kind. But after two or three more such exchanges, I suggested a meeting.

"Where?"

"I'm just round the corner from the house. You know outside the American Information Office there are some photographs?"

"Ye-es—I think so." Of course she knew; we had often looked at them together, for want of something better.

"Well, if you can slip out for five minutes, you'll find me there. All right?"

"All right. You are awful!" The telephone closed on more breathless giggling.

Needless to say, when we met we quarrelled. "You slut! You little slut!" I shouted at her. "I always thought you were no better than a whore, and now I know."

"Well, if you play a dirty trick like that, you deserve what you get."

I began to imitate her talking to the 'stranger', with that unnatural French r-sound which Greek girls affect, until suddenly she let out a scream and slapped my face. At once I slapped her back. She began to blubber and shriek out at the same time at the passers-by: "Look how he treats me! Look what he did to me!" A crowd began to collect, most of them shoe-shiners, their hands, faces and clothes streaked with red dye: but I was afraid that there might also be someone there connected with the office. So I grabbed her firmly above the elbow and propelled her forward. As we moved, she stumbled, hiccoughed and made feeble attempts to push me off, but I knew that she liked it. "Let me go, oh, let me go!" she wailed. "Where are you taking me? I'm not supposed to be out. What will she say? She'll be back any moment, and then I'll lose my job. Oh . . . oh . . . You're hurting, you're hurting, you beast."

I was both triumphant and furious. I had a key of the office, which I was not supposed to have—all of us had copies—and I rapidly unlocked the door and thrust her into the darkness and silence. "Ai! Ai! Let me out! Let me out!" she yelled, butting me in the stomach, until I slapped her again. Then half weeping, half giggling, using one hand to brush her matted hair away from her face while with the other she pinched and pulled the lobe of my left ear, she collapsed in a shuddering, tângled heap against me. After that it was easy. I took her down to the basement, so that no light would show. At first she pretended to be frightened of me, of the empty building, of walking down the stairs, of a cockroach, of the duplicating-machine, of anything and everything. But soon that passed.

We were in the middle of our love-making when we heard the creak of someone descending the stairs and a voice, at once gruff, formidable and apprehensive, demanding: "Who's there? Who is it? Come on, who is it?"

I flung up the window which backed on to a narrow yard where we kept the garbage-bins, but I had forgotten that it was barred. Fortunately I had already switched off the light. Eva began to moan, and once again I had to clap my hand over her mouth, hissing in her ear at the same time: "Don't move! Not a sound!"

But the feet creaked nearer and nearer. In the storeroom next door, the light clicked on and off; then, as I rushed to the door, to turn a key that was not there, Lady Dora entered. She was still wearing her heavy, horn-rimmed reading glasses—presumably she had been working upstairs at the estimates which, in her own phrase, 'never came out right'—and in one hand she was clutching the brass lamp that stood on her desk, I suppose as a possible weapon.

"Spiro!" She was amazed; shocked; furious; relieved.

Eva was still pulling her clothes up or down. Lady Dora glanced at her and then demanded:

"What is the meaning of this? Spiro, what have you been doing? Spiro, I demand an explanation."

"This . . . this . . . this is my cousin," I stammered. Every girl in Greece who is neither a fiancée nor a prostitute is called a cousin. "She . . . she . . . wasn't feeling well."

Even Lady Dora, so unwilling to believe ill of any-one, could not believe that. "Take her out," she said. "We'll speak about this to-morrow. Take—her—out!" Eva had begun to sniffle. "And take this lamp with you. In the boiler-room!" she muttered. "In the boiler-room! This is not the last of this."

I did not lose my job, though I lay awake all night alternately thinking about Eva, as one does about some-one whom one has petted without a climax, and about my future. I supposed that by the next week I should be back with the gang in the park. But there I was wrong: in turn, each of the ladies told me how shocked, how deeply shocked, how disappointed, how pained she had felt on hearing the news, but it was obvious that, in every case, the predominant emotion had been none of these, but excitement. In their eyes I had ceased to be the 'nice boy' they had imagined; now I was a man, and a dangerous man at that. Secretly, they dreaded and yet hoped for a fate similar to Eva's. When I happened to look at one, because she was wearing a peculiar hat, or because her nose was too heavily powdered, or merely because I was thinking of something else, I would notice a half-apprehensive, half-expectant preening. Soon my demeanour was being dismissed with a sigh and a: "Well, what can you expect, my dear? These Greeks are all the same."

A report was sent to Irvine; and again I passed a period of dread. But when he next wrote he alluded to the occurrence with the heavily playful flippancy that, in later years, so often was his only response to my more outrageous actions. ". . . I hear you've been a *very* naughty boy, and fluttered all those poor hens almost out of their wits. Lady Dora's report is so delicately phrased that, in the words of the limerick, it is impossible to discover who did what, and with what and to whom.

Please enlighten me." There was a great deal else in the same vein. I wrote back, and beyond admitting that I had done something foolish and adding that my position had, as a result, become even more difficult in the office, I said nothing on the subject. That was a time when I was still ignorant of the true nature of Irvine's attachment for me, and I imagined that to write at length about Eva and all the squalid circumstances would only serve to lose him. But already I had guessed that he was a man for whom to know that someone depended on him was not, as for myself, cause for irritation, but for an extravagance of devotion; and it was in that vein that I therefore wrote:

> . . . I suppose it's boring for you to be bothered with my problems, but being completely alone in the world, where else can I turn? I suppose you have become for me father, mother, brothers and sisters all rolled into one. You can't imagine what it's like to feel that there is no one in the world who really cares what happens to you. I might die to-night, and no one would be sorry or even notice the difference—except old Pantelides, who would complain at the extra work in the morning! Since I lost everything, you alone have . . .

The letter ran on: it was longer than any I had ever written to him before, and longer than any I have written to him since. It was not insincere: that evening I felt homesick for my village, my mother, for Stelio. I had tried to mend some of my socks, and as I looked down ruefully at the mess I had made of them, I was consumed with self-pity. I thought of my mother's neat darning, and then of the embroidery she had been doing on the night she was killed; and after that I visualized to myself our meals all together, forgetting the quarrels between my father and Stelio, the lean days when we had nothing but bean-soup to eat, and my restless desire to get away to a big city where fortunes could be made.

Nor was there any insincerity in my affection for Irvine. Greeks are like dogs: they will come to you first because you are going to feed them, but then, even if you do not feed them, they will come to you from habit. The sense of having to belong is powerful within them: that is perhaps why they lack the moral courage ever to defy the herd. I had to belong somewhere, to someone; to whom else but him?

Irvine arrived, before any answer to my letter; and, without any intention of play-acting, I was subdued and even morose on our first evening together until he asked me: "My dear, what *is* the matter with you? You're usually so gay. What's happened? What's upset you?"

"Oh, I'm fed up, that's all."

"But why? Why? Tell me."

"Nothing." I pushed my plate aside, only half of my chicken eaten.

Irvine hated that kind of waste: "You're not going to leave all that, are you?"

"I don't feel hungry," I sulked.

"Now, come, don't be silly. I'm not going to pay eighteen drachmas for something you barely touch." It was typical, I thought bitterly, that he should remember the exact sum from the menu; another man would have said 'fifteen drachmas' or even 'twenty drachmas'. "Come along, Spiro." It was the nanny-voice now.

But I had achieved what I wanted: I was asked, before our evening ended, to go with him to Mount Athos, and, during that trip, he at last decided that, at any cost, he must have me in Athens with him.

In the Athens office, I did the same job as I had done in Salonica. My salary was slightly larger, but then life in the capital was slightly more expensive than life in the provinces. In the office, I called Irvine 'Sir' to his face and 'the old woman' behind his back, like the other Greek employees. He was a man not naturally harsh to his staff, though he was efficient and shrewd: but to me he was harsh, no doubt in an effort not to appear to favour me. I, in turn, was servile. "He's got it in for you all right," the other clerks would say with ill-concealed glee. "What have you done? How did you get across him?" I would not reply; but it gave me an odd feeling of power to know that that same evening Irvine and I would be dining together.

In those early days, while I still worked at the office, Irvine was passably discreet. We avoided Zonar's, Flocca's and the other fashionable restaurants and cafés, eating either at his flat in Kolonaki or driving out by taxi to the sea. I had got myself a room at Heliopolis, a suburb on the slopes of Hymettos, and sometimes Irvine would come out there. The neighbours asked who he was, and, in the manner of the Greeks, I bragged that he was a millionaire cousin. They believed me, because they wanted to believe me: almost every Greek dreams of the relative who comes back from the New World laden with riches, and if it could happen to me, then it was all the more probable that it could happen to them.

The room, for which Irvine paid the rent, was better than my room in Salonica: there was an inside lavatory, which I shared with the family, and a bathroom with a geyser that was heated with wood. But when he first visited it, Irvine was horrified. "Oh, my poor Spiro! Is this your little hutch? It's miserable, miserable."

I felt annoyed: irrationally, since the worse he found the room the more likely he was to pay for something better. "What's wrong with it?" I demanded.

"Oh, it's cold and damp"—he gave a little shudder—"and horribly depressing. I hate to think of you living in a place like this."

"Well—here I am. It's the best I could find. At the price."

"I must lend you some things to brighten it up. A picture or two, a carpet. . . . You must have a carpet, these boards are really hideous. And a lamp, a bedside lamp. You'll ruin your poor eyes with that overhead bulb. . . ."

Slowly, things which he had lent to me began to accumulate. There was a rug from Pyrgos, a Byzantine design of lions and birds, which he insisted should be placed not on the floor but on the wall; a Dupré engraving of Ali Pasha, a character so unlike himself who had an extraordinary fascination for him; an angle-poise lamp; some copper Turkish plates. . . . As each new treasure arrived, it would be noticed by my landlady, who would tell the rest of her family, who would then tell their friends. People began to regard me as a man with 'influence': and 'influence' in Greece is more precious than money, or beauty, or brains. A widow whose daughter had sat unsuccessfully for the Cambridge Certificate of Proficiency in English came to ask me if I could do anything about it; a young man, with ambitions of emigrating to the States, begged me to 'speak for' him to my 'cousin'. In Greece one does not say that something is impossible: one says that one will do what one can, and then, quietly, one does nothing at all. That was how I now dealt with these requests.

One night, after Irvine and I had been to an open-air concert by the lake at Vouliagmeni, it was past twelve o'clock by the time we had prepared ourselves a supper at his flat, and I got up to leave. "Oh, this awful journey!" I groused. "It really is a bore. I dare say

I've missed the last bus anyway. I'll have to try to get a seat in a taxi."

"Would you like to stay?"

"Stay? What do you mean?"

"Well, why not? Provided you're—you're out of the flat before the woman comes. I think that would be wise, don't you? In order to prevent gossip."

Irvine proceeded to treat me with all the consideration he would have shown to one of what he called his 'visiting firemen'. I did not want a milk-drink so soon after supper, but he insisted that I have one. Then there was a lot of fussing as to whether a hot-water bottle should be placed in the bed or not—this, in spite of a temperature in the seventies. Finally, I was forced to borrow a pair of his pyjamas.

So much solicitude both puzzled and embarrassed me, and I said to myself: "Well, here it is. Now at last it's coming." After I was between the sheets, he entered in his pyjamas and, perching on one end of the bed, smoked a Turkish cigarette in a holder as he talked to me. Irvine was a person who always spoke of what interested him, rather than of what was calculated to interest his hearers, and if any subject interested him, it was likely to become an obsession. He had been reading the first volume of a *History of the Crusades* by an acquaintance of his, and there was some point—it was so trivial that I have forgotten what it was—on which he found himself in violent disagreement. He had discussed it in the interval of the concert; on the bus and during supper. He began to discuss it now.

I grew sleepier and sleepier. If he did what I expected him to do, I was prepared to submit: but to this tedious disquisition I could not submit much longer.

Fortunately, he broke off at last: "My poor Spiro! You're half-asleep, aren't you? But you do see the point,

95

don't you? I cannot understand a scholar who is usually so fastidious about his sources . . ." Five minutes later, he was at last saying good night.

"Sleep well, my dear! You've got all you want?" He bent over me, taking my hand in both of his. Again I told myself: 'Here it comes, here it comes!' But he did not even kiss me.

I was relieved, of course, and puzzled: but also, I must confess, a little uneasy. What did he want from me? That he should want nothing was something impossible for a Greek to believe.

The nights that I spent at his flat became more and more frequent. Irvine always kept up the pretence of disliking to be with others; but like so many of his pretences—of not caring what other people thought or said about him, of having no regard for appearances, of hating both America and England—this was really a kind of self-defence. In reality, he craved company. When I got up to leave, he would always try to detain me; and if he failed in that, he would at once demand: "When shall I see you again?"

Often, either intentionally or unintentionally, I was cruel, saying off-handedly: "I *may* be able to look in on Wednesday evening, I really can't be sure."

"Oh, well, I have nothing to do then, so I'll keep the evening free."

If I were late—and I rarely bothered to be punctual— I would see him, as I came up the hill, leaning out of his window, one end of his handkerchief usually stuck in his mouth. When he saw me, he would pluck out the handkerchief and wave it frantically, as though afraid that I might not find the way. Sometimes he was cross, as mothers are, when they have been imagining that their children have been run over or kidnapped. "Spiro,

Spiro! " he would then exclaim. "It's not the lateness that I mind, but the not knowing. Couldn't you get to a telephone? Is that so hard? Just a little 'telephonaki'." The -aki I should explain is a Greek diminutive, which Irvine perpetually used in conversation with me, though seldom with others. I hated it: above all when he called me 'Spiraki'.

Eventually, the suggestion came that I should live always in his flat; and it was characteristic that he should put this to me as if he was asking a favour. "You're so clever about things like fuses, of which I know nothing. And you've learned to mix such excellent Martinis. And then there are all those wretched refugee callers, who *will* come round here to ask for favours instead of seeing me in the office. You're much harder-hearted than I, you'll be able to deal with them so much better."

"But what will the woman say?"

"Need she say anything? What's it to do with her?"

It was typical of Irvine to be at one moment as reckless as this, and at another as cautious as a spinster in a Greek village. He had, on various occasions, spoken of me to the maid as 'a friend', 'a cousin', 'a nephew' and 'an employee'. I knew that she disliked me—one dependent is always jealous of another, and I had stopped at least half a dozen of her rackets. I also knew that she had drawn her conclusions, and one could hardly blame her if they were the wrong ones; I should have drawn the same myself.

Now I had the best bedroom. Irvine said that he preferred the other and smaller one, because it was less noisy to look out on a yard instead of the street; but I did not believe him. To make such sacrifices was a consuming need for him. I started to borrow his clothes, to use his razor, even to wear his shoes. To do so did not, at the time, seem to me odd, because in any poor Greek

97

family such borrowings are usual: Stelios and I had shared our best pair of shoes, a tie and a silver identity disk (how lucky that we had had the same initials). It is only now that I see how deep must have been Irvine's affection for me that he never protested. Gradually all his best clothes, including the overcoat I am wearing, made their way from his bedroom to mine. Sometimes he would say: "Now where did I put those links? . . . Oh, you're wearing them." As I began to take them off, he would protest: "It doesn't matter, it doesn't matter! I'll roll up my sleeves."

Irvine, with his mania for improving those nearest to him, had insisted on my taking lessons during the evenings at the British Institute, and even let me off half an hour early from work in order that I could do so. Like many Greeks, I have a natural aptitude for languages; but, being lazy, I had picked up, haphazard, a mass of spoken English which I had never tried to write. The classes bored me, even though they provided the opportunity of flirting with a number of pretty girls. I had a Greek woman-teacher, who was fat, ugly and sarcastic, and no lesson passed without my being insolent to her, to the titters of the girls and the protests of the men, most of whom were very serious indeed. Gradually I began to stay away, taking myself to a cinema or lounging in the streets instead. I missed one lesson in a week; then two; then even three.

One such evening, it was pouring with rain, and Irvine, who had been using the office-car and knew that I had gone without either an umbrella or a rain-coat, called at the Institute to fetch me. He asked for my class, and waited patiently outside until it was over; but I was not among the students. The director, whom he knew, happened to pass at that moment and asked if he could help him.

"Yes, I'm looking for a young friend of mine." Irvine, in his innocence, often blurted out such things without realizing that, in Greece at least, they might compromise him. "I was told his class was in room six, but he doesn't seem to be here."

"We'll ask Miss Sakellariou." My teacher had just appeared, surrounded as usual by the few serious-minded students who preferred to toady to her rather than to rag her as we others did. "Oh, Miss Sakellariou, have you got a student called—what is his name, Mr. Stroh?"

"Polymerides—Spiro Polymerides."

"It's rather difficult to answer that question." Miss Sakellariou opened a file, and at once a number of sheets of paper—letters, compositions, notices of lectures, library-reminders, bills—swished to the floor. Four men in frayed brown suits and glasses stooped to claw at them, while Miss Sakellariou arranged her other glasses on the tip of her bulbous nose. "He's on my list," she said. "So in that sense I've got him. But—let me see"—she peered at her register—"seven absences out of the last ten classes: that's the score."

"Seven absences!" Irvine exclaimed. "But that's impossible."

"That boy will have to turn over a new leaf, if he expects to pass the December examination. A shoulder to the wheel," Miss Sakellariou said. She was an expert, not on grammar, like most of her colleagues, but on idioms, teaching her students to say things like 'I've got the hump', 'It's raining cats and dogs', or 'Our holiday went like water off a duck's back'. "Yes, he'll have to pull his socks up, won't he, sir?" The director particularly disliked being called 'sir'. "Well, I must fly." The idea of anyone as ungainly as Miss Sakellariou flying was as absurd as the slang. "B 6," she added, on that note of deep, mysterious triumph with which clerks in

Intelligence in Greece after the war used to refer to their branches. " Bye-bye."

" Good-bye."

All this I heard from Irvine when I got home.

" It's monstrous that I should pay for your lessons," he railed at me, " when you just don't bother to attend—and tell me lies into the bargain. What was all that about doing the Continuous Present? You know how I *hate* to be deceived." I knew nothing of the kind; indeed to be deceived, whether by himself or by others, often seemed a fate which, so far from avoiding, he deliberately courted. (That is true of so many Americans resident in Greece. ' They love me' is their theme; ' they respect me'. Then when at last they discover that they are, in fact, being exploited, like Irvine they give way to temper.)

" Monstrous," he went on, " monstrous, absolutely monstrous." I had not seen him so angry since the incident of the ikon: I began to feel apprehensive. But then, suddenly, he broke off: " Oh, for God's sake remove that coat of yours. And those shoes. Do you *want* to get pneumonia? You have this weak chest, and then you do these foolish things, like going out in the rain without a coat or umbrella." Irvine was always harping on my ' weak' chest, which was not weak at all, with the same regularity that he complained about the workings of his little intestine. It gave him an excuse to fuss me.

He followed me into the bedroom, and went on: " If there can be no trust between us, then obviously there can be no friendship. Can there? When I think that I'm paying out a hundred and thirty-eight drachmas a month—and that ninety-four for books only last week— well, not unnaturally, it makes my blood boil." This last phrase was hardly well-chosen; Irvine always went white when he was enraged—' curdle' rather than ' boil' would have been a better verb.

"Oh, you don't understand," I said wearily, unlacing my shoes.

To be accused of not understanding always wounded Irvine—did he not often boast to his friends that he and I had 'a perfect understanding'?

"What don't I understand?" he now demanded. "Well? What, what?"

I jumped to my stockinged feet: "What sort of life do you imagine it is to work in that basement all day, packing and unpacking parcels, and then to have to give up an hour and a half of one's evening to sit in a stuffy classroom? Have you thought of that? Sometimes I'm dogtired, my brain hardly works. At my age, it's natural that I should want to go and play a game of cards or—or billiards, or go to a cinema. You say you want to understand me, but you never think of such things. I don't believe you were ever young."

Irvine shrank before this attack, backing away from me as I advanced. "I only want to make something of you," he said feebly. "You know that, until you get some qualifications, you'll never have a better job. Will you? It's only of you I'm thinking."

"Well, think of me a little more sensibly, that's all!" I threw off my sodden jacket, and then clawed at my shirt.

"You're soaked to the skin!" Irvine exclaimed. "You must have a bath. I'll go and run it."

"I don't want a bath."

"Don't be silly." Irvine went into the bathroom, and in his nanny-voice called out, above the swishing of the taps: "Now hurry up! Get those clothes off."

While I soaped myself, he sat on the lavatory-seat, eyeing me mournfully, in silence, through a haze of cigarette-smoke. At last he said:

"Perhaps I was wrong."

I did not answer.

He got up and scrubbed my back vigorously with a loofah. Then he sighed: "Of course it's difficult to study and do a job at the same time. You mustn't think that I'm unsympathetic. Perhaps it would be better if you gave up the job."

"And how would I live?"

"Oh, I expect we could manage. My tastes aren't expensive. With a little saving here and there . . ."

I was overjoyed; but I was careful not to show it.

"What shall I study?"

"I'd like to send you to the University. Yes, that's what I'd like to do. I don't know why I didn't think of it before. With your brains and character, *and* a University degree, well, there's no knowing what you mightn't do. The Foreign Office, anything." He broke off: "Now don't lie too long in there! Come on! Out you get! Come on, Spiro! Spiro!"

. . . B-r-r-r! Only five o'clock, and it's beginning to get chilly. For the last three weeks Mrs. Bacon has been saying that the evenings are drawing in and that before we know it the winter will be on us, but this is the first time I've really felt it. It was stupid of me to sit out here for so long, letting my feet and hands get frozen. That's what comes of having no nanny-voice to warn me —'You'll pay for it to-morrow'. . . .

The young man is putting his fork and spade in the trolley. He dusts off the knees of his overalls, goes to the tree to unhitch his rucksack, and then, giving me a quick, venomous look, begins to push away. Twice he glances back at me over his shoulder. He seems to be apprehensive: is he afraid of me? Who does he think I am? A member of the O.G.P.U.? Or merely a Park Inspector?

A woman emerges, coughing, from the mist collected, instead of the usual crowd, about the Guinness clock.

She has a string bag in one hand, and the leash of a dog twisted about the other. The dog is plump, a mongrel, with a red, tacky tongue hanging down from its mouth, and short, straining legs from which the feathers trail. "Naughty boy! Naughty!" she gets out between the coughs. "Don't pull! Naughty! Naughty!"

She reminds me of Helen Bristow: tall, like her, with the same protruding eyes—one would think both she and her dog were suffering from an excess of thyroid—and the same plain, bony elegance. She glances at me, before the mongrel drags her on.

Mischievously I whistle, on a single, low note.

At once the dog stops, and instead of being pulled, she now has to pull. "Whiskey! Wicked boy! Naughty! Oh, come on, blast you!"

I whistle again, at the same time tucking my chin lower and lower into my coat collar. The dog executes a few steps of a polka, and then skids round her legs and tries to make towards me, all but lassoing her to the ground. Through the gathering mist I can hear her swearing at it. "You bloody dog! My God, you bloody dog!" The dog cringes, its flopsy-bunny ears dragged back, and whimpers as the end of the leash descends. Though I whistle yet again, it no longer listens, but trots obediently behind its striding mistress. I get up and follow them.

I try whistling, and I try coughing, and then I walk along scraping my feet on the ground, as though I were skating. But still she does not turn. Only as she negotiates the iron swing-gate, thrusting it from her with a clang and pushing the dog's rump with an exasperated "Oh, go on, you idiot!" does she cast back a brief, apprehensive, defiant glance. I hasten my pace.

But at that moment she sees a bowler-hatted figure hurrying along on the opposite pavement, his silhouette, umbrella over arm and brief-case in hand, looking like the photograph in that advertisement for body-belts for men. She begins to croak, coughing simultaneously: "Charlie! Charlie!" The dog squeals and wriggles and eventually bolts across the road dragging its lead behind it. She lengthens her stride.

She and the man embrace, and then she takes his arm and says something to him which makes him look over in my direction. I try to be nonchalant: put my hands in the pockets of my overcoat, kick out at an empty ice-cream carton, begin to pick my way over the pavement, taking care not to step on the lines, and whistle 'One Rainy Sunday'—Irvine's favourite Greek song.

How silly I'm being! She's forty, if she's a day, and looks as if her body had been constructed from wicker. But she reminded me so much of Helen; for a moment I thought it was Helen—forgetting she was dead, one hand still clutching the empty tube of sleeping-pills which she had sent me out to buy. . . . No difficulty about that in Greece. "What would you like, sir? Soneryl, Luminal . . . or there's this new Swiss drug, highly recommended." Highly priced, too: but it did the trick all right. One's always reading in the Greek pages of sluts being taken to the hospital after swallowing an over-dose of quinine or a bottle of aspirins. They never die, probably don't intend to. I suppose that, unlike poor Helen, they can't afford the 'highly-recommended' drugs which are guaranteed not to produce after-effects of 'dizziness, nausea or headache'. . . . I remember once in a tavern near Omonoia Square (you pronounce that Ammonia; Irvine always used to make one of his feeble jokes that it was called after the public-lavatory there) a soldier and his girl began quarrelling, until he suddenly picked up his beer-mug and bit into it. He began to spit blood and glass, while the girl screamed, the crowds screamed and he screamed that he wanted to be left alone, he wanted to die. Of course he didn't want to die: he took care not to swallow the pieces, you can bet your life! I often saw him there again, at first with the same girl and then with another.

. . . There's Mrs. Mumfitt going up the stairs ahead of me. The English always despise the wops and dagoes for never washing, but no woman in Athens would wander about smelling like that. Even her cat would be ashamed to be in that condition. If I go up very quietly and very slowly perhaps she won't see me. Oh, hell!

"Good evening, Mr. Polymerides." She always pronounces my name as if it were 'Polly-Me-Rides'.

"Good evening, Mrs. Mumfitt." I feel like adding: "Don't point those breasts at me. They might go off." She's squeezing the left one as if she were judging marrows at an agricultural show.

Biting on her sand-coloured moustache, she says:

"So you're up to-day."

"Yes, I'm up. The old legs feel pretty weak."

"I thought you must be up and out. First the milkman was ringing, and then someone from the Jiffy Cleaners, and then someone, I don't know who he was. You're very popular!"

I open the door and, giving her a sickly smile, slip hurriedly through. "Oh, Mr. Polly-Me-Rides!" she calls, but I pretend not to hear.

I feel giddy and weak, as if I were going to faint or vomit. Stayed out too long. I throw myself down on the bed, without bothering to take off my overcoat, and fumble for a cigarette.

Oh, hell, hell, hell! I haven't any left, and I haven't any money.

IV

FRIDAY

CHRISTO has just been in to see me. He was on his way from one job to another, and since he was passing he thought—in his own words—that he'd 'look up an old pal'. Greeks are quick to pick up the habits of the place in which they find themselves, and Christo at once suggested that we should 'go round the corner for a pint'.

"Not with this bloody bladder of mine. It would be murder."

"Well, you can have a tomato-juice, old boy." There's something wrong about being called 'old boy' by someone with lips the colour of muscatel grapes, a hooked, fleshy nose and crinkly hair which looks as if it were made of black plastic. To-day he was wearing a blue pin-stripe suit, which puckered into creases over his shoulders, a stiff collar nipping a tie with a knot the size of his thumb-nail, and black shoes which, in spite of the high burnishing he had given them, were none the less as wrinkled as unsoaked prunes.

It was hard to believe that this was the handsome, arrogant boy, slouching at Zonar's bar in blue jeans and an open-necked silk shirt or grappling with a policeman during a Cyprus demonstration. He and his wife Maureen (who dislikes me) have a house called 'Santorin' just outside East Croydon, where they live with their two brats. On Sundays they drive to ' the coast '—they never say ' the sea '—and on Saturdays Maureen's mother looks after the children while they go out either dancing or to the cinema. Maureen teaches at what she calls a ' Dames' School '.

Christo, who has become a caricature of the English commercial traveller—he travels, himself, for his uncle-in-law's confectionery business—could not settle down to talk until he had first got a laugh or at least a word out of the barmaid at the pub to which he dragged me. I waited impatiently, kicking at a stool. The beer had left a line of froth along his neat moustache, as if he had just shaved: it got on my nerves.

" Well, cheers, old man," he grunted, tipping up his second glass. " All the best."

"*Yassoo,*" I said in Greek. It seemed ridiculous that we should be speaking English to each other.

" What d'you think of that? " he asked, nodding his head in the direction of the girl. I pulled a face. " You've always been a choosy bastard, haven't you? " He pressed the top of his cigarette-case, and pressed it again and again, muttering " Damn, damn, damn," until at last a cigarette shot up. There was a lighter attached to the other end. " Nice little toy," he murmured. " A chap we know got me one in Italy."

" How's the family? " I asked.

" Oh, fine, fine. Maureen's very busy, of course. You must come down one day." He had been saying this ever since Kiki and I had got married. " How's Kiki? "

" I wish she didn't have to work so soon before the baby arrives." Then I began to say some rude things about Kiki's mother and father, which I could see upset poor Christo: he has that respect for money and power

107

which is so common in Greece among people who will obviously never achieve either.

"What about you? Can't you get a job?"

"I've been ill in the first place. And in the second, I'm having all this trouble with the bloody police. I've got to be careful."

"You should have married an English girl, old boy!"

Christo was disappointed when he had first arrived in England with Maureen and discovered that her family was not rich as he had imagined; and he was envious when I married a daughter of old Vrissoglou—every Greek knows old Vrissoglou, as they know Onassis and Niarchos and Bodasakis. There was therefore a certain suppressed triumph in his tone.

"Oh, there are disadvantages to being married to an Englishwoman, aren't there?" I said, hoping to insult him: he had always been touchy.

He peered into his beer-mug, colouring as he did so. "All this business about English women being cold, it's a lot of bull-shit. I can tell you, I've had a damn sight more fun during these last three years in England than I ever had back home. Why, only yesterday evening, as I was driving through Balham——" I knew that as he told his squalid little story, his annoyance with me would pass, and I was glad of that. It had been silly of me to make that remark: after all, wasn't I hoping to borrow some money off him?

I listened, as one beery anecdote flowed into another. We used to talk like this to each other in Athens, bragging about the Swiss cabaret-girl, the South American widow or the Embassy wife with whom we had slept the night before. It had seemed fun then; now it was boring, and even distasteful. No Greek I have ever known has been improved by transplantation to England. A film of grime seems to settle on olive skins; and some kind of moral film seems to settle with it.

At last, in the greasy trough between one story and another, I bent forward and said softly, in Greek: "You know, Christo, I want to ask you a favour."

At once, as he belched and wiped his lips on the back of his right hand, a sour, furtive expression came over his face. "Yes? What is it, old man?"

"You couldn't—I suppose you couldn't . . . the fact is Kiki and I are virtually broke." That wasn't quite true. Kiki had been paid the day before. But who knew when I should next see Christo? And after all, her seven pounds a week didn't go far. "If you could manage to lend me the odd fiver . . ."

Christo drew a deep sigh which was almost a groan, opened his plump legs wide, and then put his empty beer-mug down on the table. He shook his head from side to side, theatrically lugubrious. "Haven't got a bean," he said in English. "Honest. No can do. S'matter of fact, Maureen and I are going through a bad patch ourselves. She *will* go to a dentist who isn't on the scheme, and that bridge of hers knocked me back a pretty penny. Sorry, old boy." These last three words were added in Greek.

God, the bastard! When he had paid for our drinks, I had seen the notes stuffed into his wallet. In the old days I was always lending him money, which he never paid back. Irvine disliked him, but in spite of that I often took him back to the flat for a meal or insisted on his coming along with us when we drove to Phaleron or Vouliagmeni. If it hadn't been for my asking Helen Bristow to ask him to her party, he would never have met his cow-wife Maureen.

And, in that case, where would he be now? You don't have much success at Zonar's bar when you've passed thirty and begin to look like an Armenian carpet-dealer.

I said nothing, drawing moodily on one of his cigarettes which I held between fingers that were trembling with rage.

"Cheery-bye, dearie," he called to the barmaid.

"Bye-bye, sir." She flicked with her duster at the counter, and waggled her bony shoulders.

Christo began to ease his bulk into the driving-seat of his Morris Minor, belching as he did so. Vindictively, I thought of Maureen having to submit to him: I liked the idea of that. Made for each other—and for no one else.

"Shall I drive you round the corner?"

"No, I'll walk."

"See you soon."

"I'll see you dead first. You swine!" I suddenly shouted. "When I think of the money I . . ." But I was walking away so fast that I knew he could no longer hear me.

. . . And now here I'm sitting, staring out of the window. God, that bloody Christo!

His father and his uncle used to own a little drapery-store in Hermes Street, but that was too good for him. He was registered as a student of engineering at the Polytechnic, but rarely attended classes, managing to pass from one year to the next by a combination of cheek, dishonesty and influence (one of his mother's sisters was married to an ancient Professor who had once been Prime Minister for a week). Christo spent his days on the beach, tanning and exercising his body beautiful, and his evenings at the fashionable bars showing his body off. But like all the young men of that circle, gifted with youth and a certain animal charm, few brains and no money, he was consumed more and more by boredom. The rowdy practical jokes which we played on each other, the drinking and card-playing when any of us had a wind-fall, the feverish quest for rich men or attractive women : these things might palliate, but could not cure, that ennui. Like so many of us, Christo turned to politics. Five years earlier he would have been one of those people whose fanaticism prolonged the agony of the Civil War; as it was, he threw himself into the organization of 'demonstrations' against the British. Soon he developed that schizophrenia so common among Greeks when they attempt to think politically, and saw nothing odd in being entertained by Irvine or Helen Bristow on the eve of leading a troop of shouting students to jeer and fling stones outside the American or the British Embassy. The Polytechnic professors were as much afraid of him as of the movement, and he knew this, and seized eagerly at the power which their fear thrust into his hands. The seal was put on his leadership when he received a number of bruises and a broken rib in a scuffle with the police. Christo became a hero; whereas the policeman who had lost an eye in the same scuffle was rapidly, and conveniently, forgotten. It was Christo who led a sortie to smash up the trams, because they were powered by the British Electricity Company. "Why don't you also smash up your mother's cooker?" I asked him on that occasion. But to that, needless to say, he could not find an answer, merely shouting at me that I was 'a bloody spy of the Intelligence Service'. (We were just entering on a period when 'British spy' took the place of Com-munist—which had in its turn taken the place of Fascist —as a term of abuse.) On another occasion he was responsible for smashing a number of the windows of the Norwegian Legation, explaining later that he had mis-taken the Norwegian flag for the Union Jack. In a country where the politicians conduct themselves like journalists, the journalists like students, and the students like brats in a kindergarten, it was not surprising that he achieved such popularity.

Maureen had come out as a governess at one of the Embassies: but she soon rebelled against being treated alternately as a confidential adviser and as a domestic servant, and having achieved her object of having her fare paid out to Greece, she handed in her notice and took a room of her own, where she used to give private lessons. She's a big-boned woman with aquiline features that will make people say when she's old: "What a beauty she must have been!" But she's no beauty now. Her voice sounds as if she were talking at a point-to-point. She lived round the corner from Irvine and me, and we used to avoid walking past her window for fear of being called in. "Hi, there!" she'd bawl. "Hi! Hi!"

"Good evening, Maureen." Irvine has the exaggerated politeness of all real misogynists. Then he would give a little bow, smile, and prepare to walk on.

"Come and have some bacon and eggs. I'm just cooking some for myself."

"Thank you, but we've long since had our breakfast. Thank you all the same."

"Well, a cup of coffee then."

"No, really, thank you very much."

"Or shall I make you some tea? Real Earl Grey you know! Given me by an admirer, though you mustn't tell anyone that." It was not the kind of news that Irvine was likely to pass on to his friends.

"Actually, we're in rather of a hurry——"

"Oh, nonsense! Would you prefer some Cointreau? Or just a lemonade? I've got some fudge I've just made. I know that Spiro loves fudge, with that sweet tooth of his." Like a mud-pie, Maureen's chocolate fudge used to crumble into grit as soon as one touched it: I loathed

112

the stuff. "By the way, Spiro, you never gave me back that tin in which I sent you your last instalment." It was a tin with the Queen of England on one side, and the Duke of Edinburgh on the other. Irvine's maid had been using it for biscuits. "Now come on! Let's have a ten-minute chin-wag. I want to hear all the gossip."

Reluctantly we entered, and at once she put a hammer into my hands: "Now be a good lad and put up my line for me. I can't ask Professor Gavrielides to do it—he's my next pupil—and anyway I don't imagine he'd know how."

"Well, what have you been doing with yourself, Maureen?" Irvine asked politely, as he removed, between finger and thumb, a pyjama-top that lay across the unmade bed and then lowered himself slowly at Maureen's invitation to 'take a pew'. There was only one chair in the room, and I was standing on it.

"Oh, what haven't I been doing!" Maureen kept up a pathetic pretence of leading a life crowded with adventure: which sometimes made her hearers wonder why, in that case, she was so often to be seen gazing from her basement window. "Lots of lessons of course—seventy-six hours of them last week."

"What energy!" Irvine murmured. Of course he did not believe her. "You must be getting rich."

"I was—until my burglary. . . ."

"Your burglary?"

"Oh, didn't I tell you?" Helen Bristow had had a burglary a week before; and anything that Helen had, Maureen usually wanted too. A long story followed, while we waited patiently for the drinks we had been promised. Then Maureen went to her cupboard.

"Oh, damn! That swine Anathassiades has swigged all the Cointreau, and the only lemon I have seems to be

growing mould. At least I *think* it's mould—isn't it?"
She rubbed a thumb-nail over the surface. "'Fraid so.
Now what am I going to give you?"

"A cup of coffee," Irvine suggested.

"It won't be real coffee."

"Anything you like, my dear."

Maureen put a saucepan on to the gas-ring, after she
had borrowed a match from me to light it. Then she
said: "I don't think much of your friend George
Constantinides."

Constantinides was a shy, handsome, ambitious lawyer
whom I hardly knew at all.

"Why?"

"Well, you know I'm preparing him for his Foreign
Office Exams, don't you?" We nodded, although we had
not known it. "The only time I could squeeze him in
was in the evening at ten. Well, he behaved himself at
his first lesson, but at his second . . . I had to tell him
to leave. Oh, I sent him off with a flea in his ear all
right!"

If an English girl invited a Greek to her bed-sitting-
room at ten o'clock at night, it seemed to me that she
deserved whatever she got. But, still, I did not believe
this story; I had heard too many such stories from
Maureen already.

"It strikes me that Greek men have only one thought
in their mind—sex, sex, sex. Believe you me, brother,
I'm sick of it! Why, in the bus the other day, when I
was coming back from Glyphada, there was this evzone,
and he kept pressing himself closer and closer to
me. . ."

Christo had not fallen in love with Maureen; but in
our circle we had all so often spoken of our plans to marry
either an American or English heiress and leave Greece
for ever, and here he had his chance. Maureen was

114

always talking about 'Daddy—he's rather a big industrial bug, I find it all so boring', and at the same time dropping remarks like 'when I was at school in Switzerland' or 'Uncle Fred promised me a hunter, but I asked for a trip to Italy instead'. But, apart from the glamour of wealth and social status, Maureen was blonde so that men whistled at her in the street when she was alone, and stared at her when she was with Christo. That flattered Christo's vanity.

As soon as they were engaged, she became as violently partisan as he in her politics. She would attack me with remarks like: "I'm not surprised that all your Greek friends say that you're a traitor."

To which I would reply: "Your English friends might say the same of you."

Often she would join in the demonstrations, and it was after one such occasion that we had our worst quarrel. I had wandered into a coffee-bar called the Brazilian, often frequented by foreigners, because I was trying to find a girl I had seen coming out of the American Express when I was too late for a dinner-date to stop. A fat young man in a duffle-coat, with a crew-cut, was standing in the doorway, one hand raising a cream-cake to his mouth while the other held a plate under his wobbling chin. He did not move to let me pass, though I said "Excuse me" first in Greek and then in English. I pushed past him, unintentionally jogging his arm so that a gout of cream splattered on one of his worn suède shoes. "Damn you!" he shouted in Greek, with a great deal else about people not looking where they went, and his shoes being utterly ruined, and was that how people behaved in my village? Greeks like to taunt each other with that last insult: no one lives in a village who can afford to live in a town.

I took no notice, but continued to peer from group to

group. Absurdly, a narrow waist and some long blond hair made me think that I'd found her, until a closer inspection revealed that what I was looking at was the back of a male German photographer who had once designed for Irvine some Christmas cards that looked like the more expensive kind of travel-brochure. Suddenly a voice said:

"Well, here's Mr. America!" It was a stupid, over-developed young man who had always borne a grudge against me for giving him the nickname 'Mr. Muscles': for some reason he thought that an insult.

Maureen, who was in tartan-trousers with a Mykonos scarf tied, charwoman fashion, over her hair, looked up from the straw at which she had been sucking as avidly as a baby at a teat. "Oh, hello," she said, as if she had just cut open a peach and found a maggot inside it.

No one was more effusive than that.

Maria behind the bar had meanwhile begun to prepare me my special, a mixture of coffee and chocolate, and though I hadn't intended to stay, I weakly decided to do so. Maria was touchy, and she'd been useful to me in the past, passing on messages and hints to women I wished to know. In return I was expected to flirt with her loudly enough for the rest of the shop to hear. "Well, Maria," I said, at a loss for a compliment, "you know who's got my vote for Star Ellas." Everyone in Athens at the time was talking about this beauty-contest.

I sipped from the glass she handed me, while Maureen's voice boomed through my head like a bad attack of sinusitis. "Alex was absolutely heavenly. There was this old boy saying '*Mais je suis Français, je suis Français*', trembling with terror, and Alex kept shouting at him in Greek, which he obviously couldn't understand: "Say 'Cyprus for the Greeks, Death to Eden', or we'll tip your car over." She whinnied with laughter, and the youths whooped and cackled around her, slapping their thighs.

"What I loved," Mr. Muscles said slowly and seriously, "was Christo unhitching the arm-thing of the tram."

"Yes, yes," the others agreed excitedly, while the fat boy in the duffle-coat asked in a voice throaty with pastry and cream: "But weren't you afraid of being electrocuted? I should have been terrified."

More cackling and whooping. "And all those people sitting there as if the arm-thing would get back of its own accord and the tram would start moving!" Maureen giggled hysterically, tears forming in the corners of her blue eyes.

"You're a wonderful shot, Maureen, I will say that," Alex put in in Greek. "You must have conked that policeman on the head at at least three metres range."

"Oh, that's the result of having been to boarding school in England. We played cricket in the summer."

"I must say the poor bastard looked amazed. He couldn't believe that bloody great rock had come at him from you, but there didn't seem to be anyone else from whom it could have come."

"I see that you've been having another picnic, Maureen," I said in English. "I can't wait for the day when you're either laid out with a truncheon or carried squealing on to a boat to be deported." I said this as if in joke, but Maureen knew that I was serious. She had now taken her straw out of her glass, and was twisting it round her forefinger as though it were a bandage.

Giving it a sharp tug, so that it broke, she said: "Where's the boy-friend?"

"Who do you mean? Your boy-friend's beside you."

"I meant yours."

"You know, Maureen, whenever you've taken part in one of these shows, you have the oddest look afterwards."

It was true. "As if you'd just had some pretty successful sex."

Maureen crimsoned, plunging her hands deep into her camel-hair jacket and thrusting out her legs. "Do you ever think of anything else?"

"Not often. Do you?"

"What do you mean? Christo, I will not be spoken to like this. I *will* not have it." She swung round on her stool, hunching her shoulders.

At that moment I wanted to hurt her as much as I could. "If you had a bit of successful sex, I don't suppose you'd be out with these hooligans. A woman of your age!" I added, remembering that Maureen was sensitive about being six years older than Christo. "It's absurd."

"Christo, will you please tell him to . . . ?" But Christo, as I well knew, was a coward: once already, when drunk, we had fought with each other, jumping out of a car on the road between Marathon and Athens, and he had later had to have three stitches along the line of his jaw. Seeing that he wouldn't interfere, Maureen now jumped up and shouted: "Don't talk to me! Do you hear? Don't talk to me! You—you bloody little pansy."

'Pansy' was the one word which I least liked anyone to call me. I knew that it was hopeless to expect others not to believe that I was Irvine's lover, but I was determined that there should be no doubt about the roles we each played. Perhaps that was part of the reason why I was so greedy for women. Now, in a fury, I jerked up my arm and the chocolate-and-coffee spattered over her face and the shoulders of her jacket. "You're so fond of throwing things at other people! How do you like that?" I demanded, as I pushed my way out of the shop.

I was convinced that her party would run after me and start to beat me up. But those that were not engaged in calming her down, contented themselves with merely gathering in a little knot outside the doorway, from where they screamed: "*Pousti, Pousti*" (that's the Greek for pansy), and a number of other offensive things.

An old woman who used to offer gardenias or roses for sale to any young man, preferably a foreigner, who was entertaining a girl for the first time, hobbled across my path, so that I almost fell over her. "Damn you!" I shouted. I'm not sure if I meant it for her, or the youths, or them both.

At that same moment I saw Helen Bristow walking towards me.

I had first met Helen through Jock, her son by her first marriage. Jock had come out to Greece while waiting to begin his military service. He had started by being an object of derision to us because of his Edwardian clothes: so that when he walked past the tables outside Zonar's, a bowler-hat too small even for his small head tipped over his eyebrows, and his trousers, too narrow even for his narrow legs, corrugated horizontally from ankle to knee, we usually used to greet him with cat-calls, whistles and cries of "Oh, I say!" or "Bad form, sir!"—these last taunts picked up from the scruffier of the members of the American Mission. Jock took no notice. He lived in a kind of dream, except when driving cars, playing bridge and poker, or flirting with women. Even when he was taking part in these occupations he seemed to be dreaming; but his skill at them proved that he must be really awake. He had had an insignificant career at Harrow, and it seemed likely that his career in the future would continue to be insignificant, short of his becoming a racing-motorist, a bridge-champion or a gigolo.

He came into Zonar's bar, as distinct from walking up and down outside it, at exactly seven o'clock each evening, and to the fury of the Americans would in five minutes be in conversation with the women that they had been ogling for the last half an hour. This was due, however, not to any charm of his, but merely to the naïve obtuseness of the Americans who refused to believe that the women were, in fact, whores. He would buy drinks, peppermint or banana liqueurs for the women and a series of gin-fizzes for himself. Then he would put an arm round the fattest of the collection, and massage one of her breasts with bony fingers which might have been those of an old man, while with his other hand he gave a sharp pinch to the buttocks of the girl on his other side, usually provoking a delighted squeak or giggle. The Americans in their blue jeans and sweaters would stare in disgust at his stiff collar, at least two inches high, his fancy waistcoat, and turned-up cuffs. Sometimes they muttered to each other that he was 'homo', but that was only jealousy: no one could have been less queer than Jock.

He had a small, triangular, pink face, with reddish gleams over his prominent cheek-bones and over a pointed chin that dimpled when he smiled. His hair, which was fine and blond, was already receding. He was always having expensive treatments for it, but apart from slightly varying its shade, they appeared to achieve nothing. The phrase he most used was 'I couldn't care less': which seemed to sum up his character.

His mother adored him, chiefly, I suspect, because she had adored her first husband, a subaltern in the Indian Army who had been murdered by *dacoits*: Jock was their posthumous child. She had some money of her own, and she lavished this on him no less freely than her love. Conrad Bristow, her present husband, a rich tobacco-dealer who spent much of his time up in Macedonia, regarded the boy with a sardonic indifference. He was not jealous of him, which would have been natural enough; nor was he fond of him. He used to talk about 'poor old Jock', as thought he himself were the younger of the two; and certainly his was the greater vigour.

I used sometimes to be invited to the large house in Kifissia. Conrad obviously distrusted me; but then, I told myself, if he had not learned to distrust all Greeks he would never have made his fortune. He was a thick-set man, with a faint north-country accent, whose restlessness at parties manifested itself in never being able to carry on one conversation with one person but having to obtrude, in turn, into every conversation that was taking place around him. A pipe, whether lit or unlit, was rarely out of his mouth, or a glass out of his hand. He was well dressed, and his shoes were hand-sewn; but for all that his appearance always seemed somehow rough and unfinished.

He adored Helen, even if he was brutal to her affectations, and her inability to make up her mind; curiously he did not seem to resent her affairs with other men, of which, being so astute, he certainly must have known. This tolerance was not due, I discovered, to any consuming interest in boys, or nursemaids, or cabaret-girls (as the Athenian gossips asserted, turn and turn about), but to the fact that all his energies were absorbed by his quest for money and power. When a new figure appeared on the political scene, he would woo him as if he were a beautiful woman; indeed he might woo a beautiful woman merely in order to meet the political figure. Greek politics are as unsatisfactorily complicated as French politics: Conrad must have been one of the few foreigners, inside or outside the Embassies, who understood them thoroughly.

One evening Jock and I had been at Kifissia for drinks, before going on to a party given by a Greek known all over Athens by his Christian name 'Sotiri'. Few people knew his other name, which was Papadopoulos—the Greek equivalent of Smith. Sotiri described himself as an 'agent': whether for houses, which he supplied exclusively to members of the foreign colony, for servants, for whiskey, gin and other such black-market goods, or for commodities even more dubious and expensive. He had what, in Athens, is called a 'garçonnière', and in England a basement, one large room with a small room off it, both of them crammed with quantities of gilt furniture, looking-glasses, paintings of sleeping shepherdesses being woken by the rough kisses of shepherds or of opulent-bosomed women rising from their baths, lamps with pink shades, boxes of Jannina silver containing either ancient chocolates that appeared to have been stricken with leprosy, or soggy cigarettes, hand-embroidered doilies, sheep-skin rugs and a smell of eau-de-Cologne. He would lend his key to this den to diplomats who would send him a case of spirits afterwards, to wealthy or influential Greeks in return for a favour, or to young men whom he fancied. If need be, he would arrange for a girl to be waiting in the flat: from her, he would expect at least twenty drachmas.

He was not a sinister character, as all this might suggest; he was not even a distasteful one. I found him kind, fundamentally stupid in spite of all his cunning and, like most procurers, oddly lonely and forlorn.

This evening he was giving what he called one of his 'balls', but Jock and I naturally did not tell Conrad or Helen this, pretending instead that we were going to the cinema. Stopping the car at a wine-shop on the corner where we had to turn down an alley to Sotiri's flat, I went in and bought three bottles of Samos wine. Greeks like their wine to be either resinated or sweet, and, since Jock did not like resin, Samos seemed to be the only alternative.

122

When we rang, a curtain of red damask was drawn back from the glass-panelled door, and a boy's voice asked shrilly in Greek, "Who it it? Who's there?"

"Two guests," I replied.

Then we heard Sotiri call out: "Oh, it's Spiro and the Englishman. Let them in!" The boy who opened the door shivered a little as he stood back for us to enter, massaging his left arm with his right hand: not surprisingly, since he was wearing nothing but a silk-scarf tied round his loins. A portable gramophone, placed on a marble-topped table the bandy legs of which terminated in gilt hooves, was blaring dancing-music. Sotiri held my hand in his for a long time, peculiarly high, as though he were about to execute a minuet with me, and alternately asked how I was, without listening for my answer, and gave instructions to the boy about where to put the bottles of wine we had brought. He was clad in a dark-blue suit which he had had made during a visit to Italy, the jacket cut so high that his prominent buttocks thrust out from below it.

A glass of banana liqueur was pushed into my hand by a girl wearing a towel fastened with two safety-pins, and a gold fillet in her hair. She then began to dance, sedately, with an elderly first secretary from one of the Scandinavian Embassies. All round us people were dancing: in evening-dress, in lounge-suits, in underclothes, in fancy-dress, men with women, men with men, women with women, or men and women by themselves. On cushions against the wall bodies lay out as though in a mortuary, slowly deliquescing, the one against the other. Jock began to give his nervous cough and smile simultaneously as a pert little girl, who had been saying that she was sixteen for the last seven years, sidled up to ask: "You mambo, yes?"

"I'll have a try." The two of them swept off.

Sotiri had been looking at his watch every few minutes, with a preoccupied, vaguely anxious expression on his flat, white face. "What's the matter?" I asked. "What are you waiting for?"

"Oh, my surprise. I'm going to keep it till eleven."

At all of Sotiri's 'balls' there was one of these surprises: a retired film-star perhaps ("You remember such-and-such, don't you?" Sotiri would say, mentioning the name of a film so old that no one could possibly remember it); a boy or a girl of what Sotiri would call 'Classical perfection' in spite of a snub nose, Slav cheek-bones or Mongolian eyes; a minor royalty; an ice-pudding which he boasted that he had prepared himself, though everyone knew that he had got it at a discount from Flocca; on one occasion even some indoor fireworks which set light to the overlong blond hair of Irvine's German photographer.

"What's it to be this time?"

"Wait and see."

A functionary from the Court, a pale, tight-lipped man with gold-rimmed glasses holding in place eyes that otherwise looked as if they would pop out like ping-pong balls and shoot across the room, was stationary before us, rocking back and forth, one hand inside the slit at the back of the dress of his dancing-partner, a child of about fifteen with far from clean fingernails and smudged lipstick. He was hissing something at her, as he hissed instructions at Court, while his hand explored downwards:

"You're just a little tart," I heard. "Aren't you? Just a nasty little, precocious little tart. Out for what you can get. Aren't you? But I like you, I really rather like you. You'd sleep with anyone for twenty drachmas, wouldn't you? I bet you would. Ten perhaps. That's the sort of slut you are. But I like sluts. Yes, I like little sluts like you. Probably you're a thief—if you get the chance. Eh? Do you thieve? Don't mind admitting it! I've nothing against a little thief, when it comes to going to bed . . ."

The girl, through all this, appeared not to listen, her green eyes focused on a silver-framed photograph of Sotiri himself, much younger and thinner, shaking hands with Venizelos.

Jock returned, mopping his brow with a silk handkerchief, and tore off first his jacket and then his black tie. "Christ, it's hot." He gulped at a glass of the banana liqueur and then choked and pulled a face: "What the hell's this flipping muck? Is that all we're to get to drink? What's become of those bottles of Samos?"

I knew Sotiri's habit of putting away the more expensive drinks brought by his guests.

Jock's girl returned. "You samba, yes?" she asked.

"Wasn't that a samba we just did?"

"No, that mambo. Now samba."

"Anything you say!"

Prematurely the party was reaching its climax. A trouserless old general, who had only just failed to be executed after the 1922 disaster, was whirling round in what appeared to be a Scottish reel, his arms extended, his shirt-tails flying, and his blue-veined legs knocking against the chairs, tables and other guests, while he let out a constant, high-pitched warble. Fortunately he was wearing a pair of y-fronted pants. A Greek actress lay full length on the floor beside the fireplace, while a young man poured into her open mouth a glass of something fizzy. She made a gargling noise, gulped, and suddenly ejected most of it into his face. Neither he nor she seemed surprised. Seated on a sofa next to me were two Englishmen in glasses, whom I had met somewhere, probably at one of Irvine's cocktail-parties. They were wearing flannel trousers and sports coats with leather patches at the elbows. They sat on the edge of the sofa, their arms crossed over their stomachs and their narrow shoulders hunched as if in an attack of colic. One was saying to the other: "No, honestly, you're quite wrong about that line. You see, it's a subjunctive—that gives the idea of doubt. You must translate it ' *may* '."

"H'm, h'm," the other said, still unconvinced. Then he blinked down at the corpse who had rolled over his feet. "I must ask Hood what he thinks," he said, drawing a pipe from his breast-pocket. He withdrew one foot, and the girl's head slumped to the floor; the Englishman seemed to be in two minds about removing the other foot, for fear of causing her partner the same inconvenience, and eventually left it where it was, taking out what looked like some nail-clippers which he jabbed into the bowl of his pipe with an expression of aggressive vigour.

Sotiri had disappeared into the other room, and when a middle-aged American woman tried the door, either out of curiosity or because she had mistaken it for the lavatory (I had heard her asking a number of guests for 'the Boys' Room'), she was at once repelled by the acolyte, now giggling instead of shivering, who had first let us in. She reeled away, muttering: "Shouldn't be allowed, scandal, what the hell," until she tripped over someone's legs and collapsed on to the floor, where she grunted, raised her head to peer around her, and eventually went to sleep.

"This party's gone dead," Jock swayed up to say. "How we going to liven it up—eh?" He hiccoughed disagreeably into my face, and repeated: "Eh?"

"Perhaps Sotiri will do that."

The acolyte emerged from the other room, switched off the gramophone to the outraged protests of the dancers, and carried it off in his arms, to place it behind a curtain. "What's up? What are you doing? Hey!" People shouted in various languages, but the acolyte only smiled, picking his way daintily over the cushions, glasses and outstretched legs to rejoin Sotiri. There was a lull, followed by cries of "Ready, ready, ready!" in the doorway to the other room and then taken up throughout the whole flat. The acolyte clapped his hands:

"Ladies and gentlemen!" he shrieked. "Ladies and gentlemen! Silence please!" Gradually everyone fell silent, except the American woman, who opened her eyes to mutter: "What's this? Where's Lydia? What's happened to the bitch?"

"Ladies and gentlemen! To-night we present the famous Italian *diva* 'Katina dei Colli' (in Greek there was a crude pun there), who will sing 'One Fine Day' from *Madame Butterfly*." He jumped on a chair with incredible agility, screaming "Signorina Katina dei Colli", and then, Ariel-like, leapt off again and darted to the curtain to turn on the gramophone. Sotiri emerged to resounding applause.

He was wearing a kimono of a brilliant shade of puce, crossed over what were presumably two cushions, and tied at the waist with a sash that appeared to be made of the same gold cord that he used for his curtains. His pudgy little feet bulged out of a tiny pair of Chinese embroidered slippers as, hands in sleeves, he took little tripping steps towards the curtain behind which the gramophone stood. His wrinkled, painted purse-hole of a mouth might have found itself in the centre of a horse's bottom; his face was dead-white. Somebody seated on the floor peered under the skirts of his kimono, at which Sotiri shot out a hand and, his face wholly impassive, gave him what must have been a painful slap on the ear. "Shame!" he trilled, contralto in Greek. Naturally he was bald, but now on his head he was wearing a black wig with two knitting-needles stuck, like hat-pins, through it, so that one almost imagined that they pierced his scalp.

He took the stance of an old-fashioned operatic soprano, legs straddled and hands clasped, threw back his head, closed his eyes, and then silently opened his purse-hole mouth as, from behind the curtain, the music started. It was a brilliant and well-rehearsed parody, and when a drunken youth attempted to join in, in a quavering falsetto, he was instantly silenced by the others.

" Bravo! Bravo! Bis! Bis! " There was a tumult of clapping and cheering. Sotiri, inserting his hands once more into the sleeves of the kimono, turned jerkily from one side of the room to the other, nodding his head, like some hideous mechanical toy. Jock snatched some roses from a vase and presented them to him with a low bow. Sotiri simpered, buried his face in the blooms, and then broke one off to stick in his wig.

" *Traviata!* " people now began to shout. " *Traviata! Do us Traviata!* "

" No, *Aida, Aida!* "

" *Lucia di Lammermoor!* "

Sotiri teetered off into the other room, from where we could hear him calling: " Marino, where are you? Come here! Come and help me! " in a voice the gruffness of which seemed obscene after what we had heard before. Marino was the acolyte.

The joke had been a good one; but jokes in Greece only become good if they are constantly repeated. We saw Sotiri, in a costume that appeared to have been crocheted out of beads, in the last act of *Aida*; we saw him in tartan as Lucia; we saw him, lying on the sofa in a pink night-dress flowing with purple ribbons, as he grotesquely mimed the death of Mimi, spitting into a vast vase and helping himself to cough-pastilles, half a dozen at a time, which he then ejected as he launched into his next high note.

"This is becoming a bore," Jock said.

"An awful bore."

"Let's go."

"But we must say good-bye."

"Oh, it'll be hours before he finishes. Come on." He caught my arm and pulled it, while the American woman, moribund on the floor, raised her head and said, presumably to us: "Sh, there! Sh!"

Both Jock and I had drunk too much; and the cold night air, after the fug of the party, had the effect, not of sobering us, but of making us more tipsy. Jock flapped his arms like a cabby, at the same time swaying gently backwards and forwards, as he asked: "Shall I go back and fetch the girl?"

"What girl?"

"Only one girl. Girl that danced the tango, and mamba, and shambo with me. Girl in blue dress."

"No, leave her, Jock. There are plenty of girls outside. Let's drive to Peiraeus."

He made feeble attempts to get the engine started, but contrived to stall it on each occasion. "No, you try," he said. "Olympia won't play for me to-night. See if she . . ." We changed seats. "Ah! The wizard's touch. See how she throbs! Hear that purr of p-p-pleasure! Christ! Am I going to be sick?"

"Where shall we go?"

"Bouzouki. I want Bouzouki. Lots of Bouzouki."

We set off towards Syngrou Avenue, and having once hit it, I sent the speedometer over to fifty, sixty, seventy, eighty, as we whizzed towards the sea. "Attaboy!" Jock cried, fumbling with his window. "Wheee!" he screeched, putting his head out as we shot past a police-man on point-duty. "Darling, I adore you!"

We swerved right when the sea glittered before us. As boys in the village Stelio and I had so often dreamed of driving some huge car headlong through the night, and now the dream had become a reality. The lights of on-coming vehicles seemed to spray us like tracer-bullets. "Bango!" screamed Jock. Then suddenly he began to yell: "Stop! Hey, stop! Tsitsannis, we're passing it! That's where we want to go."

"Tsitsannis is further on."

"Balls! Stop, stop! Hey, stop, damn you! Go back!" Suddenly he grabbed the wheel, fumbling at the same time for the brake, his body crashing against mine and bouncing away, as we swerved from side to side of the road. In a drunken fury I struck him across the mouth: "Let go, you bastard!"

"Back! Back!"

At that moment the 'bus came towards us. I was con-scious of soaring and then of plunging down, down, down, my mouth and nose full of something choking and searing. . . .

"What is it, dearest? Why are you staring like that?"

"Oh, nothing. Nothing. I just feel pretty bloody, that's all."

She comes to me and tries to put her arms round me, but I push her, gently yet firmly, away from me, saying: "Relax. That's all right, relax."

She sighs and begins to unbutton her coat and take off her hat. "I'll have to have this coat let out again. You know I'm sure it's twins. I really am enormous." Her lips are trembling, because I spoke to her like that. She flings her coat down, although she's usually careful with her clothes, leaving it half on a chair and half on the floor; then she crosses to me again. It's odd: when I can't bear to be touched by her and she knows it, it makes her all the more mad to touch me.

"What is it, monkey?" she cajoles.

Monkey! Christ!

"Nothing, nothing, nothing."

"Did you miss me all day?"

"H'm, h'm. But then I had Christo to cheer me up. The bastard!"

"How are they both?"

"As much in love with themselves as ever. Maureen says we must go down and see them some day. No date fixed."

"She's an odd girl."

"She's neither odd nor a girl. She's an unpleasant bitch, that's all, of a kind you can find anywhere."

"Don't talk like that, darling." She puts her lips to my forehead, and they feel rough and dry: this wind, I suppose. "Please don't. I hate it when you're bitter. It doesn't suit you, you know. England's made you bitter."

"England—and a lot of other things." She knows that I mean marriage as one of the other things, although I do not say it. But she continues to try to cheer me up.

"Guess who I met in Swan and Edgars?"

"Who? And what were you doing there anyway?"

"Oh, I went there for a sandwich and coffee."

"Good God, haven't I told you that you *must* have a decent lunch? You must!"

"Truly, a sandwich is all I need at midday—in spite of all this business of eating for two." She's on the arm of my chair, leaning so heavily against me that my shoulder has begun to ache. "Truly. You mustn't worry about us, monkey."

That monkey again! "Well, you've still not told me who you met," I remind her.

"Drusilla Aaronson—do you remember her at that Somerville Dance? Oh, but I was jealous."

"Haven't a clue who she is," I say truthfully.

That pleases her of course. "Don't be silly, darling! You danced with her for the best part of four hours. You *must* remember her. Well, she's working as a model, and she's doing most frightfully well. She was in Paris for three months last year. And I thought—or, rather, she thought—that instead of working for dreary old Pavlakis, well, why shouldn't I also try the same job? Not now of course. I wouldn't be much use now, would I?" she smiles down ruefully at her swollen figure. "But after he's born, some months after. What do you think, darling?"

"Well, frankly, my pet, frankly, I don't think you're —how shall I say it?—I don't think you're quite—well —quite the type." I drawl out the words, curling a lock of hair at the nape of her neck round my finger as I do so.

She gives me a push, jumping up as she does so. "Oh, you're beastly, beastly! I know that you think that I'm ugly—and—and that I haven't got a figure—and—and . . . Well, I just wonder why you married me! That's all!"

"It should be obvious. Boob that I was."

She rushes out and I can hear her sobbing in the kitchen, as she bangs about with the saucepans in which she's going to prepare our supper.

Oh, why did I say that? And why did she have to fly off the handle? So sensitive, so stupidly sensitive. But I'm a brute. I used to make Helen cry like that too. Irvine, sometimes.

"Hey, sweetie! Sweetie! Can't you take a joke? Sweetie! It was only a joke. . . . Oh, damn you! If you want to sulk, then sulk! But hurry up with that supper! Hurry up! I'm hungry!"

V

SATURDAY

I HAVE just returned from having lunch at the café round the corner. Mrs. Bacon, who was in to clean, said that she would fry me a couple of eggs and some sausages, but having had to listen to her talk at me off and on from eleven o'clock to half-past eleven, I decided to go out. She's a tall, heavily-built, handsome woman, who combines left-wing opinions with a nice sense of class. I fascinate and yet irritate her because, being a foreigner, I cannot be easily 'placed'. To-day she began to probe:

"Yes, it'll be a load off our minds if Hal gets his scholarship. Of course, what with those six weeks in bed having his hernia operated, and then all that trouble with that teacher who had a down on him, one can't really say for sure how he'll make out. But it'll mean a lot to us. There's nothing like a good education, is there? . . . Now in Greece, what kind of system would you be having there?" Mrs. Bacon uses the word system often, usually applying it to politics or to health, her two favourite subjects.

"Oh, much the same as here."

"And would you be having those public-schools—places like Eton College and Harrow College?"

"Yes, oh, yes."

"Now what would they be like? Do you have all this old-school-tie stuff? I'd have thought Greece more democratic than England. That's my impression."

"There are rich people and poor people."

"Same as everywhere. Except behind the Curtain."

"There, too, I expect."

"Ooh, this dust! I couldn't bear to live in Battersea, not after Highgate. The air's so clean up there, I notice it at once. It's this power-station of course. I expect you miss your home in Athens." I did not answer, in spite of the upward inflection. "Was it a flat?" she pursued. "Do they have flats, I mean?"

It was good to get away from all this, into a corner of 'B. Odell, Café', even though that was depressing enough, with a languid girl in a flowered overall, her hair still in curlers, swabbing at the linoleum-covered table with a sour-smelling cloth, while she used her other hand to clutch to her bosom the aluminium salt-cellar and pepper-pot and a chipped cut-glass bottle of vinegar. The coffee was octoroon-colour, and the fried potatoes had that mealy taste which comes from long keeping. Only the crisp bread was appetising. As usual after a bad meal, I now have dyspepsia.

I came home thinking of meals cooked by Irvine or prepared under Helen's supervision. They would exchange what he called receipts and she recipes, and often, when they were together, would bore me by discussing for half an hour on end the preparation of something seemingly as simple as a pilaff or a moussaka. Helen's food was usually better than Irvine's in reality, though, when described, his seemed to be the more exciting. Irvine ate, as the Greeks live, largely in the imagination.

Thank God, Mrs. Bacon appears to be about to go. She's put on her electric-blue felt hat, tucking her hair under it as though she were folding bedclothes under a mattress, and now she's rattling her umbrella about in the stand. "Well, I'll be off," she says. "I want to have a look in at Pontings to buy Jean a new plastic mac. That's the third I've bought her this year. Always tearing her clothes on something or other. She's becoming a real little tom-boy. Shall I take my money? It's thirty-five shillings owing, isn't it?"

I'd hoped she had forgotten: but Mrs. Bacon doesn't forget a thing like that. Now that she's gone, I remember that Kiki said I wasn't to pay her for that day she didn't come because she had one of her children in bed. Of course Mrs. Bacon forgot *that* conveniently. How tired I am of having to think about these small sums of money! It was not like that in the old days; then, all I had to do when my pockets were empty was to say so to Irvine or, later, to Helen. Often, both of them would chide me: "You silly boy! If you're broke, why don't you tell me?" after I had dropped some obvious hint. Then I used to pretend to look ashamed, and would mumble something like: "Well, it's not exactly pleasant to live on the charity of others." When Helen and I went out to dinner together, she would always slip a handful of notes into my pocket, and if, after I had paid the bill, I attempted to give her the change, she usually said: "Oh, keep it, my dear, keep it!" Sometimes I did really feel guilty; but then I told myself that both she and Irvine enjoyed the feeling of my being dependent on them, and since they enjoyed it, well, what was the use of depriving them of the enjoyment?

At first, after Jock's death, Helen hated me. She had already decided that I was a bad influence on Jock, having heard rumours about me, of which there were many, from both her Greek and her English friends. I was 'that boy kept by that American', 'that little crook', 'that gigolo'. She told me all this later, and we laughed about it together. 'Of course, really all the women who say such things about you would be thrilled if you made a pass! I used to say such things myself—and look how mad about you I am! Oh, yes, you're quite a topic of conversation at those dreadful canasta parties. You're like a film-star: far more people know you than you could possibly know." As you will see, she liked to lavish flattery as well as money on me: although she could also be sharp, for that was her natural character.

"I suppose I ought to go and see Mrs. Bristow," I said to Irvine during the first days of my convalescence. "I must do it as soon as we get back to Athens." We were staying at a watering-place called Loutraki, and at that time I was chiefly worried about a gash on my cheek which I was afraid might leave a scar, even though Irvine assured me that a scar would be attractive.

"Yes," Irvine said. "Yes. I wonder."

"Why?" I asked, peering at myself in the looking-glass in our bedroom and fingering the mauve, puckered flesh.

"We-ell . . ."

"Irvine, you really must change that shirt. It's filthy." From absent-mindedness, rather than any love of dirt, and perhaps also from meanness, Irvine never changed his clothes until they were visibly soiled.

"Yes, yes, I will."

"You were saying about Helen."

"Ye-es. . . . Well, you see, it's like this, my dear. You know how she adored Jock? He was everything to her. And this—this accident. . . . Well, it was unfortunate that you were at the wheel. And unfortunate—from her point of view of course"—he gave a small nervous giggle—"that he was killed, not you. I think she—she rather blames you," he concluded.

"Blames me! But if Jock hadn't been so drunk and tried to take over the steering-wheel——! "

"Yes, I know, I know. But of course—well, naturally —for her that's *your* story."

"It's the true story."

"I know, my dear, I know. Don't get so irritable with *me*. I'm just trying to explain to you what Helen must feel. It's not surprising, really, that she should decide —well—that she should decide that she doesn't wish to see you. Is it? Well, is it? "

This was a challenge, like the challenge of being told that some woman did not find me attractive; and as soon as we got back to Athens, I decided to go and see Helen. I did not telephone to her first, because I thought she would probably refuse to receive me, and I chose a time, in the late afternoon, when I knew that Conrad would be at work. Now I was pleased that the cut was still livid and swollen, and my face still pale and bony: I guessed, and guessed rightly, that this would appeal to her and touch her.

I found her in the front garden of their house in Kifissia, giving instructions to their hunchbacked gardener, who was potting some plants. She was a tall woman, and she stood, her shoulders flung back and her head high, one gloved hand on her hip while the other held a pair of secateurs. Her legs, in their ribbed woollen stockings, were wide apart. The wind had whipped colour into her normally pallid face, and her blue eyes were sparkling.

When the gate clanged behind me, she turned round, saw who it was, and seemed to be about to bolt into the house. "Hello," I greeted her, as nonchalantly as I could, while I advanced across the lawn.

"Good afternoon." There had always been a note of asperity in her voice, except when she was talking to

Jock or to the innumerable ragged old women, one-legged men or scabby children who came to the door to beg, and that note was now especially pronounced.

I stood awkwardly, waiting for her to say something else. At last I remarked: "This is really my first major outing. I hear you—you came in to see me while I was still under morphia. I didn't know. Thank you very much."

"The doctor insisted."

Later she told me that her love had dated from that moment when, stricken with grief, she had stood beside my unconscious, bandaged body: but she had not known it at the time, imagining that she felt nothing but loathing for me.

"I'm—I'm terribly sorry. . . . I mean . . . I feel I'd like to explain."

"Oh, please don't let's discuss it. I'd much rather not discuss it."

She walked towards the terrace of the house, and I followed behind her.

"I know you think that I—that I was to blame. . . . You do, don't you? Everyone tells me so. But honestly —well, I want you to hear my story. That's only fair, isn't it?"

She turned: "I don't wish to discuss it, Mr.—Mr. Polymerides." In the past she had called me Spiro. The cold had forced tears into her eyes, and one now trickled down the side of her long, handsome nose, as she repeated: "I'm not interested."

"It might just as easily have been I who was killed."

"It might—but it wasn't."

Suddenly, I was aware that she was squinting at the scar on my forehead, and pretending at the same time not to squint at it. I touched it with the fingers of my left hand, on the back of which there was another scar. She looked at that too. "Well, come in," she said. "But please don't talk about it. Please."

It was a beautiful house, built by a Smyrna merchant who had then gone bankrupt, and Helen had filled it with beautiful things. There was an open fireplace, so rare in Athens, piled high with logs, and a low table on which were laid out the silver things for tea. She rang for another cup and plate and then, softening a little in her manner, asked:

"How's Mr. Stroh?"

"Oh, Irvine. Fine, fine."

She cut me a piece of one of the two cakes on the table, and I wondered why they were there: she herself ate nothing. She held her large, capable hands out to the fire, and said in her deep, yet musical voice:

"You've got thinner."

"Oh, I'll put it on again."

The telephone rang, and she went across to it. Soon she was saying in a cross voice in Greek: ". . . but I must have it by this evening, I'm afraid. As you promised. Yes, you promised. No, I'm sorry, I must have it this evening. Yes, yes. I can't help that. This evening. By seven o'clock at the latest. At the latest. Well, I can't help that. I must have it. . . ."

When she had finished, she banged the receiver down in exasperation, and burst out: "Cretins! Why *do* they promise to get things done, when they know that they can't? It's so stupid, so pointless. And it was such a tiny job, one strut of a bridge-table which has to be fixed. We've used that carpenter for years and years." She threw a log on to the fire. "He'll be lucky if we use him again."

As she passed in front of me to return to her chair, by some miscalculation of the space between me and the tea-table, she had to brush against my legs, and I noticed that at the contact she drew in her breath sharply and made a quick grimace, as one does when one suffers a sudden shooting pain.

"Well," she said, "did you enjoy wherever you were? Someone told me where you'd gone, but I've forgotten. Delphi?"

"No, Loutraki."

"Vile place."

"The hotels are good. And there was no one there."

"When we went, they all looked like monkeys. Monkeys playing bridge and canasta. Or stuffing themselves with greasy food. We left at once, and motored on to Patras. There the people still looked like monkeys and were still stuffing themselves, but at least they weren't playing cards." Helen was one of those English people who see nothing tactless in making remarks of this kind to foreigners. The foreigners themselves are either flattered, because they are being treated as if they were English, or insulted. When I protested on such occasions she would exclaim: "But I don't regard you as a Greek!"

"Then what am I?"

She would laugh: "I don't know. But you're not a Greek."

Slowly she softened, until, leaning forward in her chair, she asked: "Well, have you recovered? You have some nasty scars still, but otherwise—are you all right?"

"Oh, yes, yes. Thank you."

There was an embarrassed silence, and she began to speak about Irvine:

". . . I adore him, I absolutely adore him." Helen tended to go to the extremes of either adoring people or regarding them with contemptuous loathing. "Though I know that he's no use for me at all, since I'm a woman. But he's always so courteous and kind. And he knows such a lot. His knowledge is really encyclopædic, isn't it? And even his little meannesses, which upset other people, don't upset me. Most people are generous in small things, and mean in big ones. Irvine is just the reverse."

So we continued to talk; till suddenly she asked: "Tell me, Spiro, where do you live? I've never known."

"Oh . . . near Irvine. Near there. I have a room."

I was astonished that a woman who knew so much about everybody did not know that I stayed in Irvine's flat. Or was she being disingenuous? Weeks later I asked her, and she replied: "Oh, I'd heard gossip about that, of course. But I never believed it. It never struck me that Irvine would do anything so foolish. Especially since these purges have started." It was typical that Helen should have heard about the purges long before Irvine or I or any of our American acquaintances.

When I got up to leave, she said, off-hand: "Well, pass by some time. You know how to find us now, don't you?"

It seemed an odd thing to say when I had been brought so often to the house by Jock.

The next Saturday, when I returned from my English lesson, Irvine announced:

"Oh, the Bristow woman telephoned. They're driving to Ramnous for a picnic to-morrow, and want us to join them. I said that we'd planned to go to the morning concert."

"Ramnous would be more fun."

"With them?"

"It's Economides conducting. You know that you always say that he reminds you of a duck having a bath."

"But the Haydn variations, I'd like to hear them."

"You've got that Beecham record. While we have this spell of fine weather, it seems a pity not to——"

"Well, let's go somewhere alone together."

"In a crowded 'bus? You know what Sunday's like."

"I could get the office-car."

"And pay for it? Why?" That, I knew, would be the strongest argument with Irvine. There was a silence, while he deliberated.

"I find her rather tiresome," he said at last.

"She knows that." Helen did not know it, but since Irvine morbidly shrank from hurting anyone's feelings, I pretended she did. "She thinks you think her a bore."

"Well, she is. But I quite like her, have nothing against her. Did she really say that?"

"Yes, the other day."

"I don't know where she got the idea. I'm always quite polite to her. Aren't I?"

"Not always."

"Yes, always, Spiraki!"

"You have an off-hand way of saying things to people sometimes. You don't realize it, you know."

In the end Irvine telephoned to Helen and told her that, after all, we should like to accept the invitation. I heard him from the hall: ". . . no, no, you must let me make the Scottish eggs. You can bring the *pâté*. No, I insist. I have a receipt which Robert gave to me, I want to try it out. Ah, that's a secret. Wait till you taste them."

The Bristows had had two cars, the American Ford which Jock and I had smashed, and a Landrover in which we now set off. Helen drove, tensely and with a great deal of cursing under her breath at pedestrians, traffic-policemen and the gears. Conrad and Irvine talked politics, and I said nothing.

". . . I can't think why Papandreiou hasn't gone

further," Conrad was saying, with the worried air of a father discussing his son's career at school. "After all he was the best Minister of Education that Greece has had for years. And he's certainly the most brilliant man in Greek politics."

"The most brilliant man, but not the most brilliant politician," Helen put in dryly. She was bored by Conrad's obsession with politics, and yet, since she was an extremely intelligent woman, her remarks on the subject were normally far shrewder than his.

All through lunch, which was excellent, Conrad went on discussing the career of Papandreiou. Eventually Helen said to me, "Let's go and explore". Irvine was aware that we were drifting away and watched us unhappily; Conrad was not.

"Oh, how tired I get of all this political nonsense! As if it meant anything at all in this backwater."

"Football doesn't mean much either—and yet people quarrel about it."

Helen had a Leica camera, and was experimenting with a colour-film. Everything she did, she did efficiently, and she was now so careful to work out each of her exposures with a meter that I began to understand what Conrad had meant when he had said to her, testily, earlier in the day: "I used to think that Baedeker bores were hell to travel with, but camera bores are worse." She photographed me against the jagged base of a column, my smile becoming more and more false as she kept saying "One moment, one moment," and changing the stops. "That'll be nice," she remarked, when she had at last taken the photograph. "Your olive skin, and your red shirt, and the white of the column. And the sky and sea behind."

"Shall I take you?"

"Oh, no, I hate to be photographed. Unless it's by a

143

Cecil Beaton or an Angus McBean. Then I know that it'll be flattering."

"You don't need to be flattered.".

"At my age?"

"Come on. Let me take you."

"Oh, all right." She slipped the camera off her shoulder. "But put this strap over your neck, won't you? In case you drop the camera."

I put out my hand to grasp the strap, but she herself raised it, and eventually I ducked my head underneath. There was something clumsy about us both. Her hands rested on my shoulders, the fingers long and bony, with one enormous stone above her wedding-ring. She said in a rapid, irritable tone: "No one has the right to be as handsome as you."

I am used to women paying me compliments, and I am seldom at a loss for a graceful retort. But like some schoolboy of seventeen, I now merely grinned at her sheepishly.

"I should hate to fall in love with you."

"Why?"

"I don't think you'd give me much of a time. Would you?"

"Try it, and see."

"Shall I?"

Suddenly she put her lips to mine. It was a lightning kiss, and when I attempted to prolong it, putting out my arms to drag her towards me, she cried out: "No, no! Take care of the camera. Take care. Don't be such an idiot."

We walked on, taking it in turns to stumble over clumps of asphodel, hidden chunks of marble, or rabbit-holes.

"You're very vain," she remarked, peering down at her feet.

"Why do you say that?"

"Oh, I can see it. Like all Greeks. You know that you're not particularly clever, and not particularly efficient. But you don't care. You're beautiful, and that's enough. Isn't it?"

I disliked the tone, sardonic and combative, in which she had spoken.

"Well, you're arrogant," I said.

"I? How?"

"You think most people are monkeys," I said, laughing.

"Do I? Well, they are! Most Greeks, at any rate. Clever and charming monkeys."

"You shouldn't say that to me," I said, half joking and half cross. "I'm a Greek, after all."

"Oh, you! . . . Anyway, if you're a monkey, you're a very pretty one."

That adjective 'pretty' made me crosser.

"Now photograph me," she said. "But from far away, so that my wrinkles don't show."

When we returned to the others, they had drunk nearly a whole bottle of Naoussa wine between them, and Irvine, whose head was weak, was already slightly tipsy. He pirouetted and pranced, like some mechanical doll, as he helped to pack up the picnic-basket, talking all the while in an over-pitched, over-precise voice. He was making a comparison between politics in fifth-century Athens and politics in modern Greece, digging away at the subject with his usual dentist-drill persistence.

Helen drove even more abominably on our return. As we came swaying along the muddy track which joined the main road, an old woman emerged from some bushes, spinning with one hand while with the other she clutched the rope of a goat. The goat, terrified by the oncoming

145

car, reared on its hind legs, but Helen, instead of slowing up, merely began to hoot. Leaping sideways, the goat tugged its halter loose from the hag, and bounded down the hill-side. The woman shouted and then gestured at the car, showing us the palm of her wrinkled right hand, the fingers extended, and at the same time thrusting out her tongue.

"She's put a curse on us," I said.

"And well deserved," Conrad muttered. "God, you do drive badly. And inconsiderately. That poor wretch will be chasing her goat for the rest of the day."

Helen did not seem to care, and though I disliked her for not caring, I also admired her. I suppose I'm ruthless myself—certainly I'm often told so—and ruthless people tend to admire ruthlessness in others. Anyway, at that moment I was reacting from Irvine's sentimentality: if it had been he who frightened that goat, nothing would have satisfied him short of going off in pursuit of it himself, and he would have been mentally wringing his hands over the incident for the rest of the day. As it was, he said mournfully: "Poor old thing! She looked at least a hundred." Had he been a little less frightened of Helen, he would certainly have asked her to stop.

From then on we had a series of small mishaps. We got out at a café, and Helen, backing the car, managed to scrape the mudguard along a wall. She took out her camera to photograph a view of Euboea and discovered that her yellow-filter had dropped out of its little purse. Then the clasp of her bracelet came mysteriously apart, and, though Conrad twisted it back and forth in exasperation, until she cried out "Oh, leave it, leave it! You'll only make it worse," he was unable to get it to work again.

"You see, the evil eye," I said.

"What do you mean?"

"That woman. She's put a curse on you." I half-believed it: in the Greek villages there is no one who does not believe such things.

"Oh, what a bore," Helen said, and she *sounded* bored. "How do I protect myself?"

"It depends on the strength of her magic. We'd better start with blue beads. If they fail—and they often do—we'll go on to something more complicated."

Irvine began to talk about primitive magic: one of those disquisitions of his which seemed to be rehearsals for lectures he would never give, rather than attempts at conversation.

When we got home, he was oddly fretful.

"What a tiresome day!"

"Didn't you enjoy it? I did."

"Yes, I could see that. I used to think Bristow the greater bore of the two. Now I'm not so certain. She's such a bad-tempered woman," he added.

"You don't sound in any too good a temper yourself."

"Well, I hate to waste a whole day."

"But you love Ramnous. You know you do."

"What did you and she find to talk about?"

"Oh, this and that."

"Mostly *that*, I expect."

"What do you mean?"

"Dear Spiro. She's obviously in love with you. Isn't she? Don't you feel it?" He said it in the tone in which patients reveal their more alarming symptoms to their doctors.

"Rubbish."

"Oh, no, not at all. You wait and see."

I met Helen, by accident, in the street two days later. She was looking astonishingly handsome as she strode down Hermes Street in a mink coat, her head as always held erect above a crowd most of whom she dwarfed.

"My blue beads," she said as soon as we had greeted each other. "You must get them for me. Things are still going wrong. One of my maids has German measles, and the lights fused three times in the course of last evening."

"Sounds bad. I may have to take you to a witch."

"Let's try the beads first."

I walked her down to Monastiraki, where there is a row of wooden-shacks outside which dangle bridles, halters, girths and saddles. There is always a smell of the country there, although one is in the middle of the city, and most of the people who pass are dressed as peasants and have the slightly bewildered, sleep-walking peasant look.

We found a string of beads, with a leather cross attached at each end. "I can hardly wear it," Helen said. "Can I? That kind of blue is really not my colour."

"Unless you wear it under your dress."

"So lumpy and uncomfortable. In my bag, perhaps?"

"Yes, why not?"

"What do I owe?"

"Nothing."

"Is it a present?"

"Of course."

"But why?"

"Because I want it to be."

She slipped the beads into the purse of her bag, and then said: "Well, Spiro, that's very sweet of you. Now I have something to remember you by." On a lower note she added: "As if I should forget you."

The following day she telephoned to Irvine, to ask where I could be found.

148

When I spoke, she announced at once: "They've worked."

"What have worked?"

"The beads. I won a hundred and eighty drachmas at bridge last night, I've found the brooch I thought I'd lost, and Conrad has had to go off on a tour to Macedonia."

"Good," I murmured.

"When shall I see you?"

"Oh, I don't know."

"Thank you for that enthusiasm. . . . Well, when?"

"When would you like?"

"Now?"

"Now?" I repeated: it was barely twelve o'clock.

"Come and have lunch with me."

"But I'm supposed to lunch with Irvine."

"The fairy godmother? Oh, put him off! Can't you think of an excuse?"

"It'll be difficult."

But it was never difficult; Irvine believed anything I told him. I produced some story about having met some cousin of mine, who was a sailor on a ship which had docked at Peiraeus for the day, and at once he agreed: "Oh, but of course you must go and see him." I hated Irvine for being so easy to deceive, just as, on the telephone, I had hated Helen for being so easy to humiliate.

The lunch was excellent, and we had a bottle of hock instead of a Greek wine. "I don't know why I'm giving this to you," Helen said, in that tone which was half-joking and half-insulting. "You won't realize how good it is."

"Why should you think that?"

She laughed, and leaning forward, put a hand over mine, as though in an attempt to take the offence out of her words: "Because no Greeks know a good wine from

149

a bad one. Even your bottled wines are wildly variable.
Look how a Naoussa '43 tastes, in one bottle like the best
Burgundy, and in another like vinegar! And that awful
Mavrodaphne which you all adore—invalid port, that's
all. I remember when Professor Emmanuelides returned
from a Conference at Oxford last year. He maintained
that he had brought back with him some excellent 'English' wines. It was only when we went to dine with him
that we realized that he must have shopped for them at
the local chemist's!" There was something hard and
crude in her mockery, and yet it appealed to me, in spite
of my annoyance. This was to be the pattern of our
relationship in future: when she was not humiliating
herself, she was busy humiliating me.

As she handed me my cup of coffee, she demanded:
"Why do you wear that appalling ring?"

"It's not appalling. What's wrong with it?"

"It looks so vulgar. I'm surprised Irvine has never
told you so." Irvine had, in fact, often remonstrated
about the ring; and it was more out of obstinacy than
anything else that I had persisted in wearing it, even
though I acknowledged to myself that his objections were
valid. It consisted of a modern cameo, the colour of a
blood-orange, of a helmeted Greek warrior set in heavy
gold.

"What's vulgar about it? No one in England would
wear such a thing, but what has that got to do with it?
This is Greece, not England. You're so insular! You've
lived abroad for years and years, and yet you still expect
everything to be exactly as it is back home. That's
typically English, of course."

"Yes, you're right. I suppose I am insular." There
was a throaty, vibrant tenderness in her voice as she con-
ceded the point. "You mustn't take me too seriously,
though. . . . I like to tease."

When we had sat talking for half an hour, she suggested that we should go out for a drive. "It's such a lovely day. Oh, these winter days in Athens—there's nothing like them anywhere else in the world."

We drove out until we reached the end of the new road, then uncompleted, between Vouliagmeni and Sounium. An old shoe lay on the road beside a puddle that glistened in the sunlight; an empty cigarette-carton lay beside it, some wrapping paper, and a crust of bread. Further on a concrete-mixer seemed already to be sinking beneath the chocolate-surface of the newly-dug extension of the road. No one was in sight.

Helen clicked on the radio. "Bach," she said, as the clanging, jigging sounds of a harpsichord came out. "The Italian Concerto."

I couldn't stand it, and hurriedly pressed another button.

"Oh don't! Spiro, no! No!"

"Yes, yes!" I said.

"Bully." She relaxed against the seat and then put her hand on my knee. She sighed. "We have nothing in common. Have we?"

"Except this." I leant over and put my lips to hers.

She allowed me to kiss her only momentarily, giving a quick flick of her tongue, and then pulling her head away, laughing coquettishly, in the manner of a woman of a different class and age. There was something nauseating about it, and I demanded brutally:

"Why do you do that, when you know that you like it?"

She scrambled out of one side of the car, and I out of the other. She kicked at the stone which lay in the road, and then, plunging her hands deep in the pockets of her tweed coat, began to walk down the grass slope to the sea. There were three flying buttresses of rock, purple

151

and veined like newly-cut steak, and under each there was shelter from the wind. We lay under the third, where the sea was so loud, echoing as if in some empty hall, that we had to shout if we wished to speak to each other. But we had little to say.

We lay under our coats, shuddering a little from the cold and our excitement. Helen's body, strong and firm from exercise, was of a kind that one never meets in Greece. Peasant-women's bodies are equally muscular; but at that age they are scraggy and scrawny and twisted with child-birth and toil. The women of the middle-classes get marshmallow soft: that is how their men prefer them. Helen was forty-five at least, and hers was the most beautiful and the most responsive body that my hands had ever touched.

She gazed up at me at the end, stern and yet wary; I began to feel uneasy.

"Well," she said, "no good can come of it."

"What do you mean?"

She began to pull up her brassière, and clumsily I tried to help her.

"Do you think that I can't see that you're hard, and selfish, and mercenary?"

"Well, you're hard too."

"Oh, not hard enough for you, my dear Spiro."

We walked back to the car in silence, our arms linked.

Irvine had never been jealous of my affairs with women in the past, but he was jealous of Helen. Unconsciously he had always regarded me as his own work of art; and now it was as if someone else had picked up a brush and begun daubing at it. When he had questioned me about Stassa, the girl who took coats at the Argentina, or about Lydia, who was a typist in the American Naval Mission, or about any other of the women with whom I had slept,

I had been completely frank with him, because I had divined that in this way I provided him with some peculiar kind of titillation. He would pretend to be shocked, with exclamations of "You wicked boy!" "Oh, the poor creature!" "No, Spiro, you really have no conscience!" and so on; but in fact he was delighted. In the case of Helen, however, I was as secretive as possible. I did not tell Irvine that she was my mistress; I even denied it angrily when, from time to time, he made the suggestion. But he knew I was lying: Irvine always knew my inmost feelings, as I knew his.

About three weeks after that drive when we had lain together shivering under the flying buttress of rock, Irvine fell ill with influenza, which was followed by laryngitis. He lay on his side, his knees almost touching his chin, except when he was asleep, and then he lay on his back. However often I, or the maid, straightened his bedclothes, they were always either about to slip to the floor or wound, like swaddling-bands, about his pink, infantile body. He blew his nose noisily, and cleared his throat as if he were gargling with castor-oil. The soups he was brought were always either too hot or too cold; the books either ones he had read, ones he did not wish to read, or ones that were so closely printed that they tired his eyes. He was afraid of illness, but he embraced the fear with the exhilarated abandon of someone on a switch-back: indeed, it was only when he discussed his temperature or the doctor's last visit that he rallied at all.

He liked me to sit with him, but, after five minutes of having me at his bedside, would either grow peevish, begin to read or draw the sheet up to his chin and fall, or pretend to fall, asleep. He had not shaved for a number of days, and grey-white bristles, like those of an extra-hard toothbrush, stuck out from his pointed chin.

"Would you rather I didn't go to this concert?" I asked. The tickets were his, and I had told him that I had invited Christo in his place, although, in fact, I had invited Helen. Anyone else would have suspected I was lying, since Christo was the last person who would be willing to spend two hours listening to classical music; it was odd enough that I myself should be going, now that I was relieved of the obligation of accompanying poor Irvine.

"Oh, no! I shall be quite all right. Irene is doing some ironing and will be here for at least another two hours. It would be a shame to waste the tickets," he added. Kempff was playing, and Irvine had already grumbled about having had to pay thirty-five shillings for each. "Tell me all about it when you get back. But don't be late."

Helen greeted me in the foyer: "It's as mad for me to be seen here with you, as for the fairy godmother. Everyone one knows seems to have come. I've just said hello to the Ambassador. How lucky you didn't arrive five minutes earlier!"

Maureen, in a tartan skirt and beige twin-set, passed with a nod and a crooked smile: she would like to have cut me, but she had an acute sense of the importance and power of people, and she knew that Helen was both important and powerful in the foreign colony. However, I was sure that this knowledge would not prevent her from gossiping about us as soon as she was out of earshot. I watched her: she was ascending the stairs to the gallery, taking them in twos and threes as if she was climbing the Lycabettus, while three youths, whom I knew by sight only as the members of a swimming team, pursued her less athletically. At the landing she paused and, glancing down at us, made some remark. The three youths squinted, one of them with his mouth open, and then two of them began to laugh. The other merely widened his gawp.

Helen used to suffer from bouts of restlessness, and this was one of such occasions. The music was superbly played, even if it had obviously been chosen for an Athenian audience: a great deal of Beethoven and Liszt, and even more of the composer whom Athenians call 'Sopin'. But Helen, not I, was the one who intermittently wriggled, looked around her and sighed on this occasion.

"What's the matter?" I whispered to her, between items.

"I can't sit still."

"I can see that."

She slipped her hand under the arm that separated my chair from hers, and then rested the back of it along my thigh. Now she was quieter, but in the interval she hurried out before the applause was over and then, in the still empty foyer, turned round to urge me: "Let's go."

"Go?"

"I don't like to be seen by all these people who know me. It's madly indiscreet."

"Are you ashamed of me? Everyone knows that I was a friend of Jock's."

"Everyone knows a great deal else about you too. Come on." She grabbed my arm and pulled me towards the door, as some students came clattering down the stairs from the gallery. I followed her out, without protesting further: after all, I was not so fond of classical music, and the seats were at once hard and yielding, like beds in the worst kind of hotels.

Helen climbed into the car, and at once started an altercation with a policeman, who told her that she had no right to have parked where we were. "I don't understand a word, not a word. Don't understand. No understand," she reiterated in English, although she understood perfectly well.

The policeman waved his arms, as if he were attempting to repel an attack by a swarm of bees, shouted and grew red. Then he gave up. "All right, all right. Make tracks," he shouted in Greek. He even grinned. Needless to say, Helen understood that idiomatic 'Make tracks' all right. She chuckled:

"When friends of mine arrive in Greece and ask me if they ought to learn the language, I always tell them to do nothing so foolish. If one can't speak a word, one is given the same licence as an idiot."

"Where are you driving?"

I had assumed that she would be making her way either home or to Zonar's or the King George Bar. But we were now rushing out along Syngrou Avenue towards Phaleron and the sea.

"Aren't we going to eat something?"

"I mustn't be late. I said I'd be back as soon as the concert was over."

"He won't come to any harm."

"He hates being left alone, when he's ill in bed. I mustn't be late," I repeated.

"Rubbish. We shan't be very late."

"Please, Helen!"

"Rubbish."

We turned right, towards Peiraeus, as Jock and I had turned right on the night of our accident, and as we made our way along the sea-front of New Phaleron, much more slowly now, Helen began to hum the tune of the 'bazouki' song which we could hear being bawled, amplified at least a hundred times, after the Greek fashion, in one after another of the neon-lit taverns. It was 'The Girl Wants the Sea!' One heard it everywhere that winter.

" Where are we going? "

" You'll see."

She turned down a narrow side-street, and then another, and then a third, and stopped outside a tavern which was no more than a wooden and corrugated-iron shed. " You like sea-food, don't you? " she said.

" Yes."

" Well, you get shrimps here that are bigger than any-where else in Athens. And fried mussels, and ink-fish. Good wine too." She began to lock the car, and having done so, slipped her arm through mine. " There are other advantages as well, my dear."

There were three cast-iron tables on the bare wooden floor of the room which we entered, each covered with a blue check table-cloth, from which the colour had run in streaks, almost as though by design. An old, unshaven, bloated creature with a swollen upper-lip sat, in an apron, at one of the tables, with one arm dangling over the back of a chair on his right and one leg supported on the strut of a chair on his left, while he sleepily opened and shut his eyes. A woman was frying something in a pan on a charcoal stove, while a boy, who could not have been more than nine or ten, in an apron reaching to his ankles, sliced some potatoes.

On the left side of the room there was a partition, open along the top, with three wooden doors set into it, like lavatories at a barracks or school. Helen, wholly un-embarrassed, greeted the old man and the woman, obviously knowing them, and then pointed at the furthest of the doors. The boy scuttled across to it, and pushed it open, his wet hand leaving a mark on the cracked green paint like the trail of a slug. Helen, to my annoyance, began herself to order the meal, and it took a long time. She smelled the oil, and prodded at the eye of a fish, gleaming on an aluminium platter, with the bent prong of a fork which the old woman handed to her. She picked up a cray-fish and examined it, creaking its joints, as if it were some antique. She even rejected the white bread she was shown, and insisted that the little boy be sent out to get some brown.

Then she led the way into our partition, and shut the door, slipping the bolt across. She laughed. "You look thoroughly peevish."

"What a place!" I exclaimed. There was a cast-iron table like the tables outside, three straight-backed chairs, and along one wall a bunk covered with a mattress and three grey cushions.

"Wait till you taste the food. I promise you—it'll be delicious." She took off her fur-coat, and sat down on the bunk, patting it as she said: "Come on. Relax. But before you do—be an angel and tell the old boy to put some more wood on the stove." When I returned, she repeated: "Come on, sit down. Sit down."

I sat down, but on the edge of the bunk, not leaning far back, as she was, with her head against the wall. "How do you know this place?"

"Oh, it's well known. Isn't it?"

"I've never been here before."

She laughed. "I imagined that you must have been here hundreds of times. Where do you take your girls?" I did not answer, leaning forward with my hands clasped. "It's convenient for me. Being a foreigner, if I go to a hotel, I have to show my passport."

Her frankness infuriated me; although, of course, I had never supposed that I was her first lover.

"You've been here often?"

"Of course not, don't be silly." Now she sounded cross.

"Who first brought you here?"

"You wouldn't know him. An army officer, who has

a wife and five children." She seemed to enjoy the bit about the wife and the five children, smiling as she mentioned them. "He's in Salonica now. He was very sentimental, and something of a bore. But a dear, all the same."

There was a knock at the door, followed by a second, louder knock, after which Helen and I both shouted simultaneously: "Come in!"

The boy set out the knives, forks and glasses on the table, and then went out and scurried back with the bread and the wine in a carafe which looked like a hospitable-bottle.

"It's all so squalid," I said.

"Not at all. It's perfectly clean. And the old boy and his wife couldn't be nicer."

"I can't understand how someone like you—someone who——"

But the boy returned at this moment with two plates of fish-soup, and Helen cut in: "Let's eat before it gets cold." She moved on to one of the straight-backed chairs and rubbed her hands together, smiling down at her plate: "Smells marvellous," she said. "I'm famished."

She was right: the food in that shack was as good, in its own way, as any I have ever eaten at Flocca's or Costi or the Grande Bretagne. The wine, in spite of its ambiguous appearance, matched it superbly. It was impossible to continue to be disapproving.

When at last we had finished, Helen wiped her mouth on her paper napkin, gulped down a whole glass of wine, and then went and stretched herself out on the bunk, with her fur-coat over her feet, from which she had kicked off her shoes. "Come," she said.

"They'll hear us."

"Tell them to put on some music. Bazouki music." She smiled. "That's loud enough, isn't it?"

I did as she commanded: then I came and lay down beside her.

When we at last went out, I was amazed to find the outer room had filled up with people: a party of sailors, an obviously bourgeois gathering of businessmen and their plump, cow-like wives, a solitary navvy, two soldiers dancing the butchers' dance together. I had heard nothing, and neither had Helen. When we saw that it was already twenty past ten, our astonishment was even greater.

Helen insisted on coming to see Irvine.

"But if we arrive together, he'll be terribly upset. He'll know at once what we've been doing. I didn't even tell him that I was going to the concert with you."

"All right, you go first, and after twenty minutes I'll come round."

"It's so late."

"Don't be silly. We'll be there before half-past. You know Irvine never goes to sleep before midnight. Even when he's ill. The last time I visited him was when we were returning from the theatre, and that was well after eleven."

I continued to protest, and she to insist. I could not understand her eagerness to see him, even at the risk of arousing his suspicion: it never occurred to me at the time that perhaps, whether consciously or unconsciously, she might wish to arouse his suspicion.

"Well!" Irvine exclaimed as I entered his room. I had previously called out from the hall, while taking off my coat, but had heard no reply. "You're a nice one, I must say."

"I'm sorry, Irvine." I went to the bed and first picked an empty tea-cup and a copy of the *New York Times* off the floor, and then began to tug at his bedclothes which, as usual, were half cascading on to the floor and half tangled around him. "I met Vazeri"—this was a Germanophile Greek youth who had recently inherited a shipping fortune on the death of his father—"and he asked me round to a party he was giving for Kempff. It seemed too good a chance to miss. I hurried away as quick as I could. You're not angry, are you?"

"Not really, my dear. But you did seem to be away for hours and hours and hours. I had to get up and fill my hot-water bottle myself."

"Does it need filling again?"

"No, my dear, thank you. Come. Sit down." He patted the eiderdown. "Sit down. Come." The gesture and the words reminded me of Helen on the bunk, and I felt a dumb shame. "Was the concert good?"

"Marvellous."

"I thought it would be. Oh, I could kick myself for not having been well enough to go with you. How did he take the second movement of the Appassionata? Did he take it as slowly as he usually does?"

"About the same." I had no idea whatever.

He continued to ask me questions like that, and I continued to say "Yes", "No", "Oh, of course", at random, until the bell tinkled.

"I wonder who that is?" Irvine said.

"I wonder."

When I opened the door, Helen said in a loud voice, obviously for Irvine to hear, "Hello, Spiro. How's the patient?" and then at once put her mouth to mine, swaying in my arms as she kicked at the open door with her foot. Embarrassed, I pushed her hurriedly from me, though I would like to have kept her exactly where she was.

"Irvine, my sweet, are you any better? I've brought

161

you some flowers, which Spiro must put in a vase for you at once. Here you are, Spiro." She gave me the bunch, and then seated herself on the bed, where I had been sitting. "You *look* better," she said. "Are you?"

"Oh, yes, I suppose so," Irvine whispered without conviction; he could never really believe that he would recover from any illness. "I suppose so. My voice is coming back." He had begun to ease his body up, tugging and pushing irritably at his pillows, wriggling, and kicking with his legs. "Let me help you," Helen said.

"Where have you been?" he asked, when she had at last got him settled.

"Oh, at a boring dinner. Business contacts of Conrad's. The American Rubber Federation, something like that."

"Then you weren't able to go to the concert."

"No. Wasn't it a bore? I was so looking forward to hearing Kempff again. But Conrad insisted. So, like a dutiful wife, I gave in to the wishes of my lord and master." She was lying effortlessly and, as I thought, with utter conviction.

"I was asking Spiro about his tempo in the second movement of the Appassionata. Schnabel used to take it so much faster. I remember I once heard Paderewski play it one week in Geneva, and Schnabel in Berlin the next. The comparison was interesting . . ." Irvine was off on one of his lectures: but he gave it drowsily as if, for once, he were as much bored by what he was saying as myself and Helen.

When she got up to go, Irvine said with an exaggerated courtesy: "You'll see our guest down to the street and into a taxi, won't you, Spiro?"

"Oh, I have the car."

"Ah, you have the car. Well, then, you'll see our guest into her car, Spiraki my dear?"

"Does he suspect something?" I asked Helen on the stairs.

"Of course not. Don't be silly. And what if he does?"

"I wouldn't like to hurt him."

She gave her contemptuous chuckle: "That's odd, coming from you."

"What's odd?"

"Worrying about people's feelings."

She unlocked the car door and then leant inside to take something out of one of the pockets. "For a beautiful boy," she said, putting into my hand a small cardboard box.

"What is it?"

"Open it and see."

I opened the box, and found inside a pair of cufflinks. By the dim Athenian street-lighting, I could not make out what were the stones, but I certainly never supposed that they were genuine, or the gold solid gold. "Well?" she demanded.

"Thank you," I muttered. I did not wish to accept them; I felt cheated, humiliated and ashamed, as I had never felt when accepting presents from Irvine.

"What's the matter? Aren't the rubies big enough?"

"But I . . . I can't . . ." I stammered.

"Of course you can. You will." She climbed into the car, and pulled the door shut. "Good-bye, sweetie," she called: the tone seemed one of mockery, though it may have been only my mood at that moment that made me suppose it was. I put the little box into my pocket and returned up the stairs.

Irvine said: "Well, I suppose I'd better take my temperature. Can you find the thermometer?"

I hunted about the room, and eventually found it under a pile of his clothes.

"You'd better wash it," he said.

As I held it under the tap, he eased himself up on his elbow, cleared his throat, blew his nose and then, in his hoarse whisper, said: "Well—what about the truth now?"

"What do you mean?"

"Oh, Spiro, Spiro, Spiro!" He shook his head from side to side. "Do you suppose that I'm so easy to deceive?"

Brutally I replied: "You always have been."

"You were with her, weren't you? She just came here to crow over me. That was all. To crow over me. I saw it at once. You even smell of her scent, you smell of it now. Don't imagine I'm jealous, I'm not, I'm not!" The whisper grew louder and louder, the muscles of his throat taut and strained, and his breath coming in snorts and whistles through his nose which was, itself, inflamed from so much blowing. "Have I ever been jealous of your friendship with any other women? Have I? Have I?" I regarded him stonily. "But she's—she's so old and . . . and . . . Oh, it's all so squalid. I hate to think of someone like you wasting himself on a—a *hag* like that." He brought out the word 'hag' with an extraordinary hatred and venom.

"There are people who say that I waste myself on you," I said, advancing to the bed, with the thermometer held out.

"I don't understand, I just don't understand you. Why should you—you practise these—these cheap deceptions? Why should you? What's the point? I don't see it, I don't see it. Oh, it's all so *messy*. There are things about you which—which baffle me completely. Sometimes you're so gentle and good and kind, and then it's as if a devil got into you, and I feel that I mean nothing—nothing at all to you . . ."

I almost pushed the thermometer into his mouth to make him shut up. He continued to stare up at me until, suddenly, to my horror and disgust, I saw the tears welling up in his eyes and beginning to trickle sideways down to the pillows. He mouthed on the thermometer for a while, twisting his lips, and then pulled it out, thrust it on to the chair beside his bed, and turned over and away from me, his left hand pulling the sheet over his head as if it were a cowl.

"Irvine," I said sharply.

There was no reply.

"Stop that. Oh, for God's sake."

Then I went into my room and began to undress. When I had put on my pyjamas, I remembered the studs, and still muttering to myself "Idiot! Silly fool!" as I'd been doing ever since I'd left his room, I got the box out of my pocket and again raised the lid. They were beautiful. Helen was right: I would certainly keep them. But in some extraordinary way all the tenderness I had felt for her as we had lain, exhausted in each other's arms on the bunk in the shack, had been destroyed by the gift. I felt at that moment that I would never experience the same tenderness for her again.

I heard a shuffle and padding in the hall, and rapidly pushed the box and its contents into a drawer. Irvine came in, bare-footed, with his eiderdown over his shoulders: his face was crimson and glistening with fever and the tears he had shed.

"I'm sorry," he whispered. He began to cough, and then sneezed. "Forgive me. Please forgive me, Spiro."

"Why are you out of bed?"

"I—I didn't know what I was saying. When one has a temperature like this, one—one says things one doesn't mean. . . ."

"Get back to bed. You're mad to be up." I began to

shove him back into his bedroom, and though he protested, I knew that he enjoyed it. "Do you want to get pneumonia? You know what the doctor said."

I exaggerated my indignation, scolding him as a mother scolds a child. That was what he wanted from me, and I was willing to give it.

. . . Hell! There's that bloody cat again. It's got into the flower-pot with the antirrhinums in it, and keeps scratching, glancing around, and then giving a hurried curtsy when it thinks I'm looking elsewhere. Its ears are as thin as autumn leaves; the tip of one seems to have frayed away altogether. It has its mouth slightly open, as if it were grinning in sardonic contempt, while the one eye which is not covered by a cataract glimmers like a lump of amber in the autumn sun. Where's my shoe? Oh, good shot, good shot! That cracked it over the side of the head all right. That squawk was more like a frightened parrot's. My aim must be improving.

The bell has begun to ring, and even before I get to the door I seem to know that it's going to be Mrs. Mumfitt.

Curling-pins, the size of small torches, gleam out of her dull, black hair. She holds the end of a ragged kimono together across her swelling bust, with hands that look as if she had just been doing the week's washing, to judge from their pancake texture. The moment she sees me, she lets fly:

"You've done it once too often!" She bellows at me like a heifer that's just come into season. "Come into my flat—come on! Just come and look at him! Just come and see what you've done to him! He's trailing blood wherever he goes! I'll get the police on to you for this, and the R.S.P.-C.-C.——" She splutters away on that C for a while like a machine-gun, and then explodes into a roaring "A!" pushing her face up to mine so that I almost feel as if my chin were being tickled by the down on her upper lip.

I draw on my cigarette and then blow out the smoke, so that her head is enveloped in a blue cloud. I know that will madden her. "You come in here first, and see the damage that pussy has done to our antirrhinums." I don't think she knows what antirrhinums are, so I go on: "What's the good of our trying to grow things on our balcony if that — cat of yours then comes and scratches them up." The word I say before cat makes her recoil as if I had slapped her. She bellows:

"Don't speak to me like that! How dare you! Kindly remember that some people were not dragged up in the gutter! You—you—you . . ."

"Yes?"

"You—you, Levantine!" I think she must have some idea that a Levantine and a libertine are one and the same thing. "Aren't you ashamed of yourself? Letting your poor wife slave away to keep you, in the condition in which she is, while you sit at home all day with nothing better to do but torment a poor defenceless creature that never had any cause to harm you. You call yourself a man! A man!"

"How would you like it if I climbed over on to your balcony and used your potted tomatoes as pussy uses ours? Eh, Mrs. Mumfitt?" I again blow smoke out into her face.

She begins to cough and flap her hands before her face, letting go of the two frayed ends of the kimono to reveal a pink slip through which the nipples point like the teats of a baby's bottle. I feel an impulse to pinch them.

Perhaps she senses this, because she begins to back: "You wait!" she menaces. "You haven't heard the last of this. My patience is exhausted. It takes a lot to get me angry, but when I'm angry, I see red, I can tell you! . . . Brute! " At that she slams the door. From inside I can hear her calling in a voice that has suddenly become tender and maternal. " Kittykins! " the diapason throbs. " Kittykins! " (The creature must be at least ten years old.) "Come here, lovey! Come to Mumsey-wumsey! Come here, darling! Did the horrible dago man hurt us then? Did he? Did he then? That's right. Oo, the poor, poor earums! Oo, oo! Mummy's going to put some Dettol ointment on to that. And then we shall have some liver as we like it. Yes, that's what we shall have—some liver as we like it. Yes, that's what we shall do. We shall have some liver, and the giblets from the chicken on our own little plate. . . . Yes! That's what we like, isn't it? Yes! Yes! Yes! "

VI

SUNDAY

IT was lucky that Kiki had returned home before the policeman arrived. In the first place I was still in a temper with Mrs. Mumfitt; and in the second we Greeks tend either to hector or cajole the police, and in England that seldom works. Kiki was perfect.

The policeman was a blond young man with an abnormally long, thin neck and long, thin fingers, the nails of which were far from clean. He said "Mr. Polly-me-Rides" to Kiki as she opened the door, and at the same moment Mrs. Mumfitt pushed her face round from behind his shoulder and said: "Yes, he's in all right, he's in. I know he's in." The cat was squirming in her arms, as she rocked it from side to side.

Kiki said: "Yes, come in, won't you? But would you come without——?" She smiled at the policeman and indicated Mrs. Mumfitt with a raising of her eyebrows.

Mrs. Mumfitt protested, of course; I had seen her protest in exactly the same way when she was once queueing up behind us at the Chelsea Classic, and we were the last to be let in and she the first to be left out. But the policeman, like the commissionaire on that occasion, would not yield.

"Oh, darling, there's a police officer here to see you," Kiki called out. "I'm afraid it's something to do with poor dotty old Mrs. Mumfitt." Kiki was clever to make light of it. "Come in, officer, won't you? I'm sorry the place is in such a mess, but my husband's been ill and I have my job."

The policeman mumbled something about his wife also doing a job, while he peered round the room as though he expected to find bloodstains on the walls.

"I expect it's that cat, isn't it?" Kiki prompted. "Oh, dear! The trouble we've had with it. And it's not as if we disliked animals. We're devoted to them. We're always quarrelling about whether to have a dog ourselves. My husband thinks it's cruel to keep a dog in London, but after all, we've got the park just opposite. What do you think?"

"Well, a small dog," the policeman said.

"Oh, of course, a small dog. We couldn't think of a large one. It would cost too much to feed."

"Oh, they cost you a fortune, big dogs. A pal of mine has a boxer, a German boxer, that's what they call it—it eats him out of house and home."

"Well, I'd love to have a boxer," Kiki said. "That's the kind of dog I love. But in London it just wouldn't be fair. Would it, darling?" She turned to me.

Like most Greeks, I value animals for their usefulness, not for their friendship. If Kiki and I lived in a Greek village, I'd keep a dog to bark and even bite if anyone tried to steal from us. I'd kick it and starve it in order to make it savage, and I wouldn't allow it into our house for fear of ticks and fleas. I'd be as fond of it as of my oil-press or my tractor—if I were lucky enough to have a tractor. But in Athens or in London a dog would be out of the question: what would be the point?

However, needless to say, I did not confess to all this in front of that Bobby.

Kiki was soon showing him the pots on our balcony,

and I could hear his voice: "Well, flowers brighten the place up, don't they?" And then, "We're lucky, you see, having this strip of garden we share with our neighbours." My God, what perfect ladies these British police are!

". . . Of course it's more than a little disheartening when one goes to all that trouble to plant seeds, and then to water them, and suddenly, one day, that cat slips over and scratches them up. It makes my husband see red. But he didn't mean to *hurt* the cat, just to frighten it off, that was all."

"You'll have to do something about those caterpillars," the policeman said as he came back into the sitting-room, followed by Kiki. He had to bow his head a little as he stepped over the threshold, and for a moment I thought that he had a hairy caterpillar curled up on the back of his neck, just above the collar of his tunic: then I realized that it was a large mole, like the one on his chin.

He sat down on a straight-backed chair, and got out a note-book, rapidly flicking over the leaves with fingers damped with spittle, as though he were counting banknotes. He took down our names and the address, and a lot else that seemed to be irrelevant and then, having refused a cup of tea, made his way out. As he clattered down the stairs, in an obvious hurry to avoid being summoned back by Mrs. Mumfitt, we could hear him whistling 'Down Mexico Way'. Kiki began to hum the tune herself, and then broke off.

"Well, that's that," she said.

"You were marvellous."

"I don't imagine that we'll hear any more of that little story."

"You've obviously inherited your father's knack with the police!" Old Vrissoglou is always getting tangled with the law over tax-evasion and other fiddles of that kind, in Greece, in England and in America, but somehow he always manages to squirm out again: I suppose that's the secret of his fortune. But Kiki doesn't care to be reminded of his peccadilloes; if I hadn't at once put my arms round her, she might have been cross. "They're so cosy, these English bobbies," I said. "One feels so safe with them."

"He was rather a pet, wasn't he? And such a good-looking boy."

"Good-looking! Are you completely crazy?"

Kiki began to cover my face with small kisses, pressing herself closer and closer to me, but at that moment I was not thinking either of her or of the policeman, but of being interrogated after Helen's death. That was far from cosy, far from safe. I remember how I was passed from room to room, from one officer to another until, as a variation, the room would remain the same, but the officer would change. I felt, all the time, that I was a child let loose in a lunatic-asylum. For a while, I would be wheedled and coaxed with cigarettes, cubes of Turkish-delight or gritty cups of coffee; then I would be slapped, not hard, but as a child is slapped in a fit of irritation; then something, which I knew to be untrue, would be repeated to me, over and over again, as though in the hope that if the grown-ups said it often enough the child would accept it; then a futile attempt would be made to catch me out on some entirely irrelevant point: ". . . How old are you? . . . How old were you when you first went to school? . . . How long did you stay at school? . . . How old were you when you left school? . . . How long ago was that?" culminating in a triumphant pounce: "You're lying, you're lying! The figures don't agree." There was one sergeant who spoke with the rough ch-sounds of the Cretan villages—if any accent should be called *chi-chi*, that should—and he took me back and back over my story with the dogged stubbornness of someone who keeps re-doing a sum in the hope that eventually two and two will be five. The facts were unalterable: Helen had died some time between two and three o'clock in the morning from an overdose of sleeping-tablets taken at eleven o'clock in the evening, when she had asked the maid to bring her some hot milk; and I had been playing poker from nine until dawn. But that Cretan sergeant longed to alter the facts. He loved the phrase: "Now let's go back over all this once more," and we all went back repeatedly: I, the maid, the doctor, Christo and the other boys with whom I had been playing. He'd have liked me to have killed Helen, one could see that: he had that hysterical Cretan desire for violence. But he couldn't make his dream come true, and then, in exasperation, he would slap my face and shout at me: "Liar, liar, liar!" But, in between such spells, he was kind, wonderfully kind: he even offered me a Pall Mall cigarette from one of the packets he had been given by the wife of an American Colonel whose car he had helped to start in Constitution Square.

Well, perhaps he was right; perhaps I did kill Helen. Before her death, I used to have dreams in which we were nagging at each other, as we often used to do; and then, in a fury, I would leap at her, and seize her by the throat, shaking her back and forth, back and forth, until I woke up, drenched in any icy sweat. Sometimes she would be lying beside me, and she would say: "Darling, what is it? What's the matter? Another of your nightmares?"

She was always jealous; and it seemed to give her some kind of savage, self-hurting pleasure to reveal that jealousy to me or even to our friends. I would seldom have been conscious of the difference in our ages had she not reminded me of it. I do not think I would even have committed infidelities, were it not that, by her endless suspicions and her frantic possessiveness, she seemed herself to drive me to them. "Stop looking at that woman, or I shall walk out!" she would suddenly exclaim venomously in a restaurant, when I was looking at no one at all; and at once, as though I knew that subconsciously it was this kind of suffering that she craved, I would begin to look. "I haven't much to offer, compared with her," she would then say with a terrible self-abasement. "Nineteen years old, blonde and busty, and not a brain rattling about in that doll's head of hers." I remember now one evening when Conrad was away and we had been making love at the villa. Since I had been tired by a day on the beach, there was a lassitude in my love-making, which Helen had at once noticed, and taken as a sign of indifference. At once, she jumped off the bed and pushed her arms through a wrap, folding it about her as she flounced into the bathroom. I went after her and found her standing, in the gloom of the late dusk, tears trickling down her cheeks, before the big looking-glass. I stood behind her and kissed first the nape of her neck and then, easing away the wrap, her bare shoulder. "Oh, get away!" she cried out. "I'm hideous—hideous," she wailed. "Look at me." With one hand she pushed her hair up and away from her face. "I'm old."

At that desire awoke in me, as though the flame had been set to it by her complete humiliation. I turned her round violently, and we stood face to face, thigh to thigh, our bodies straining against each other. She began to try to say something which sounded like "Don't, don't, don't", but the words were muffled by my own mouth. Then I made them out, reiterated over and over again: "Don't leave me, Spiro, don't leave me, don't leave me, don't leave me." Her nails were digging into my arms now, as her cat once clawed me when I climbed up a tree to fetch it down. . . .

That summer, while Conrad and Irvine worked, Helen and I went almost daily to the beach. She preferred Vouliagmeni and the rocky bays beyond it, where we could alternately lie alone in each other's arms and bathe alone, for hours on end. I, being a Greek, and therefore gregarious, preferred to go to Bati's, where there were two tiers of cabins in a semicircle round a beach crowded with people. Walking over the sand Helen had once trodden on a lighted cigarette-end, carelessly thrown down, and she had hated it ever since. On another occasion, when the wind was blowing from Peiraeus, where the American fleet was anchored, we found ourselves smeared with oil and had to spend hours swabbing ourselves with wads of cotton-wool soaked in paraffin. There was a restaurant, and often I used to say to Helen: "Why go to all this bother preparing a picnic lunch, when they can prepare something for us?" But she could rarely be persuaded not to bring food, and on such occasions she always complained—the meat was 'off', the potatoes greasy, the bread stale. We used to drive up in the car, and between us we used to carry down to our cabin (which we avoided sharing with others by giving a generous tip to the attendant) all the brightly-coloured paraphernalia of picnic-baskets, rugs, magazines, towels, under-water swimming equipment, cameras and changes of bathing-dress, which Helen always insisted on bringing with her. I myself was used to going to the beach with a slip wrapped up in a towel, and nothing else.

The Greeks are obsessed with appearances: what is important to them is how a thing looks, not what it is, and it is therefore even more important to look rich than to be rich, just as it is more important to carry around a gold watch that does not work than a trashy one that does.

You will see Greeks arrive on the beach loaded with gleaming picnic-baskets which contain nothing but bread, cheese and olives, their bodies strung about with thermos-flasks, the water in which is not even iced. When later, an English or American family drives up, and drags out of a dusty station-wagon a tattered army blanket, a rucksack, a bulging string-bag, and a number of damp, or shrivelled, bathing-costumes, such Greeks are always puzzled: they decide that foreigners are misers. But Helen was different. Her car gleamed extravagantly, and her equipment gleamed to match it. Admiringly the Greeks goggled at her, as I spread out the nylon sheet with its pattern of sailing-ships and gulls, and she then placed herself on it, and began to rub her already golden skin with oil. Youths would gather about us, and some of them I knew. They were most of the members of the Zonar's set, and they spent the day cultivating their bodies as a farmer cultivates his land. When Helen clicked open her gold cigarette-case one would at once rush forward with a lighter or match; when she wanted her Lilo they would pass it back and forth between them, blowing into it until their faces were crimson—thus saving me the trouble of having to inflate it for her. They moved with a studied grace, and assumed poses, their arms round each other's shoulders or the head of one resting in the other's lap, which were studied in their carelessness. Helen pretended to be irritated by them, and would always speak to them with an ironical contempt: but I am sure that she was flattered. After all, she was a married woman, and already in her forties. " I do wish they'd stop gaping! " she would exclaim. For all of them she had nicknames, far from complimentary, although they themselves regarded them as such: Fido, the Beetle, Ginger, Jean Marais, Pimples—some of them come back to me. All round us there were girls younger and prettier than her: but not one of them had that glamour of foreignness and wealth which is so potent for the Greeks, and not one had Helen's assurance.

One day our little audience seemed to be oddly shrunk and inattentive. Pimples or Jean Marais or the Beetle would make a few desultory remarks, trickling the sand through his fingers or fiddling with the catch of the picnic-basket, and then, mumbling something inaudible, would wander off. Helen soon realized that something was amiss; and though, when the crowds were thick about us, she never ceased to complain, yet now I could see that she was puzzled and cross. "What's the matter with them all?" she demanded eventually. "Do you suppose it's something to do with C-Y-P?" Like many English people, talking English among themselves, Helen had got into the habit of spelling out the first three initials of the island.

"Oh, God, no."

"They're definitely unfriendly."

That was not true—they were not unfriendly, they just did not care; and I had guessed already that their reason for not caring was that they had found something more rewarding to care about. One by one they had been making their way up the stairs which led to the terrace outside the upper tier of cabins, but from where we were placed it was impossible to see what was happening to attract them. Helen saw me peering and asked irritably: "Well, who is it this time?"

"No one."

"Then what are you ogling at?"

"I'm not ogling."

She stretched herself out, and adjusted a pad over her eyes: her body looked superb. She put out a hand and groped for mine: "Anyway, it's nice to be by ourselves

177

without all those chattering, staring youths around us."
Her fingers were slightly greasy from the oil she had
applied to her body, and there were small, gritty particles
of sand stuck to them. "Why doesn't Irvine bathe?"

"He doesn't like the water. Why doesn't Conrad?"

"Too busy."

"Poor Irvine," she sighed, with obvious satisfaction.

"Poor Conrad."

Helen was an expert swimmer, but she rarely exerted
herself. We swam out to the wreck of what had once
been a diving-platform, now collapsed and poking
jaggedly out of the sea, its surface here abraded with rust
and there slimy with sea-weed. There was a notice,
'Danger, Keep Away', but I began to clamber up, scraping some skin off the sole of one foot as I did so. "Don't
be silly, Spiro!" Helen called. "Spiro!" The note of
obvious anxiety had the effect of spurring me on.
"Spiro! Oh, Spiro, you bloody idiot! Come down."

I had now reached the topmost point and, balancing
precariously, was preparing to dive (I can dive beautifully), when a loud-speaker blared out from the shore:
"Attention! Attention! It is strictly forbidden to
climb up the diving-platform. It is strictly forbidden . . ." At that I dived.

Helen swam towards me: "You silly show-off!" she
cried. "Now there'll be trouble."

"Nonsense."

"Of course there will."

"Nonsense."

I swam underwater to her, and, when I rose to the
surface, had her, struggling and tearing at my hair, over
my shoulders.

When we reached the shore—Helen pulling off her
bathing-cap and shaking out her hair, one arm linked in
mine—a loutish member of the Harbour Police, with

legs shorter than his arms and feet longer than either, leant over from the upper terrace, and shouted down: "Hey, you! Yes, you! Come up here! Come on!" He had white gaiters which, on those legs, seemed to reach almost from ankle to knee, and a great black moustache which, when he had nothing else to do, I had seen him comb with meditative affection. I knew that I was due for some childish sarcasm and bullying, and I knew that I could also get the better of him. "Excuse me," I said to Helen.

"I suppose they never taught you to read in your village," he greeted me, and at once a crowd, thirsty for a scrap, began to collect around us.

"Oh, I've finished the gymnasium. They taught me to write too. You ought to learn—it's lots of fun."

There was a great deal more of back-chat of this kind: boring to record now, but greeted with enthusiastic laughter at the time. There was Christo there, and soon, one by one, all the rest of our little group had gathered: for them a pointless altercation like this was even more fun than a pointless flirtation with some stranger. They applauded each of my sallies, partly because they knew me, but chiefly because the Greeks, unlike the English, have no respect for authority. Suddenly the little harbour policeman lost his temper: he began to shout, alternately at them and at me, threatening us and our families with arrest, with beatings, with venereal diseases, with having to submit to the more outrageous perversions, with years in hell-fire. During this outburst, I glanced away from his face, working red and shiny behind the vast moustache, and saw a young girl, of seventeen or so, sitting awkwardly forward in a deck-chair, her plump hands between her plump knees, as she laughed at the scene. This was Kiki. Next to her was a fat woman, whose shiny, creased, yellow body looked as

179

if it had been made of china, which had been broken and then stuck together. She had a hair-net over her black hair, and otherwise was wearing only high-heel shoes and a bathing-costume.

At last the fuss subsided, and I went along to the shower-room, where Christo had preceded me. He was not taking a shower, but was hauling himself up and down by the arms from the beam which ran along above the three compartments. Like those women who when they have nothing to do or say or think about automatically begin to knit, Christo on such occasions would automatically begin to exercise himself. At a party he would suddenly go down on the ground and execute fifty press-ups on end; waiting for a 'bus, he would astonish the passers-by by going through the movements of skipping without a rope, or touching his toes.

As I came in, he lowered himself for the last time from the beam, and lovingly ran a hand over his gleaming, golden pectoral muscles and shoulders, as he said: "You amused the Vrissoglou girl."

"Who's she?"

"You know—the daughter of old Vrissoglou. They live in London, but the mother and daughter have come here on a visit. She's not bad looking. Her dowry should be enormous, she's the only daughter. I wouldn't mind marrying her—that would solve most of my problems. Wouldn't it?"

"I'll beat you to it. You wait!"

We joked about this girl, in the way that Greek men usually joke, but neither of us ever conceived that she would one day become my wife. Yet we had a precedent for it: only the previous summer, we had all joked in a similar fashion about an ageing American film-star, and to our amazement, when he had left once more for Hollywood, he took one of our group with him.

When I had finished my shower, I strolled along the terrace and placed myself near to where Kiki and her mother were sitting. The mother was dozing, her chin sunk on to her raddled chest, so that her neck collapsed into three little sausages, like the three smaller sausages at each knee. Her hands were tiny, and they were encrusted with rings. A copy of *Harper's Bazaar* lay over her belly. Kiki was reading or pretending to read—I remember that I squinted at the title on the spine, and made out the words *Vanity Fair*, a book then unknown to me. Suddenly she glanced up, and her eyes met mine; then she hurriedly looked down again, but there was a faint smile at the corners of her mouth.

She was too plump and too graceless to be really attractive: Helen had spoiled me for those things, as for the black hair which in those days Kiki, like most Greek women, used to allow to flourish under her arm-pits and along her upper lip. Her breasts and haunches were those of a hamamissa as depicted in the Greek equivalent of 'Men Only', and her hands and feet were, like her mother's, minute. It is extraordinary how, by taking thought, a woman can add, not perhaps a cubit to her stature, but attributes to herself which she never before possessed. Nowadays, Kiki's body is like the body of an average English woman of the same age; just as then it was like the body of an average Greek girl. The curves have gone, and with them the contrasts between the smallness of the extremities and the amplitude of the torso.

Suddenly a gust of wind blew the copy of *Harper's Bazaar* whirling across the terrace, and I raced to catch it. Mrs. Vrissoglou woke up as I brought it back, and I noticed the gesture with which she felt the rings on her fingers, as though to reassure herself that all of them were there, even while she smiled at me and said in

Greek: "Thank you so much. How kind of you! " In
English, she then said to Kiki: "If you want another
bathe, you'd better have it now. We must leave in "—
she glanced at the little platinum-and-diamond watch on
her wrist—" in exactly half an hour."

Kiki once again pressed her plump hands between her
plump thighs. "Can't be bothered," she said. "The
water looks so dirty."

"Oh, it's not dirty to-day," I put in boldly. "When
the wind's in that direction, it's always clean, always."

Mrs. Vrissoglou looked me up and down, and I think
she liked what she saw: in later years she would often
confide in me about her romantic youth—there had been
a French engineer working on some electrification
scheme, a Swiss diplomat, a young Greek doctor who had
himself died of tuberculosis in which he was specializing.
. . . She had not left Vrissoglou for any of these, and,
given a second chance, she would not leave him now;
but she liked to think that she would. Regret for
her, as for so many women, was the most voluptuous of
pleasures.

"You come here often then? "

"Oh, yes, at least twice a week. Other days we—I—
go to Vouliagmeni or Glyphada or even to Megalo Pevko.
Do you know them? "

She shook her head, not upwards, in the Greek style,
like a shying horse, but from side to side, and answered:
"I hardly know Greece at all."

"But you're Greek, aren't you? "

"Oh, yes, I'm Greek."

To my annoyance, as we went on talking, I was aware
that, one by one, the 'group' had started to gather
around us. Christo was the nearest, whistling aggres-
sively, as he used the railing of the terrace as a bar on
which to show off his gymnastics. ' Jean Marais ', whose

blondness, it was often said spitefully, was not natural, had stretched himself out on a deck-chair near at hand, closing his too-small eyes, but for which he would have been the beauty he imagined himself to be. 'Pimples' was picking at his face. 'Ginger' whispered something to him, and they both began to giggle; then 'Pimples' whispered it to 'Jean Marais', stooping over him and putting his lips to his ear, with the tenderness of a lover giving a kiss. 'Jean Marais' gave his high-pitched cackle.

Suddenly Mrs. Vrissoglou began to scream at them in Greek: "What is all this? What do you think you're doing? Can't two decent women sit in privacy without a number of bum-boys"—she used a word which is even cruder and more forceful in Greek—"spying on them. Go on, leave us, leave us! Get away! Leave us! Otherwise I shall complain to the police! I warn you! I shall complain to the police!"

They at once made off; but from the other end of the terrace, their courage reviving, we could hear them making rude noises, giggling and jeering.

Mrs. Vrissoglou's outburst had been that of any village mother anxious to protect her daughter's honour. On such occasions—and there were many—one forgot the Daimler car, the holidays in Cannes or Venice or Salzburg, the dinner-parties with too much good food and too much bad conversation, the box at Covent Garden, the membership of the Curzon Street Bridge Club, the subscription to the Times Book Club, and merely remembered that, like so many members of Greek Athenian or Greek London society, Mrs. Vrissoglou had had peasants for ancestors. But, in a moment, she had changed back again, as she asked, with the experienced hostess's air of feigned interest: "Do you live in Athens, Mr.——?"

"Polymerides," I said. "Yes, I live here now."

"My daughter and I are here on a visit. Just two months. I thought it disgraceful that she knew so little about her own country, and decided we must do something about it. She wanted to go back to Italy herself— didn't you, dear? She's mad about art. Oh, it was all I could do to tear her away from Florence last Spring. And when we were in Paris, instead of coming along with me to help with my shopping, she was always off to the galleries." She went on in this vein, grumbling and yet obviously proud of the things about which she grumbled, just as later she was to grumble, and yet boast, to me about her son: he was such a reckless driver, he did not know the meaning of fear, she was sure that he was fonder of his Jaguar than of any of them. Kiki was, needless to say, embarrassed—this was her habitual state when in the company of either her father or mother— and she took the copy of *Harper's Bazaar* off her mother's lap and began to turn the pages.

". . . Yes, she's got this idea into her head that she wants a career. She's set her heart on going to Oxford, nothing else will satisfy her. Well, her Daddy's given her everything else she's ever wanted, and I expect he'll give her that too. I dare say we'll see her a professor before we've finished!"

Suddenly, I was aware that Helen had appeared at the top of the stairs at the other end of the terrace, fully dressed, with a beach-attendant following laden with her paraphernalia. She carefully made a point of not looking at me, said good-bye in an over-brisk, over-jolly voice to the group of boys, and then continued on up the next flight of steps. "Excuse me," I said, and began to run after her, even though there was a large notice saying that it was forbidden to go out into the street in one's bathing-slip.

She was already in the car.

"What are you doing?" She did not answer. "Helen, what are you doing? What is all this?"

Suddenly she shouted, staring, not at me, but at a 'bus which was approaching: "Oh, go on back to that slut! I'm not interested, I'm not interested."

"I merely picked up a magazine which had blown off her mother's lap," I began, but Helen cut in:

"Do you know how long you left me alone down there? Do you?" She held out her wrist, and jabbed at the watch on it with her extended forefinger. "Thirty-five minutes, thirty-five minutes! Oh, no, my dear, I don't hang about that long for you or for anyone else. I'm sorry. If you come to Bati's for your little pick-ups, you must drop me before you come. Got it?"

The car began to move off, and I ran for a time beside it, protesting: "Helen, do be sensible! For God's sake, Helen." Then it accelerated, and I realized that I was running down the road in nothing but a slip, that the soles of my feet were smarting from the hot gravel under them, and, worst of all, that the harbour policeman was shouting behind me.

As I passed him on my way back, he began: "What do you think you're doing? Don't you know that——?" But I yelled in his face:

"Oh, go to hell!"

I thought, immediately afterwards, that he would put me under arrest; but to my amazement that was the end of it.

From that moment Helen and I started to quarrel, not sporadically and half-heartedly as in the past, but continuously and savagely. I was not in love with Kiki. I did not even find her as attractive as Helen: but I was flattered that she was so obviously already in love with me. I was repeatedly told by Christo and the others how

185

lucky I was and how rich I would be, and, as always, there was the additional incentive of Helen's jealousy to spur me into doing the things which she feared I would do and did not wish me to do. I was clumsy about concealing my meetings with Kiki because, I realize now, I subconsciously wished that Helen should know about them. Our relationship had always been one of mutual cruelties and, once a relationship has set in that mould, it is hard to transform it. Helen herself became wilder and wilder, and more and more hysterical in her scenes of jealousy and rage.

A climax came five weeks after that day when I first met Kiki at Bati's. She had been due to leave in three days' time, but then, in order to fit in with the arrangements of old Vrissoglou, who was meeting them in Zurich, it became necessary for her and her mother to take the first 'plane that they could get. She telephoned to me at Irvine's flat to tell me of the news.

"I must see you before we go. I must. I've been trying to get hold of you all morning."

"It's difficult," I said; and then I thought, wondering, how I was to get out of my promise to spend that afternoon and evening with Helen.

The silence was so long that eventually she demanded: "Are you there? Spiro! Are you still there?"

"Yes," I said. "I'm just trying to work it out. It's difficult," I repeated. "I've got this man I'm supposed to see about a possible job—it's a chance I oughtn't to miss."

"Don't you feel that you oughtn't to miss me? Oh, Spiro, who knows when we shall see each other again?"

"All right. I'll fix it."

I hadn't realized that Irvine had come into the hall from his bedroom while we had been talking. He stood, pretending to read the newspaper which I had brought in with me, but in reality listening to our conversation. When I rang off, he said:

"Helen?"

"No."

"Kiki?"

"Yes."

"She telephoned three times this morning. I didn't know you were back, or I'd have come and told you. They're leaving, apparently sooner than they expected."

"Yes, by the night flight."

"Are you going to see her?"

"Yes."

"But I thought you were seeing Helen this evening?" He had been sour at breakfast that morning when I had told him that I would not be able to go to the theatre with him, because of this date, and he was sour now as he reminded me of it.

"I was."

"You've put her off?"

"Not yet."

"But you're going to?"

"Yes."

I knew that he wanted to say: "You're willing to put her off for your Kiki, but never for me," but he restrained himself, no doubt fearing I should lose my temper, as I so often did when he tried to scold me. "You're priceless," he said. "If I were one of those wretched women I wouldn't put up with it for a moment."

"You put up with quite a lot."

"Anyway, I think you've made the right choice," Irvine said, ignoring this remark.

"What choice?"

"Well, better the young than the old. It's more

187

dignified, and you lay yourself open to less comment. Even though she *is* so rich. Don't you agree?"

I think that Irvine knew that, at that moment, Helen's hold on me was far stronger than Kiki's: the older woman, not the younger, was his real enemy, and it was from her that I must first be prised away. He went on: "Poor Helen! she's aged so much recently. She was looking quite haggard at the Levidis dinner-party. And for once her dress did not suit her. Have you noticed how the less women have to show the more they want to show it? I thought that at any moment a tit would pop out. Yes, poor dear, I'm afraid you're making her suffer. Not that I didn't warn her. But that's so like a woman: she was convinced that *she* could manage you. Well, she's learned her lesson now." He said this last sentence in a tone of odious self-congratulation, which all but persuaded me to give up Kiki that afternoon and keep to my original engagement. In any case, it would not be so easy, I knew, to excuse myself; in Helen's present state of suspicion and hysteria, no story, however true or plausible, was likely to be believed.

"What job?" she demanded, when I had finished spinning my tale.

"Oh, something that Irvine has in mind for me. An American businessman who wants a buyer here. Hand-woven fabrics, peasant-pottery, copper- and silver-ware, that sort of stuff. You know."

There was a silence. Then: "Do you honestly expect me to believe that little story?"

"You can believe it or not, just as you choose. It happens to be true."

Again there was a silence—this was odd, I had expected a spate of recrimination. "All right. I'll believe it. Yes, I'll believe it." There was a terrible weariness about the tone, and a hint, I thought—though it was hard to tell over the telephone—of suppressed tears. "So I shan't be seeing you?"

I relented. "Well, I'll try to get away early. We're meeting for a drink and dinner. Americans usually eat early, don't they?"

"Try and come."

"Yes, I'll try."

"I was looking forward to this evening so much."

"I'm sorry."

"Spiro, try and come. Please try and come."

As I went into the sitting-room, where Irvine was writing letters, he began to sing gaily:

> "'How happy I'd be with either
>   Were t'other dear charmer away——'"

and then broke off: "Well, what did she say?"

"She took it pretty well."

"What else could she do? Poor wretch!" Suddenly his jollity had gone, and he looked genuinely unhappy at the thought of Helen. He picked at the nib of his dip-pen, muttering: "Damn!" Then he held up a sheet of paper: "Look! I shall have to do that again. That piece of fluff has ruined it." I noticed that the letters of the last word were thick and crude compared to the fine-drawn beauty of those that had come before.

"Is that necessary? What is it, a letter?"

He nodded, and, taking another sheet of paper from the box, began laboriously to make a copy. I was tempted to go and stand near him and then pretend accidentally to jog his arm; I wanted to see if he would then embark, yet again, on a new sheet. But I restrained myself.

Kiki and her mother were staying with some cousins,

representatives of old Vrissoglou in Greece, who had a large, bare, uncomfortable, expensive flat near the Palace; it was there that I went to pick them up. We set off for the airport in a cortège of seven American cars, as if to a funeral, and Kiki managed to escape sitting between her mother and a young man in the Greek Foreign Office, the son of old family friends, who had been wooing her ever since her arrival, and instead jumped in front beside me. She took my hand in hers, and squeezed it, and then gripped my knee, all the while chattering away, to lull the suspicion of the others. As our caresses became more and more imprudent, her comments and laughter began to be pitched on a wilder and wilder note of unnaturalness.

Once in the airport, we were separated by innumerable, dark, plump, balding men in blue pin-stripe suits, the jackets of which were draped almost to the knee, women in black against which glittered their diamonds, feathers and teeth, youths who attempted to look American or English, and girls who attempted to look Italian or French, all chattering, and laughing, and kissing each other, no one listening, all carrying on those simultaneous monologues which pass for conversation in Greece. Kiki's eyes would meet mine momentarily over a bobbing plume, between two T-shirts, from behind a flash of gold teeth, then I would lose her. A man passed calling out: "Souvenir! Souvenir!" and swung under my nose a small evzone-doll, made from wool, which was suspended by a piece of elastic from his nicotine-stained forefinger.

Everyone seemed to be pressing presents on Kiki and her mother, and I had none. "How much?"

"Twenty drachmas."

"Ten."

"Fifteen."

"Thirteen."

"I'm a poor man."

"You're a thief. Thirteen."

"Fourteen."

"Fourteen."

Kiki was delighted when I pushed my way through to her. "Oh, Spiro, Spiro! How sweet! I shall wear it in my button-hole for luck. I'll fasten it here. May I kiss you for that?"

"Why not?"

There was laughter and clapping as she kissed me, decorously, first on one cheek and then on the other, and then she herself began to laugh: but the laughter was forced, as all her gaiety had been forced, and I began to wish I was not there.

For the wife and daughter of old Vrissoglou there seemed to be no customs or passport formalities; the chauffeur had been despatched, and now he returned with an official who cringed up to Mrs. Vrissoglou and began: "Excuse me, madam, but a word, just one word. The husband of one of my cousins has applied for a job at Mr. Vrissoglou's office in Patras, and if it would be possible . . . if you could perhaps mention . . ." He undid the top pocket of his greasy tunic: "I have the name here. This is it, madam."

Mrs. Vrissoglou took the card without looking at it, and put it in her bag. "I'll see what I can do." She turned away at once, and did not listen to his nauseating whine of gratitude. ". . . may the Lord bless you and yours . . . my children will be taught to honour your name . . . good journey . . . success . . . prosperity . . ." I felt furious that poverty and corruption should have reduced a decent man to this: a shuffling, grinning idiot, backing away from this over-dressed, over-painted, over-fed woman as if she were royalty.

"Well, good-bye, Spiro."

"Good-bye, Kiki."

"Write to me."

"Of course."

"And I shall write to you. Don't forget," she added in a whisper.

"Never."

Suddenly she leant forward and, in front of them all, kissed me on the lips. Then she hurried up the gangway, waving a hand but not looking round, and disappeared from sight. I felt that they were all staring at me: some with astonishment, some with envy, some with anger, some ingratiatingly as if in apology for having ignored me before. It was as if, by one of those accidents so frequent in Greek political life, a back-bencher had suddenly found himself elected Prime Minister. Soon, I felt, some wretched Customs official would be cringing up to me.

Helen had obviously been crying: her features looked swollen and therefore unattractive, and she had powdered too thickly. Sometimes such pathos would make me feel repentant and tender; more often, as now, it irritated me towards some further cruelty.

"Well," she said listlessly, "so you've come."

"As you see."

As I began to comb my hair, dishevelled by riding back in an open car belonging to one of Kiki's male cousins, Helen placed her arm round my neck and then raised her lips to my cheek with something of the furtive timidity of a child asking to be forgiven. Then I was sorry for her. I slipped the comb back into my breast-pocket and took her in my arms.

For a while we were happy; but she could not leave it like that. Between embraces on the couch in the sitting-room, she had to squirm away from me to ask: "Well, did you get it?"

"Get what?"

"The job of course."

I had forgotten completely about the job, and I betrayed it. "Oh, it's—it's not certain," I stammered. "We just discussed the possibilities, and then he said that he would let me know."

"Liar." Suddenly she sat up on the sofa, wrenching out a cushion that had got doubled up beneath her.

"What do you mean?"

"Oh, come off it, Spiro, come off it. I know when you're lying. I'm not in love with you for nothing." As she said that last sentence, her lower lip came outwards and then began to tremble, and her eyes filled with tears: as though, I thought at the time, an invisible dentist's drill had been placed in her mouth. "Oh, I'm so tired of all this deception. If you knew how tired I am."

"And I'm tired of all your ridiculous suspicions—this possessiveness—sick and tired of it. I feel as if—as if I were suffocating. One seems to be living in a prison all the time."

"Oh, no. I'm the one that's in a prison, I'm the prisoner. You're free, my dear, you're free as the air." She put her forehead down on the arm of the sofa, twisting her body round, and from the shaking of her shoulders, though she made no sound, I knew that she was weeping.

"Oh, for God's sake!" As when Kiki weeps, it filled me with rage; really there is nothing more exasperating than the seemingly avoidable sufferings of others. One wants to say: 'Pull yourself together; control yourself; snap out of it,' imagining that the will can still dictate these courses to the overwrought emotions. "For God's sake! Oh, this hysteria."

She went on and on crying, while I picked up *The Times* and then *Punch*, strolled to the window, smoked a cigarette, mixed myself a drink, and, in between all these things, either tried to coax or verbally slap her out of this mood of wild despair. "Well, I'm going," I said at last. She did not look up, perhaps she did not even hear me. But as I opened the door, I heard a muffled: "Spiro! Oh, Spiro!" Her face was still down on the arm of the sofa, but she was extending a hand, as though to grope for an invisible object in the darkness. The stifled tone, her slumped and twisted body, and then those fingers looking for something that was not there, all at once had a pathos for me. "Helen! My dear! Do stop, oh, do stop!"

Perhaps she had merely wept herself out; or perhaps she sensed that now, for the first time, my sympathy was genuine. Sobbing noisily, she threw herself on my shoulder. "Helen, Helen, what is all this? Why work yourself up over—over nothing? Why, why, why?"

"Oh, Spiro, what's the good, what's the good? It was silly of me to think it could ever work. How could it, how could it? And I'm not Irvine, I can't deceive myself, I'm no good at that. I know you don't love me—well, why should you, why on earth should you?" I was going to say something at that, but she put a hand over my mouth and went on with a sigh: "It's so hopeless. If I don't lose you to that girl, I shall lose you to another. Of course I shall. Every day makes it more difficult to keep you. And anyway it's so—so undignified and humiliating, all, all this!" At that there was a fresh paroxysm of weeping, the knuckles of her left hand pressed to her mouth as though to stifle, not so much her tears, as a scream.

Slowly I soothed her: until she reached that state of

dull, heavy calm which so often follows outbursts of physical or emotional violence. She stared into the twilit garden, hunched up, while with one hand she rubbed at a sodden cheek as though to scratch some invisible insect-bite. At last she said: "You'd better go. I'm no good this evening."

"No, I'll stay."

She shook her head. "Please, Spiro. I'd—I'd rather."

"What are you going to do?"

"Try to sleep. I haven't slept properly, oh, for weeks." Again the lower lip came out and began to tremble, while the eyes filled with tears. I knew that that 'oh, for weeks' was a ridiculous exaggeration—only the Tuesday before she had slept all night beside me; but that did not seem to lessen the pathos.

"Haven't you got something to take?"

"I've run out. Not that it helps—much. I meant to get some more of the stuff when I was in town to-day. I forgot." As I went out into the hall, she said in a voice oddly normal after all the hysteria that had gone before: "Spiro, would you be an angel? Would you do something for me? I must sleep to-night, I can't have another of those nights, I can't face it. Would you take the car, drive down to the town, and fetch me a bottle of my tablets. Would you? Is that being a nuisance?"

"Of course not."

When I returned, she took the little packet from me, and began flicking with a nail at the elastic-band that held the wrapping together, as she said: "I must try not to be such a drag on you. Poor Spiro! I make you go through a lot—don't I?"

"Don't be silly."

Her kiss was perfunctory, like an exhausted child's: so perfunctory that I doubt if she had then planned what she was to do within a few hours. As I went to the car, my lips had on them the bitter, salt taste of her anguish, and I kept trying to lick it away.

It was Soula, her fifteen-year-old skivvy from Euboea, who discovered her in the morning. About a year before, Helen had missed one of her rings which she had left carelessly in a drawer after a dinner-party. The police had questioned all the staff—Helen herself had suspected her hunch-back gardener—and had then, inexplicably, announced that they wished to take the girl off for further questioning. Helen protested: if she trusted anyone, she trusted Soula, who was devoted to her. The two detectives shrugged their shoulders, and persisted that they must take her with them. Eventually they returned, bringing with them both the ring and the girl, who was now a snivelling, cowed bundle of bruises and abrasions. It turned out that she had a lover, who was a deserter from a Commando regiment at Vouliagmeni, and that it was he who had forced her to steal for him. Helen, as she herself often said, would have sacked the girl but for those terrible marks on her body: as it was, she declined to prefer a charge, and kept her. Then the imaginary "devotion" became a reality; Soula would, I am sure, have stolen a ring for her mistress too, had Helen demanded it.

The girl's reaction to the discovery of Helen's body was peculiar in the extreme, and was long discussed in Athens. She did not scream, she did not call for help. Instead, she slipped out of the house, and began to run—she was seen running by the boy who brought the yoghourt, and he called out to her, but she neither stopped nor answered. The police, not unnaturally, at first regarded her as their chief suspect, and set out in search of her. They found her in Leopezi, a village some fifteen miles from Helen's house, where she had arrived half-crazed with hunger, exhaustion and hysteria, at the house of some cousins. For days they could get nothing coherent out of her; and by then they had already lost interest in anything she might have had to tell them.

Later she got a job in the *Arachova*, a tavern frequented chiefly by soldiers and sailors, and once, when I went there with Irvine and some American tourist friends of his bent on 'slumming', she had been as much transformed by the life she lived there as once by the blows and slaps of the police.

. . . Often, when Helen had taken me to task for some act of neglect or infidelity, she would then relent, and say dismally: "Oh, but it's not your fault. You're not to blame. After all, why should you be expected to return the love of a married woman in her forties? If I were your age and you were mine, I'd probably find such devotion just as irritating. No. To use that odious phrase, I've only myself to blame."

But had she? As I sit here, in this darkening room, waiting for Kiki (there's a smell of chrysanthemums, yesterday Kiki brought home a bunch given to her by Pavlakis), and thinking of those days lying out on some deserted beach or driving the car back along the coast road through the falling dusk, one of my arms about her shoulders and her hair against my cheek, I feel as I have never felt about her before. I want her back, I want her near me; and it's as if I had myself seized the sleeping tablets and forced them down her throat, thrusting them deeper and deeper until I had choked her. I try to think of any kindness or consideration I ever showed to her. Didn't she often say: "Oh, Spiro, you're so good to me?" But now, it's odd, I can't remember one single occasion when I was 'good'. Of course I was, I know I was; but it's like when I had jaundice, and it was impossible to imagine a time when I wasn't feeling nauseated. That's how I feel now: as if I had jaundice.

She was a bitch, Irvine was right about that, and the death of that son of hers, instead of sobering her, only made her worse. She could be ruthless, vindictive and selfish. But how generous she was! And how capable, and intelligent, and strong! Not strong enough for me. . . . Oh, I hate that smell of chrysanthemums, smell of autumn, decay, death. God, the street looks gloomy. There's no one in sight except a woman limping up the steps opposite, one hand pressed to her side while the other grips a stick with a rubber ferrule at the end.

Oh, Helen, Helen, I want you. I want you. . . .

VII

MONDAY

"WELL, I didn't know that it was nylon. It doesn't look like nylon."

"It isn't nylon. It's orlon."

"Well, orlon then. I didn't know that it was orlon. I didn't know that one was not supposed to iron orlon."

"But I told you, I told you!"

"You did not!" Kiki looks at her watch, and then begins to rush about the room, opening and shutting drawers, and snatching at things. "I'm already ten minutes late. It's your fault. When you know that I'm going to be late, why must you start to nag at me."

"Well, it's a little upsetting, you must admit, when one's new shirt has a hole burnt in it. I've only worn it once."

"I'm sorry, I'm sorry! I'll buy you another."

"Do you know how much a shirt like that costs?"

"I'm sorry, I've told you—I didn't *know* that it was nylon."

"Orlon."

"Oh, hell." She pulls out a drawer of the desk so violently that it crashes to the floor. "Now look what you've made me do." Cotton-reels, letters, corks, photographs, theatre-programmes and pea-nuts litter the floor.

"Christ, what a mess! What were those nuts doing there?"

I go across to help her to replace the things, and our hands meet; at which she cries out: "Oh, Spiro, do leave me to do it myself. Leave me! You only make things worse."

She is crouched on the floor, and no sooner has she said this than suddenly she rocks back, so that her shoulders rest heavily again the sofa, and puts a hand to her forehead. Her face is mottled with curious mauve blotches, and her eyes look dull, yet frightened. "What is it? Kiki, what is it?"

"I don't know. I felt so peculiar. Just for a moment. I felt I was—I was going to faint." She smiles feebly. "Wasn't that silly of me?" She gets up slowly to her feet, and totters slightly, one hand gripping the arm of the sofa. I go close to her.

"You don't think it's——"

"No, no, of course not. It's far too soon." Now she laughs: but weakly, like someone who is tipsy. "No, I'm tired, that's all."

"You mustn't go to work."

"Oh, I must, Spiro, I must."

"No, you mustn't. Here, lie down for a little. Please. Kiki. Lie down. I'll fetch a rug to cover you." I force her on to the sofa, and she takes my hand in hers, looking up gratefully at me.

"But if Pavlakis thinks I'm no longer fit to work, he'll get rid of me. And then what will we do?"

"Now don't worry. I'm going to ring him up."

"But, Spiro, you know what he's like. He keeps suggesting that I'm no longer really up to the work."

"I'll fix him."

Pavlakis has not yet reached the office, but I leave a message with the girl—Madge is she, or Maude?—who acts as his personal secretary. " . . . Oh, she's seedy *again*, is she? Oh, I am sorry, yes, what bad luck. The second time in two weeks. . . . Well, I hope she'll be better soon, tell her not to worry. . . . Oh, yes, we'll be able to manage, I *expect*. Oh, yes, yes." When Kiki first joined the office, Madge (or Maude) tried to make a chum (I'm sure that's the word she would have used) out of her: but Kiki only wanted one chum at that moment, myself, and after she had refused two invitations to visit Madge's (or Maude's) home in Barons Court and another to 'do' a gallery, Madge (or Maude) gave her up. No doubt she decided that Kiki thought herself too good for her—that's the kind of thing that she must often decide in her relationships with other people—and ever since then, she has shown poor Kiki all the restrained hostility of a schoolmistress attempting to be fair to her least favourite pupil.

"Well?"

"That's all right. I spoke to Maude."

"To whom?"

"To Madge."

Kiki giggles: "Don't be silly. You mean Mildred."

"Well, Mildred then. What a name!"

"Her mother and her brother call her 'Dreddy'. She told me that. . . . Thank you, darling." I put a rug over her swollen body, tucking it under her, and then stoop down and kiss her on the lips. "You're very sweet."

"It's you who are sweet." She closes her eyes, and sighs deeply. "You mustn't get cross with me, if I do silly things. Because I've always done them, and I suppose that I shall always do them. That's me. I know that I should have thrown away those pea-nuts—they must have been in that drawer ever since that evening when we went to the Pleasure Gardens. I'm a slut, I'm afraid. Aren't I?"

"Of course you're not."

"It's difficult for me to be tidy. Before, you see, there was always someone to be tidy for me."

"Just as there was always someone to iron shirts. Yes, I know, sweetie. I've been horrid these last few days. It's not having any work, and feeling so bloody, and being cooped up for all those days. . . . It gets me down."

"Poor Spiro." Without opening her eyes, she gropes for my hand, and then puts it to her cheek.

"Sometimes I think that we're fools to stay in London. Perhaps it would be better to return to Athens. Being poor is not quite so—so beastly and squalid there. Is it?"

"But it would be even harder to get any work," she says.

"You know so many people. All those relations of yours."

"They're relations of Daddy's, first and foremost. They wouldn't help us, if they thought he didn't want them to help us."

"But what—what is he up to? I don't get it. I can understand his not wanting to see us, and refusing to give us money. All right. But why try to dish us as well?"

"Oh, to starve us out." She opens her eyes, and looks at me, smiling, although, God knows, there's little to smile at. "He's used to getting what he wants, always. And he wants me back. Without you."

"I see."

"That's how it is."

"Yes."

"But he's never going to separate us. Is he? Is he, Spiro?"

"Never, darling."

As if that reassurance were all that she wanted, she shuts her eyes again and, her hand still in mine, drops off to sleep almost at once. Gently I release myself, and then go and sit down in the chair opposite to her. 'He's never going to separate us. Is he? Is he, Spiro?' So often, doing these last months, I've told myself what a fool I have been: to marry for money, and then to find that the money is not there; to be saddled with a child; to condemn myself to this life of either working not at all or working without a permit, of pinching and scraping, of sitting alone in this ill-heated room, of quarrelling with the neighbours or Kiki, of telling lies to avoid paying our bills, of throwing things at that cat, of remembering, always remembering. . . . So often I've decided 'I've had enough. I must clear out.' One day, I even got as far as to begin to pack my things, while Kiki was out. But always something—the unborn child, her defencelessness, her love—seemed to prevent me. And then, because I could not do what I wanted to do, I would be savage to her; sometimes would even hate her. Her parents said that I had trapped her, but it was she who had trapped me—that's what I would tell myself. And I would remember those lines of poetry which Irvine had quoted at me in the first letter he wrote after hearing the news of our marriage. It was an odd letter to receive, hardly one of congratulation, and it sent both me and Kiki (to whom I showed it) into a rage against him.

'. . . I wish you good luck, of course I do, because I should like you always to be happy. I have seen some neutral marriages, many unhappy marriages, few happy marriages. I hope that yours will be one of the few. But I have little confidence in the blessed state: marriage was created by women, for the benefit of women, at the expense of men—that's my view, at least! How does Blake put it?

> *And if the babe is born a boy*
> *He's given to a woman old*
> *Who nails him down upon a rock,*
> *Catches his shrieks in cups of gold.*
> *Her fingers number every nerve*
> *Just as a miser counts his gold*
> *She lives upon his shrieks and cries*
> *And she grows young as he grows old.*

I have seen so many marriages like that; I hope yours will not be one. Never let yourself be nailed down upon the rock! . . .'

It was a horrible letter, because it put into words all that I dreaded: even 'the cups of gold'—were they supposed to represent the Vrissoglou money? "Horrid old faggot!" I exclaimed; and then Kiki suddenly pointed and said: "Oh, look, you've dropped something." On the floor was curled up a cheque for a hundred dollars.

Often, after that, I would find myself re-reading the letter, and I would say to myself bitterly: "How right, how right you were!" But when I myself wrote to Irvine I never suggested that I regretted my marriage: I did not want his smug 'I told you so'. Even when I asked him about the possibility of going to America and finding a job there, I always wrote to him as if Kiki would be accompanying me, although, secretly, I had decided that, if I left, I should leave alone.

Alone, without her. . . . Yet, now, as I sit here, watching her as she sleeps, it seems inconceivable. If only, like Helen, she distrusted me and feared to lose me!

That faith in my kindness, and goodness and love is what keeps me nailed to the rock; somehow, against that, I have no power. She looks extraordinarily beautiful, calm and fragile as she lies there, her thin hands crossed over her swollen stomach, and one flushed cheek resting on her shoulder. These months her skin seems to have grown paler and more transparent, so that the blue veins show at her temples, on her neck and on her wrists. If only she were less defenceless; if only someone else loved her; if only, just for once, she would see me as I really am!

I never told her that the shirt was orlon, but because I insisted that I did, she will now believe that I did, and that she herself forgot or did not hear me. Helen would have known that I was lying: but for Kiki a lie from me is unthinkable. I used to feel like that about my father; and then, when I was eleven, I caught him out in some deception so obvious that I could not ignore it, and from that moment I felt for him nothing but contempt. Will Kiki one day catch me out like that? And how will she feel?

The orlon shirt is lying on the floor by the door, with the triangular orange burn across it. "It simply stuck to the iron, I couldn't get it off," Kiki explained. "You fool!" I shouted, rushing up and tearing it from her hands. "You've ruined it." Irvine had sent it as a present, and I had been particularly pleased with it because, as Kiki herself had said in excuse, it looked as if it were made of poplin: not like that vulgar, transparent, blue nylon shirt which Irvine bought for Dino, and which had been the start of all the trouble. No one, not even Kiki, could have tried to iron that.

. . . Irvine and I had gone to *Drosia* (Coolness), a tavern in Fish Street, with two Swedish interior-decorators, both immensely tall, with the same voices that sounded as if bath-water were running out slowly through a choked waste-pipe, the same protuberant Adam's apples bobbing up and down in long, scrawny necks, and the same large hands so pink and moist that it seemed as if they had just been removed from a basin. They had remarked enthusiastically on the dancing of a man, in blue-and-white cotton trousers and a sage-green shirt whose handsome Victorian face, with its blond side-burns and drooping moustache, might have come from one of those ancestral daguerreotypes which you see hanging on the walls of country cottages in Greece. He did not dance well, but they were not to know that, since the 'zembekiko' is an art which it takes time to appreciate; but he danced wildly and joyously, with prodigious acrobatic leaps, twirls and clappings of the heels with the hands, and that was enough for them.

At the conclusion, Irvine sent over a can of wine, explaining to the Swedes that, in Greece, this was the way in which one showed one's appreciation of a dance: never did one applaud. Everyone at the other table then raised a glass to our health, while the Swedes made gobbling noises to each other like two excited turkeys. The youth grinned at us, and the gobbling became even more frenzied, until one of the two Swedes leapt up and offered a packet of Camels, spilling cigarettes over the floor in his anxiety to have them accepted.

Soon, by smiling and patting the chair beside him, Irvine had succeeded in getting the dancer to join us. As though he were interrogating a small child, he then began:

"What is your name?"

"Dino."

"And where are you from, Dino?"

"A village near Thebes."

"Which village?"

"You wouldn't know it."

"Ah, but I might, Dino. You'd be surprised how well I know Greece. Much better than my friend here." He indicated me. "Don't I, Spiro?" I nodded. "What is it called?"

"Kreokouki."

"Oh, Kreokouki, well, of course I know Kreokouki. It means Cold Bean," he explained to the Swedes, "but I've always had the warmest of welcomes there. And what work do you do?"

"I'm training to be an electrician."

"Oh, an electrician!" One almost expected him to add: "Well, fancy that!"

"I go to night school. And I'm an apprentice at the Naval Station."

"What do you get paid, Dino?" Irvine, like many Americans, had been trained to repeat a name over and over again when he first heard it, so that it should not slip his memory.

"Four drachmas a day."

"Four drachmas a day! Four drachmas!" Irvine turned to the Swedes, and said in English: "This poor boy gets only four drachmas a day. That's a shilling. A shilling a day. Can you imagine anything more iniquitous? Spiro, did you hear that? A shilling a day, four drachmas a day!"

"Oh, I don't believe that."

"What do you mean, you don't believe that? He's just told me. That's what you said, isn't it, Dino? Four drachmas a day?" he now confirmed in Greek.

Dino nodded.

"That's what he *said*, of course, but how do you know it's true? Don't be so simple."

"It's by no means impossible," Irvine countered crossly. "Wages in Greece are scandalously low, everyone knows that." He looked at the Swedes, as though for confirmation, but since they had been in the country for only three days it would be difficult to say what confirmation he could possibly have expected from them.

"Not as low as all that."

Dino leant forward, his chin resting on the calloused palm of his hand, elbow on table: in some extraordinary way one usually divines what is being said about one in a foreign language, and when he now spoke it was as if every word of our English had been intelligible to him. "I'm an apprentice, you see. I want to become an electrician on a ship, but I have to pass my examinations at the night school first and also work for a year at the Naval Station."

No one listening to him could have supposed that he was lying; and indeed I now remembered having already heard something about this exploitation of apprentices by the Greek Government. But an unconscious jealousy, already aroused as though by some mysterious fore-knowledge of the events that lay ahead, made me persist: "Well, that's his story. Take it or leave it."

"I prefer to take it," Irvine said quietly; and he then drew his mouth together into a puckered bunch, as he tended to do when he was annoyed.

"Make him to dance again," one of the Swedes said. "Please make him to dance again."

"Only if I had my camera with me! Ah, only!" the other exclaimed. "I have Leica, I have flash. Beautiful photographs!" He raised his glass and bumped it against the Greek's: "Skaal!"

The Greek, dazed yet pleased, turned to me for help: "What does that mean?"

"He's drinking to your health."

"Ah!" Dino bumped his glass back, and when retsina

shot out of both glasses at the impact, giggled uproari-
ously.

"He's nice," one of the Swedes said.

"He's very nice," his compatriot said, and hiccoughed.
"He has so much gay and so much laughter."

Dino asked: "Are they Americans?"

"No, Swedes."

"Ah, Swedes." Obviously he had no idea of where
Sweden might be; but he thought for a while and then
said: "Soup."

"Soup?" Irvine looked first at him and then at me
with raised eyebrows. I was equally mystified, until I
remembered the soup provided by the Swedish Red Cross
for school-children during the worst years of the war.

"Yes, soup," I said.

"Are you a Swede?"

"No."

"American?"

"No."

"English?"

"No. I'm Greek."

Dino stared at me in amazement. Then he shook his
head and laughed: as if to say: "Yes, I'm a peasant, I
know, and you're an educated man. But I can't believe
that."

"I'm a Greek," I repeated.

He shrugged his shoulders and laughed again, revealing large, square, white, even teeth under the drooping
moustache. "All right, have it your own way."

"It happens to be true."

"Please make him to dance again, Spiro, Irvine," one
of the Swedes interjected.

Dino danced, and the Swedes once more gobbled at
each other: "Fantastic! Beautiful! Wonderful!"

"He's not very good," I said.

"Of course he's good," Irvine burst out.

"You must learn to be objective. A muscular body, white teeth and a peasant idiocy do not, of themselves, make a good dancer."

When, sweating and grinning bashfully, Dino returned to the table, one of the Swedes thumped him on the back, much as if he were a successful athlete, while the other filled his glass to the brim with wine, so that when the Greek wished to drink, he had to stoop over it, without raising it from the cloth. He lapped, and then, picking it up, dashed it off at a gulp. With his bare forearm he wiped the sweat from his forehead, saying: "Hot work."

Some women with frizzed, erratically platinum or auburn hair had stepped out from a taxi drawn up on the other side of the hedge which separated the garden of the tavern from the pavement; they were shrieking and clutching at one another. Three American sailors bundled out behind them, two of them with their hats over their blunt, shiny noses, while the third had his hat dangling from his forefinger by its rim, as though it were a quoit.

One of the girls said in English: "Music, dancing. Come on, boys," and the others all shrieked: "Come on! Come on! Hey, Joe! Come on! Boys! Say, boys!"

Dino was eyeing them: then he looked at me, as the only person who was both of his own age and capable of understanding his language, and remarked appreciatively: "Nice pieces."

These women were certainly better than the gypsy-like hags who used to frequent the park in Salonica, but they were certainly not 'nice'. One of them, I noticed, was thickly powdered over the collar-bones where a mauve rash, the same shade as her dress, was none the less visible to the eye. They tottered past us, hugging close around them the fur-coats, which they sported in defiance

of the temperature, and swept inside the tavern, followed
by two of the sailors and a pandemonium of whistling,
cat-calls and obscenities. The third sailor, who was
obviously more drunk than the rest of his party, saw us,
and at once stopped beside our table, swaying back and
forth on his heels, while his cap whirled faster and faster
round his nicotine-stained forefinger. " Hiya, fellows,"
he said at last.

" Hi," said one of the Swedes.

" Hi," said the other.

Irvine remained silent.

" Does anyone want to buy a nylon shirt, a beautiful
nylon shirt. Eh? Eh, fellers? A beautiful nylon shirt.
Look." He took a parcel from under his arm, and then
began to unroll it on his knee, one foot having been
already raised on to the edge of Irvine's chair. " Now,
take a look at that. Have you ever seen anything like
that? "

Dino asked me, in Greek: " Does he want to sell it? "

I nodded.

" How much? "

" How much? " Irvine asked in English.

" Well, feller, I don't want to make anything out of
you. I just want to raise the wind to pay for that dame
in there. See? You name a fair price, and there won't
be no arguments."

" May I try it on? " Dino asked.

" He wants to try it on," Irvine translated.

" Sure, sure. Go ahead. Go on, go ahead."

To our amazement Dino at once stood up and stripped
off his own shirt, revealing his naked torso. Excitedly he
thrust his arms into the nylon shirt and jerked it over his
head, while the American cried out: " Whoa! Hey!
Take care! "

" Perfect," the Swede said.

"It suits him fantastically," the other agreed, pronouncing 'suit' as 'suet'.

There was something at once ridiculous and touching in the contrast between the heavy, sun-burned, muscular, peasant body and the vulgar powder-blue cocoon which appeared to have been spun in sugar around it: something ridiculous and touching too in the Greek's childish preening, as he gazed either down at himself or at his extended arm with a smile of idiotic beatitude on his features. Then he sighed and began to remove the shirt once more.

"Is he going to take it?" the American asked.

"Are you going to take it?" Irvine translated.

The Greek giggled ruefully, wiping the back of his hand across the tip of his nose. "No money," he said.

"How much?" Irvine demanded of the sailor. "I'll give you three dollars."

"But, Irvine, you don't want a shirt like that. It wouldn't suit you." The idea of Irvine appearing in such a garment was inconceivable.

"Make it four," the sailor said.

"No, really, Irvine, what possible use can you have for——"

"Four it is."

Irvine dug the dollar-bills out, one by one, from the back of his purse, where each had been placed, folded and separate.

As soon as the sailor had tottered inside the tavern, Irvine handed the shirt to Dino, as though it were a dirty dish-cloth, between finger and thumb: "For you," he said.

Dino at once ripped off his own shirt again, and put on the nylon one. I was consumed with rage.

"You'll make a hit in that in your village," I said viciously. "Or do you think you'll sell it again?"

"Yes, they'll all ask me where I got it," he agreed, beaming with delight. He felt the stuff between his fingers. "I've never had a nylon shirt before. And this is American nylon. Thank you, sir, thank you very much." He turned back to me: "Your friend is very kind, a real gentleman."

Against such ingenuousness all my sarcasm seemed to be useless, both then and later. Like the Christian Scientists, Dino believed in the goodness of everyone, but, unlike most Christian Scientists, he seemed to have come by his belief naturally, without any prior exertion of the will. He never suspected that I might dislike him, or be jealous of him, or wish to do him harm. Even when the evidence was there before him, he merely shook his head, baffled and dazed. It is difficult to wound such people: the lance breaks off in one's hand. Because I was the same age as he, and a Greek (for, at last, he was convinced of this), and another recipient of Irvine's generosity, he treated me as a chum: and if, in return, I was bitter or cold or vicious, well, I was a moody fellow, that was all, but I had a good heart. He always insisted on that: I had a good heart.

When we got up to go, it was to me that he put his request:

"I don't like to ask your friend this, I feel ashamed. But perhaps if you—if you would ask him," he whispered.

"Yes, what is it?" My tone would have deterred anyone else from continuing, but Dino, his beefy hand on my shoulder, now leant forward:

"I've been wanting to get into the Electricity Company for a long time. They haven't got a place. But if your friend—if your friend knows anyone there. . . . It's a British Company, isn't it? If your friend has any influence—if he would speak for me . . ."

"What is this?" Irvine asked, turning from the two Swedes, who were attempting a Greek dance themselves, their legs entwined round each other and their bodies bent almost double. "What does he want?"

"Tell him," I said to Dino.

"I feel embarrassed."

I shrugged my shoulders, and moved away.

"Come on, Dino. What is it? What is it, eh?"

Dino told Irvine, who pulled out his lower lip between his forefinger and thumb as he said earnestly: "Well, Dino, I'd do anything I could to help you. But, you know, the Americans and the English look at these things differently . . ." I had heard the lecture which followed many times before, but it was obvious, from his intent, respectful, surprised expression that Dino had not. "It may seem odd to you," Irvine concluded, "but really it's much the best system. In every office and factory in Greece at least a quarter of the staff have no right to be there—isn't that so? But they have *Mesa*"—this is the Greek word for 'means', or influence, and when one brings it out, a smile, guilty yet furtively delighted, usually appears on the face of the Greek whom one is addressing—"and, as you know, Dino, it is better to have *Mesa* in this country than money, or brains, or beauty or anything else. But I'll see what can be done. Perhaps not with the Electricity Company, but with one of my Greek industrialist friends. All right?"

"How can I see you again?"

Irvine took out his card; English-style, it was engraved, not printed, and there was only his name on it, so that it was necessary for him to write his address and telephone number in one corner. "There!" he said. "I've written it in Greek. You get in touch with me in three or four days. Will you do that?"

Dino nodded, peering at the card.

"You can read, I suppose?" I said.

"Oh, yes, yes. Not very well. What is this street?"

Laboriously, syllable by syllable, he made out the name. "Where is that?"

"Kolonaki," Irvine said.

"Ah, Kolonaki. The aristocracy." There was no envy, no irony, no bitterness in the comment. He turned to me, as Irvine made his way ahead of us from the tavern: "You're friend must be rich."

To say that someone is rich in Greece is a compliment: the equivalent to saying that someone is 'clever' or 'of a good family' elsewhere. I knew this, being myself a Greek, but I intentionally used the phrase to try to discredit Dino as soon as he had left us. Irvine had just said, looking after him:

"Nice boy. Don't you think so, Spiro?"

"Oh, nice enough. But I wouldn't trust him an inch."

"Why not?"

"Because you can't trust people like that. That's something you'll never learn. You're a foreigner, and that means that you're a millionaire—and a sucker. Doesn't it? You've been in Greece long enough to know that. He just remarked to me when we were leaving the tavern 'Your friend must be rich!' Offering one of his own cigarettes to Bengt"—this was one of the Swedes—"was merely a way of getting that packet of Camels. Bengt thought it charming and touching that a Greek who was virtually down-and-out should offer him his last fag—didn't you, Bengt?—and the trick worked beautifully. But it was a trick all the same."

"Of course it wasn't."

"Oh, yes, it was. I'm a Greek. I know. Those peasants have a cunning all their own—they must have, or how would they survive?" In those days I tended to talk as if I had wholly forgotten that I myself had once been a peasant too; and it was typical of Irvine's goodness that in our arguments he never once reminded me of it.

215

"You take altogether too dark a view of human nature, Spiro, my dear."

"And you take altogether too rosy a one."

"That boy was utterly honest."

"Well, wait and see."

"I'm willing to bet my bottom dollar on that."

"Wait and see."

Irvine had no success in finding Dino a job, even though he made a number of telephone calls and visits on his behalf. The English said, in effect, 'Sorry, old boy', the Americans 'Let's discuss it over a drink', and the Greeks, 'Well, yes, of course, of course, I shall probably have something next week': but, to one who had spent as many years in Greece as Irvine, all three replies were equally unfavourable. Four days after the meeting in the tavern, Dino telephoned from the kiosk a hundred yards away from the flat, in Kolonaki Square, and was told that he could come round. He stood on the doorstep, reluctant to enter in spite of Irvine's urgings, because, as he explained, he had come straight from his work and was frightened of dirtying the flat.

"Nonsense, nonsense!" Irvine took his arm, and dragged him, laughing, first into the hall and then into the sitting-room. But nothing would make him sit down.

He had on blue overalls, threadbare and stained with grease, and apparently nothing under them except a soiled khaki vest and, one supposed, some khaki pants. He looked as if he had not shaved since our last meeting, and the lids of his eyes had a rubbed appearance: one of them even, perhaps, beginning a stye. He looked smaller, older and less handsome than in the exuberance of that Sunday evening of drinking and dancing, and he was horribly ill at ease.

"Well, Dino, I'm afraid I've no news for you. I've done the best I can."

"The Electricity Company?"

"Nothing there. I spoke to the Director at an Embassy dinner the night before last. And to the Personnel Manager, by telephone."

I wonder if Dino believed this: probably not, though it happened to be true. It was just what a Greek would say, after he had done nothing at all.

"You know how it is, there simply isn't the work."

Dino nodded miserably and sighed, rubbing one of his inflamed eyelids with the back of his hand. "I suppose I'll have to go back to my village," he said slowly, at last.

"But why do that, my dear boy?"

"What else is there to do?"

Bit by bit Irvine extracted from him the information that he was no longer receiving any money from his parents who, themselves, could barely survive in their village, the father being ill; that a brother, a petty-officer in the merchant navy, used to help him until he had got engaged to a German girl, since when he had barely written; that he owed both a month's rent and the fees for the current term at the night school; that he was living on a single meal of bread and olives each day.

"Then how did you manage to go to the tavern?" I asked.

I knew what was probably the answer: he had made twenty or thirty drachmas on some odd job, and with the reckless prodigality of the Greeks had then gone to squander it. Probably I would have done the same. But Irvine, who was so prudent and thrifty, would certainly disapprove, and I wished him to disapprove.

"Oh, well, you see, it was the name-day of one of my buddies at the Naval Station, the older one with the red hair—you may remember him? It was his name-day, and he said he'd treat."

"I'll have to give him something," Irvine said in English. "Perhaps a meal first. He looks grey with hunger and tiredness."

Irvine fed Dino, who exclaimed in astonishment at the tinned Irish stew and tinned raspberries set down before him. Then he gave him two hundred drachmas and told him to call back the following week.

"My God, what lives they lead!" he exclaimed, as he shut the door and returned with me to the sitting-room.

"Their lives are not as bad as all that."

"Not bad!"

"They manage to enjoy themselves. You mustn't imagine that being deprived of tinned Irish stew and tinned raspberries is something that rankles. One doesn't miss the things one's never had."

"One misses food, whether one's ever had enough of it or not."

"Probably Dino is far happier than you."

"I doubt it."

"Have you ever enjoyed yourself as he was enjoying himself that evening at the tavern?"

Irvine shook his head. "No, Spiro, let's face it—the life of the average Greek peasant is hell. When I first came to this country I indulged in the blind sentimentality of the usual tourist: the villages were so cute, and so were the villagers; how much pleasanter to live in a shack or the side of Mount Parnassus than in an apartment in New York. . . . But I've seen too much now, and I've seen it in winter. No, no, Spiro." Irvine began to peer ruefully into that disgusting, greasy little purse of his. "But it was an expensive visit all the same."

"Self-deception is always expensive. Isn't it?"

"What do you mean?" I did not answer.

"I don't know what you've got against that poor boy."

"I've nothing against him. But I'd rather not see you exploited."

" He's perfectly honest."

" Oh, I don't suppose he'd *steal*, probably not. Not unless he were really hard put to it—or the opportunity were too inviting. But—well, he's a scrounger."

" I don't agree."

" Then why do you think he came here? "

" To ask about the job."

" And told us all about his sick father, and the brother engaged to the German girl, and his school fees, and rent, and the olives and bread? "

" I questioned him, didn't I? " Irvine placed himself on the sofa, and stared, long and unhappily, down at my shoes. " You're getting so hard, Spiro! " he said.

" You're getting so soft."

I thought it would be easy enough to eliminate Dino; had I not eliminated other possible rivals, so neatly and painlessly that Irvine had never, I suspect, even noticed what I was doing? But on this occasion Irvine displayed an extraordinary stubbornness. He had always been attracted by peasant simplicity, by poverty, by dependence, by ignorance: it had, of course, been those things which had first attracted him to me; until, with that perverseness which makes us attempt to change in the beloved precisely those traits which have caused us to fall in love, he set about making me complicated, civilized, independent, educated. I was, as I have said before, his work of art: but I was a work of art now nearing completion, whereas Dino was still the work of art that is no more than a conception in its creator's mind. It is, of course, the conception, not the finished work, that most excites the artist.

I tried to be openly contemptuous of Dino; to patronize him; even to insult him: but all these manifestations of ill-will were received with so gentle a submission that I realized that I was placing myself, not my opponent, in a

219

dark light where Irvine was concerned. After one evening which the three of us had spent together, Irvine reproached me as soon as Dino left.

"You're not fair to that boy, Spiro. He has no defences —you ought to pick on a stronger opponent."

"I happen to detest him."

"With no reason at all."

I went to the open window and leant far out into the street, my thighs trembling with fury as I pressed them against the sill. Then I turned and shouted: "He's spoiling it all, he's spoiling it!"

Irvine looked at me in astonishment. "What on earth do you mean?"

"We were happy until he came along. Now it's all different."

"Oh, don't be so silly, Spiro." He came over to me, and having put an arm round my shoulders, pinched the back of my neck. "Are you jealous? Spiro, are you jealous?" He liked the idea of that; who doesn't? "Spiro, I believe you're jealous."

"Well, what if I am?"

"But it's so ridiculous, my dear. Dino means nothing to me. I like him, I feel sorry for him. But do you suppose he could ever take your place? Of course he couldn't. He's a peasant dumb-ox, that's all." Again he pinched the back of my neck. I shouted out in fury:

"Oh, for Christ's sake leave me alone! Don't maul me about!" Then I rushed into my bedroom, where I threw myself on to the bed. Helen was dead, Kiki was gone: and I was tied to this—this awful fairy (it was the first time I had ever thought of him viciously in those terms) who hadn't even got the courage to be what he was. . . . Eventually I picked up a copy of *Thesavros* and began to read one of those Greek serials about an unmarried mother who works as a skivvy in a rich household, where her baby (who, of course, does not know her) has been adopted by a banker and his neurotic English wife. That helped to calm me.

The climax to the new situation created by Dino was not long to come. Irvine had soon started to go through with him the work, chiefly simple mathematics, which he had to prepare for his night school, and often when I came home I would find them seated at the dining-table, like teacher and pupil, text-books and copy-books open before them. "He's no fool," Irvine would say. "The Greeks have so much natural intelligence, if only they could be taught to use it. If I tell him anything, he remembers it."

On one such evening, when I came home to find Irvine explaining simple equations, he merely said: "Oh, hello, Spiro," in an offhand, please-don't-bother-us voice, while Dino contented himself with glancing up, blinking his eyes and smiling vaguely: infuriating. I crossed to the wireless and switched it on loud.

"Spiro, please! We can't possibly have our lesson against that din."

"I want to see if there's any news about Cyprus. There's talk of an agreement."

"Well, the news will have to wait."

"I suppose it doesn't matter to you that people are being shot and hounded and whipped, does it? Being an American, you can afford to ignore that kind of thing." I knew that I was talking like a leader in *Estia*, but that's how I felt: venomous, malicious, anti-everything. "Spiro, please turn off the wireless." He spoke quietly, politely, coldly. "Now, Dino. . . . Let us say that X is 16. Well, then the whole equation must read——"

I slammed the door on his voice.

I was going out to one of Sotiri's parties, and I had to

change first. When I had done so, I met Irvine in the hall, where he was putting on his overcoat, Dino beside him.

" Going out, Spiro? "

" You know I'm supposed to be at Sotiri's. I told you so this morning. I'm late as it is already."

" And I'm late too."

" Where are you going? "

" To the Canadian Embassy." That had also been discussed that morning. "We'd better share a taxi. It's started to rain."

Irvine turned to Dino: " Well, amuse yourself—look at those magazines on the table, or listen to the wireless. The drinks are in there." He pointed through the door, at a cabinet in the sitting-room. "Help yourself."

" Isn't Dino coming? "

" No. He's meeting his girl-friend at half-past seven in Kolonaki Square, and it's only seven now. No point in his getting drenched. . . . Well, good-bye, Dino." Irvine turned, so that his back was to us, drew out his wallet, and then, turning round once more, pressed something into Dino's hand.

" It's—it's not necessary. There's no need."

" Take your girl to the cinema."

As we went down the stairs, Irvine ahead of me, I demanded: " Are you completely dotty? "

" I don't think so. Why? "

" To leave that boy alone in your flat, it's crazy."

" He won't take anything."

" How do you know? "

" I trust him," Irvine said simply.

" Oh, you and your trust! "

" What was it that Forster said about the confidence-trick being the work of man, but the no-confidence trick

222

being the work of the devil? Ah, there's a taxi." **He** would not be ruffled.

Striding off into the rain, I shouted: "Oh, damn Forster!" Soon the taxi drew up beside me:

"Come on, Spiro, get in. Don't be silly."

"I prefer to walk."

"Get in, Spiro."

"I prefer to walk."

"Oh, very well, just as you wish, my dear." As the taxi swished on, it spattered my legs with water to the knee; and such was my mood at that moment that I was convinced that Irvine was somehow to blame even for that.

It was one of Sotiri's dullest parties; or perhaps I was merely not disposed to find it amusing. A Greek woman archæologist, almost a dwarf, with a bulging, shiny forehead, and a nose around the nostrils of which clustered innumerable blackheads—how did she get invited?— came and sat beside me on a sofa. I showed that I was indifferent to her, perhaps even showed that she bored and repelled me; and at once she became combative, as women so often do when they fail to attract a man by whom they are attracted. She said a great deal about the degeneracy of Greek youth, taking as her examples the couples dancing before her; but since in many cases the young were dancing with the old, either of their own or the opposite sex, I asked her: "Well, what about the degeneracy of Greek middle-age?" She bridled yet further at that: no doubt assuming, as I had intended, that I was referring to her.

Eventually a girl I knew came over to rescue me. "What's the matter with you, Spiraki? Why do you look so bad-tempered?"

"We've been having an argument," the archæologist explained, bringing out this admission with the guilty delight that accompanies the confession of a love-affair. She hugged her knees, pressing her breasts against them. "I tell him that he's a good-for-nothing."

The girl stared down at her, pityingly; then she said: "Spiro, dance with me." Soon the contact of her youthful body, closer and closer to mine, began to relax me. "That's better," she said, smiling. "But I don't blame you for looking like a thunder-cloud with that woman near you. What is she?"

"An archæologist."

"Oh. I thought she must be a gynæcologist," the girl said. It was not a joke.

Eventually a plump lawyer came over to suggest that the girl and I should join him, another girl, and two Zonar's youths for dinner at a tavern in Kifissia. All that evening I had been wondering whether it was the girl or one of the two youths that attracted this lawyer: he had so carefully divided his time between them. At first I refused; but when the girl kept saying: "Oh, come on, Spiro, come on! It'll be fun! It'll be such fun!" I let myself be persuaded.

It was in the car that I discovered the loss of my cigarette-case: the gold case which Helen had given me. I was not sure if I had used it at Sotiri's—there had been cigarettes out on all the tables—but if I had dropped it there, I knew that I was unlikely to get it back. Few, if any, of the guests would steal such a thing; but many of them, finding it, would keep it. We returned and a search was made, during which a drunk girl of about fifteen kept rushing up to me, carrying one after another of Sotiri's cigarette-boxes, each bigger than the one before, and crying out: "Is this it? Tell me, is this it?" But the case was not found.

"I'm afraid I must pass by my home, to see if I've left it there. Otherwise I won't enjoy the evening."

The girl I was taking with me climbed out of the car when we reached the block and appeared to be eager to accompany me upstairs. But I said: "Oh, why bother? It'll only take a moment to have a look round."

"Just as you wish." She pouted, and flounced back into the car, scattering gleaming drops of rain off her high heels.

The case was on my dressing-table; and it was then only that the idea came to me: just as I picked it up and slipped it into my pocket. Dino, of course, had gone, and Irvine need never know that I had returned for this moment to the flat. I went to the sitting-room and picked up one of the three cigarette-boxes, thinking of the drunk girl: but wouldn't that be too obvious? I knew that Irvine kept money in the left-hand drawer of the desk, and that, though careful even to the point of miserliness, he would often, when in a hurry, leave it unlocked. To-night it was open. I scooped out everything that was in it, except for a fifty drachma note—did I leave that out of superstition? for luck perhaps—stuffed the pocket of my overcoat, and hurried downstairs.

"Found it?" the girl asked.

"Yes, I found it."

She cuddled close to me, as I got into the car, and for a moment I thought she was going to put her hand into the pocket where the money rested. All desire I had felt for her while we were dancing had mysteriously evaporated: I found her nearness as repulsive as the nearness of the archæologist on the sofa at Sotiri's.

I managed to spend a lot of the money at the tavern to which we went—the lawyer was rich, and I vied with him in tips to the orchestra for playing this or that 'little number', as he called every tune, as well as every girl whom he discussed, in buying cigars to plug his flabby

mouth, and in ordering bottle after bottle of 'Sampania'
—and the remainder I scattered, note after note, on the
rain-laden wind, while the taxi, from which the rest of the
party had all disembarked, carried me homewards. I
was drunk; but through my drunken confusion, I was
aware—as though of a pain still dormant beneath a drug
—of my terror of ever again being sober.

Irvine had returned, and hearing my key in the door,
came out in his pyjamas, his hair sticking up in innumerable small tufts.

"Did I wake you? I'm sorry."

Irvine's eyelids still flickered against the unaccustomed
light, as he approached me. "Some of my money has
gone."

"What! What money? What do you mean?"

"From the drawer, the drawer in the desk." It was
not cold, but his whole body was shaking, while the
words came out clumsily, tumbling on top of each other
as though his lips and jaw had been frozen.

"How much?"

"Oh, three or four hundred drachmas. It's not the
sum that matters. Is it?"

"Well"—I shrugged my shoulders and sighed—
"didn't I tell you not to leave Dino alone up here? It
wasn't even fair to him. Putting him in temptation."

"Dino didn't take that money."

I was a little frightened by that. "Well, who else did?
Unless it was the woman—and she's been with you for
years. No, I'm afraid everything points to him. He
probably started opening the drawers merely out of
curiosity: and then, seeing the money there—well, it
would have been hard to resist it. And you don't even
know where he lives, do you?"

"Oh, I could find him." The shaking of Irvine's body
was becoming more and more violent. "If I had to. But

Dino—Dino—Dino didn't take that money. You know that, Spiro."

"Well, who else?" I asked. "Who else?"

Irvine's legs were short, and he had never yet possessed a pair of pyjamas, whether made for him or not, the trousers of which did not fall over his toes. Now, as he moved towards me, he almost tripped over. "Why did you take it?" he asked. He spoke like a man who is almost speechless with terror or rage; perhaps, in his case, with both. "Why?" he repeated. "Why?"

"Really I don't know what you're talking about. You've kept money in that drawer ever since I've known you—and you almost always forget to lock it. Have you ever missed anything before? Have you?"

"No. That's the whole——"

"Well, then," I flashed back, suddenly furious. "Why the hell do you suppose that to-day of all days——"

"That's what I want to know. That's what makes it so incredible. And beastly."

I hardly heard him as I rushed on: "You leave some-one in this room whom you hardly know, a complete tramp, a penniless tramp, and then, instead of making the obvious inference—the inference that anyone else would make—you have the cheek to suggest that perhaps I'm the culprit. Apart from anything else, what motive could I have, what possible motive? If I want money, you give it to me. Don't you? You may sometimes grumble, but you give it to me."

"Oh, no, Spiro, no, no." He seemed to be beseeching me, as he wrung his little pink hands together, and stared up into my face. "Do stop, do stop." Suddenly he flopped down on the box-ottoman which was the only piece of furniture in the hall, apart from the telephone and its table and chair, crossing one of his legs, in that characteristic manner, high over the other, and hunching his body over, his chin on the palm of his right hand. He twisted his mouth from side to side, his tongue flickering round it, like a dog chewing grass, and at last got out: "I know it wasn't Dino. You only make things worse by trying to put the blame on him. Don't you see that?"

"How do you know? What makes you certain?"

"I went out without my money; I had to come back. The money was there when Dino and I left together. The money was there, Spiro." Suddenly he jumped up. "If you'd taken it because you needed it, I—I wouldn't have minded so much. But to take it simply out—out of jealousy and hatred of poor Dino, well, that's—that's disgusting. It, it simply revolts me."

"I didn't take it!" I shouted into his face. "And if you think I did, it's finished between us, finished, finished, finished! I'm not going to be suspected, and insulted, and treated like a thief. I won't stand for it, I warn you. See?"

On other occasions, when I had said those words 'It's finished between us', Irvine had at once been quelled. He had known that this was the trump-card: I could always do without him (though it might be hard); he could never do without me. But now he merely stared for a long time at me, as though trying to recall a forgotten face, his pink little hands clasped over his pinker pyjama-tunic and the toes of one bare foot twitching on the parquet. Then he said: "There's no doubt about it, Spiro. Oh, what's the use of pretending? It was a shabby thing to do, a mean thing. Why do you do things like that? What harm had Dino ever done you? What harm could he ever do? Surely you didn't grudge him the odd meal, the odd fifty-drachma note? Did you?"

"Shut up!" I shouted. "Shut up! I won't listen to these mad accusations. If I hear any more of them, I'll walk out. I warn you! I'll walk out! And you won't see me here again in a hurry! "

"Spiro, Spiro, Spiro. I'm not going to say that you didn't take the money, simply because you shout at me and threaten me. Don't be silly." I was amazed by his calm, so unusual when he and I quarrelled. His voice was firm and level, the shaking of his body had stopped. Once again his eyes searched my face, as if for some sign that would reveal my identity. "I wish I understood you," he said.

"Very well," I said. "Very well. If that's how it is."

Perhaps if I had drunk less, my fury might have been less insane: perhaps if I had been less conscious of the shamefulness of my behaviour. As it was, I marched into my bedroom and began to fling things into my suitcase, haphazard, hardly knowing what I was doing: so that, later, I found that I had left out my razor, but packed two pullovers, neither of which I needed at that time of year. I expected Irvine to come in after me, to plead with me, as on other occasions when I had threatened to go: but he remained waiting for me in the hall, once more hunched up on the box-ottoman, his chin supported on the palm of his right hand, while with his left hand he massaged his ankle.

"You'd better take some money," he said, without getting up. "Wait a moment."

"I don't want your money. I don't want it."

"Very well. Just as you please." This, too, was astonishingly unlike such scenes in the past: I had imagined that, as on those occasions, he would thrust the notes into my hand saying something like: "Please take this, please! I can't bear to think of your going out penniless into the streets": even that he would tug feebly at me, in an attempt to keep me with him.

"I warn you!" I shouted over my shoulder. "You'll pay for this!" Then I slammed the door. At the time those last words had no real meaning; but later I was to recall them—as, no doubt, did Irvine—and to savour their irony.

I hurried down what was once Lykabettus Street but is now Mackenzie King Street (few things irritate me more than this Greek habit of changing street-names with every change of foreign policy), my suitcase banging against my legs. I had no idea where to go, but I counted on meeting some friends—Greek, American or English—who would be able to put me up, even at that hour. Near the bottom of Lykabettus Street, I passed Teddy's Bar, with its shop-window of tipsy dolls made out of fruit and vegetables, beginning to mildew and curl up at the edges as they perched or pranced on bottles of whiskey and gin. I had seen this gruesome show often enough before, but now I halted to stare at it. A bluebottle was buzzing against the glass at one corner: inside the ear, humorously exaggerated, of one of the reeling dolls a spider had spun a web as tight as a wad of cotton-wool. A clove-eye lay on the dusty orange crêpe, while its owner winked at me from his insecure seat astride a Pernod bottle.

"Spiraki! What are you doing? Come in, come on in! Come and have a drink."

It was Christo, who had seen me through the window, himself even more drunk than I.

"Are you going away? Why are you carrying that suitcase?"

I put down the case, without giving an answer, and eased the aching muscles in my arms and my back. I disliked this bar, at once squalid and pretentious, and even more disliked its clients, who were for the most part grey and puffy businessmen, standing in little groups and

230

making jeering remarks at the sluts who attempted to pick them up. The owner had a niece—perhaps she was not really his niece at all—a girl of fourteen or fifteen, provocatively demure and composed, who served behind the bar and attracted most of his trade. The businessmen did not jeer at her, preferring to woo her with remarks as fatuous as Christo was now making.

"Do you ever go bathing?"

"No."

"Can't you swim?"

"No." She rarely looked up, and when she did, it was only for a moment, to reveal that she had a slight, and not unattractive squint in her large, black eyes.

"What! You can't swim! Well, you must let me teach you. What about it?" She did not answer. "Eh, what about it? Shall I teach you? Shall I teach you, Anna."

"No, thank you."

"Why not? Are you afraid of drowning? Or are you afraid of—something worse?" He leant his torso, bulging out of its mesh shirt, across the bar and leered at her, his head on one side. I wanted to kick him.

"Where's Maureen?" I asked.

"Oh, Maureen. British Council. Play-reading."

"Why aren't you there?"

"Damned bore. Shakespeare, something like that. Anyway, I keep away from British Intelligence. Unlike certain other people." His mood was slowly becoming ugly, I could see.

Next to us were three men, either Americans or Greeks who had lived in America, to judge from their closely-cropped hair, their shoes and their nylon wind-cheaters in contrasting shades of grey and beige. "Bourbon on the rocks," I heard one say, as he reached across the counter for a toothpick with which he then began to excavate a back molar, an intent, vaguely apprehensive expression appearing on his slack, dull face. "Bourbon on the rocks, all round."

One of his two companions, whose cheeks were scarred with acne, said: "Believe me, brother, she hides a great deal behind that fan."

"You should know!" the third whooped. "You old bastard."

Christo raised his glass. "Here's to you, boys." His accent, when talking to Maureen, was assiduously English; now it was hideously nasal. "Are you talking about that Swedish bitch at the Argentina? Well, let me tell you——" Christo was off: the usual Greek bragging, pitched on a more and more unnatural note of crudeness deemed acceptable to those foreigners who were, in fact, little more foreigners than we ourselves. I had talked like this often enough, God knows; but now I was sickened by it. I was sure that Christo had never spoken to this dancer, let alone laid a hand on her.

"Oh, this is my pal, Spiro. Boys, I want you to meet Spiro," he broke off to say, first patting me on the back and then thrusting me at them.

"Pleased to know you, Spiro."

"Nice to know you, Spiro."

"Hiya, Spiro."

"Spiro's a good boy, one of the best. Spiro's my oldest pal." Talking to Maureen, Christo would have said 'friend'. "Aren't you, Spiro?"

I did not answer: I hated all this.

"Well, Spiro, how come you're out so late? And what about this suitcase? Are you spending your night with someone? Spiro, he's crazy about women. Women, women, women. Yes, he's a good boy, but about women he's real bad. Aren't you, Spiro?" I forced a grin which looked like a grimace when I stared across at the looking-glass behind the bar, and gulped at my brandy. "Well, how come?" Christo pursued.

"Oh, I've finished with him," I said. Suddenly I began to feel, not remote, contemptuous and misanthropic, but affectionate to Christo, tremendously affectionate, as though we had been united by the sharing of some common disaster or grief. "Yes, I told the bastard what I thought of him. My God, I'm sick of his perpetual nosing around—nosing and fussing. It's like being a slave—worse than that, a dog. He whistles, and you go to him. And if you don't go, you don't get your lump of sugar. Well, it's over, and I'm not sorry, I can tell you. If I never see him again, I shall be glad, damned glad. I don't care how hard things may get: that's the last time I'm going to let myself in for anything like that, thank you. . . . Here, let's have another round."

Christo patted me on the back, drunkenly affectionate, and we swayed back and forth together. "That's the boy," he said. "Anyway, you've nothing to worry about. Have you? You don't need an old pansy like that when you've got the Vrissoglou girl. Her father could buy him out with what he earns in an hour. You're all right, Spiraki—you're bloody well all right."

One of the three men beside us said: "What's all this? I don't get it."

"Oh, Spiro's a good boy, a good boy, but he's a poor boy. And there's this American fairy, she's not rich, not really rich, but she can keep him. So he goes to live with her, see. Well, that's no good, no good, is it? That fairy wants—well, that fairy wants what he's too good a boy to give. See? That's how it is. So he quarrels with that fairy. He walks out."

"A nice bed-time story."

"Anyway, who is this guy?"

"Which guy?"

"This guy you're talking about."

"Oh, he's called Irvine. You see him walk down the street, and you know at once. You say 'He's a pansy'. You see him walk down the street, and you say it like that. Isn't that right, Spiro?"

But what had seemed so right a moment before—the swaying arm-in-arm with this so-called 'friend', whom really I hated; the blurred, facile confidences; the drink-sodden betrayal of Irvine, my heavy feet trampling his reputation in the saw-dust of the bar-room floor, before these hideous strangers—all this now seemed all wrong. I felt panic-stricken; I felt as humiliated as if I had just received a public thrashing. Perhaps I knew already what I had done.

"Irvine stroh the Sis," said one of the three. He picked up the top of a beer-bottle, placed it on his thumb-nail, and then flicked it into the window where the vegetable-and-fruit manikins perched and pranced.

"Good shot!" shouted the gangling man with the acne-scars. One of the figures, a woman constructed out of an apple, a potato, and four carrots, had lost her apple-head which bounced on to the floor. "Watch me!" But he missed.

The third sent an arm flying; and the first, in his excitement, went and trod on it, crushing the rotten parsnip as though it were a slug, and leaving a slug-like glistening smear as he dragged the sole of his shoe across the floor.

The proprietor appeared, not sure whether to be annoyed or amused: but these were old customers, Americans too, and he decided to be amused, laughing with them in a high-pitched cackle strange for someone so large and fat and hairy.

One of the apples, into which match-sticks had been

stuck to make immense blonde eye-lashes, split open at its grin, crackling horizontally across into two halves hinged on a piece of green skin. I watched, fascinated, as a maggot wriggled slowly out from the centre.

. . . Damn, that door again! Poor Kiki swings her legs off the sofa, and sits up with a little muffled cry.

"Nothing, darling. Only the bell. Go back to sleep."

"Oh, Spiro, Spiro. I had such an awful dream. Spiro!" She puts out her arms to me, beseeching me to go to her.

"Darling, what was it? Tell me. What was it?"

"I don't know. I can't remember. But it was horrible. Oh, Spiro." She grips me to her, pressing my head to her breast, as I kneel down beside her. "I'd lost you. I think, I'd lost you for ever. Spiro, Spiro."

"Silly girl."

"And I feel so peculiar. I wonder—I wonder if I have a temperature. My head's throbbing so."

That bell again.

"Just one moment, sweetie. Let me see who it is."

"Oh, leave it, Spiro. What does it matter?"

"But I must go."

There's a man with a face as grey as his rain-coat, into the pockets of which his hands are plunged deep. He has on a trilby-hat with too high a crown, and the ends of his collar are held together with a tarnished tie-pin. He says: "Mr. Polly-me-Rides?"

"Yes."

"Mr. Spiro Polly-me-Rides."

"Yes. That's right."

"I wanted to have a word with you, Mr. Polly-me-Rides. I'm an officer of the police. I wanted to check on your residence permit."

"Oh, yes. Come in, won't you? Do you mind if we

go into the bedroom. My wife's in the sitting-room. She's not feeling too good."

"Spiro, what is it? What is it, darling?"

"Nothing. Nothing at all. Nothing. Nothing. Nothing."

VIII

SUNDAY

I T might still be summer.

The two English undergraduates who are sharing the room opposite to mine have just been in to ask me to go to the beach with them. Do they really want my company? Or is it simply that they are curious about me, or sorry for me, or anxious to have with them someone who knows the language and the town? If they were a rich, middle-aged American couple like the two I met on the aeroplane, I'd go with them of course: for the sake of a meal, if for nothing else. But they've already explained to me that they 'want to make their money last as long as possible'; and when English people say that, it usually means that they count on taking advantage of the Greek 'hospitality' about which they've heard so much. Well, they must be disappointed in me, poor boobs.

They wear khaki shorts that reach to their knees, and sweat-stained mesh shirts. The one with the spectacles also has a sniff: he's reading for the Church. "You need cheering up. You can't sit by that window all day. A dip will do you a world of good. Come on! "

"Oh, no, thank you."

He has a way of wandering about the room, examining my possessions, while he talks to me: he even peers down at an envelope on the dressing-table (from my sister's

237

husband, saying that he's terribly sorry but, business being so slack, he can't, etc., etc.), itching to ask me what's inside it.

"Well, you're a funny bird!" He gives up at last. "Isn't he, Bob? To sit in this poky hotel bedroom on a lovely day like this—look at the sunshine, man! That's a change from England. In the *Daily Telly* I bought last night they said they were having fog back home."

Bob takes out a packet of Greek cigarettes from the breast-pocket of his shirt, but he does not offer me one. "Where can I buy some Elastoplast?"

"At any chemist's."

"Oh, at any chemist's. And where's the best chemist?"

I show him a chemist's from the window.

"We need another wick for our oil-stove."

"And don't forget that you want to buy some of those amber beads that the Greeks are always playing with in the cafés."

"Yes, do tell us where we can find those amber beads."

"If you want real amber, they're expensive."

"Oh, it doesn't matter about the real stuff. Just a souvenir, that's all, to take back to me Mum."

Now that they've gone, leaving behind them a smell of sweat and cheap Greek fags, I peer into my wallet to see what I've left of the fifty pounds that old Vrissoglou gave me and the twelve I got for the ikon. There are two ten-drachma notes, a fifty-lira note, and a twopenny-halfpenny stamp, folded in two. I shall be able to buy myself a meal this evening, and a coffee to-morrow morning—and then, what? When I first arrived, eleven days ago, I went to see all my old friends and acquaintances, in the hope that one of them would find me a job. I put on my best suit, paid for a shoe-shine, and took Nicko or Stelio or whoever it was to Zonar's for a drink, or even a meal. The money went quickly: and, in return, I was

given all the old Greek promises and excuses—there had
been a post but it had been filled the day before, perhaps
next week, perhaps a friend of a friend would help, perhaps the British Embassy, perhaps the British Council,
perhaps the Americans. Perhaps, perhaps, perhaps. I
soon tired of that: and all to-day I have done nothing
but sit at this window, looking down into the square. I
never knew before that there were so many old women
tottering around with drooping bunches of flowers to press
on to tourists; so many wizened, grimy children trailing
from table to table, a crooked palm extended; so many
blind people led around by a daughter, sister, or friend
with a shrill, accusing voice; so many stray cats, peasant
vendors, gypsies with babies in their arms, lynx-like girl-
sluts, crutches, bandages. Twenty feet separate me at
this window from all of them on the pavement. To-
morrow I shall be on the pavement too.

Oh, damn, damn, damn! Damn Haralambides for
cheating me over the ikon! Damn Vrissoglou! When
the old boy first heard that Kiki had been taken off to
Battersea General for her operation, he could not have
been kinder, politer, or more affectionate to me. "We'll
have to get her out of here," was almost the first thing
he said as he stepped from the Rolls. It was inconceivable that a daughter of his should be in the public ward
of a hospital: and south of the river, too. To the doctor
he was patronizing; he was, no doubt, a clever enough
'little man' (this was, I discovered later, one of England's
leading surgeons), but he was not being paid, and therefore could not be good. We must have the 'top' man,
nothing less would do.

After Kiki, by now running a high temperature, had
been settled at the London Clinic, and we left the room
where she was about to be prepared for the operation on
the morrow, he put an arm round my shoulder:

"Look, you'd better come and stay with us. You can't manage by yourself in that hole of yours. Let's go and pick up your things for the night. . . . Now, cheer up, mother." He turned jovially to his wife, slipping his free arm through hers. "By to-morrow evening it'll all be over. You heard what the doctor said—nothing to worry about, nothing to worry about."

But Mrs. Vrissoglou went on snuffling into her handkerchief: to a peasant to enter a hospital is to relinquish one's last claims on life; and though she knew that most people who entered hospitals in England at Kiki's age came out alive, yet she was enough of a peasant not to be able wholly to believe it. "Poor little girl! Oh, my poor little girl!" She moaned with a peasant's uncontrollable grief, rocking back and forth under the leopard-skin rug, while her husband placed one of his large hands, the square nails polished to a burnish, over both of hers.

That evening we played Canasta, and Vrissoglou won greedily. The boy was bored, and sucked sweets, sighed and flung down cards without any thought. Sometimes, when he and the old man were playing together, the old man would scold him: at first quietly and coldly, in English, and then in a hot torrent of Greek. Mrs. Vrissoglou's eyes would then dart from one to the other, as my mother's used once to dart from my father to Stelio, but she never intervened.

That night I lay in a bath scented with the geranium essence that I had found on the green glass shelf above the basin, and thought of Kiki. It was horrible: I hoped that they had given her something to make her sleep, and that she was not lying awake, brooding, as I was brooding now, on the dead child within her and the ordeal of the morning. I kept running more and more water into the bath, until it began to trickle down the waste-pipe with a dry, gulping noise. How odd, I thought; it sounded just like Mrs. Vrissoglou when she had cried that morning. I began to feel sleepy, faint and slightly sick; I had stayed in too long.

We visited Kiki the following afternoon. She took my hand in hers, and at first she looked astonishingly well and happy, her cheeks seeming to be flushed, not with fever, but with the sleep from which she had woken. "Well, that's that," she said. "It's done." She was vague and dreamy—I suppose from the anæsthetic and the drugs which they had given her. I squeezed her hand.

"So it wasn't twins," she said. "It wasn't anything, anything at all." I was horrified to see tears oozing from under the eyelids which she had closed at the last words.

"Oh, Kiki, Kiki," I said. "It doesn't matter. There'll be lots more chances."

A nurse then told us that we had stayed long enough.

It was that same night that the blood-clot reached her heart and killed her; and it was as if it also killed the affection which the old boy had suddenly conceived for me. Immediately he became morose, he began to avoid me; but at first that seemed natural enough: in my grief I, also, wished to be left alone—unlike Mrs. Vrissoglou, who would clasp everyone who visited her in her arms, wailing out her sorrow. Then, on the day after the funeral, he came into my bedroom where I was dressing and said:

"May I have a word with you?"

"Of course. Sit down."

He touched his rich, black tie and then glanced down at the vast signet-ring, onyx in gold, which he wore on his little finger, as he perched on the edge of the bed.

"What are you going to do with yourself?"

"I haven't an idea."

"When do you have to leave the country?"

241

I had already told him, on the day when Kiki had been taken to the London Clinic, and he had then waved his cigar in the air as he reassured me: "Oh, never mind about that. We can fix all that for you. Trust the old firm." Was the old firm now going to let me down? Had he forgotten his promise?

"I was given until Saturday—next Saturday, that is. But if you remember, you said—you said . . ."

He scowled at his feet. "Well, of course, when I said that, things—things were rather different. Weren't they?"

"You mean——?"

He got up and went across to the window: waddling, his little paunch stuck out, and yet, paradoxically, with an extraordinary, chilling dignity. "While you were Kiki's husband—we wanted her here, and we knew she wouldn't stay, unless you could stay too. I'm being frank," he turned round to explain.

"Oh, I can see that all right."

"Now—well, again frankly, it doesn't much interest us what becomes of you."

"I see."

"For Kiki's sake——"

"You don't have to explain. But don't you think that she would—would have liked us to—to be friends—now that she's—she's . . ." But I could not go on: to a man like Vrissoglou, that sort of appeal sounds sentimental and false.

He came towards me. "I've never liked you, have I? I never wanted you to marry Kiki. You ruined her life for her. I'm not going to say that you killed her—that would be an exaggeration—but if she had married some-one else, who had been able to support her instead of sending her out to work while she was pregnant, well, I expect she would still be with us now." He put a hand up to his eyes, and I thought that he was about to break down; but he went on fiercely: "You'll have to clear out. I'll buy your air-ticket to Athens, or anywhere else you wish to go—provided it costs no more; and I'll give you fifty pounds. That's all."

"You're being very generous."

"Why should I be generous to you? Why the hell should I be generous to you?"

"The Vrissoglou millions," I sneered.

"Yes, the millions you married." He turned and walked out.

Mrs. Vrissoglou pleaded with him, but she had never in her life succeeded in persuading him to do anything he did not wish to do. She said that she would try to get some money to me, but: "He watches me, he watches me. He knows every piece of jewellery I have. He treats me like a child—I have no money of my own, you know that, don't you?" Yes, I knew it; after all Kiki and I had often enough tried to borrow off her. On the morning I left the house, I found that she had slipped an envelope containing two pound notes and a ten-shilling note into my dressing-gown pocket. 'This is all I can manage, I'm afraid. Good Lack!' The writing was like a child's, scrawled in thick pencil; I enjoyed that Good Lack, there was a nice irony about it.

Well, I've had the Lack since: lack of Kiki, lack of friends, lack of job, lack of money. On the aeroplane I got into conversation with two middle-aged Americans, a businessman and his wife, who were seated opposite to me and were filled with admiration and gratitude when I pointed out Mont Blanc. At Rome they asked me to have lunch with them—the wife had eaten nothing on the plane itself, for fear of 'throwing up'—and when I refused, they insisted on buying me at least a 'negrone'. "Well, I must remember that on our return-trip—a

243

'negrone'," the man said. "Now write it down, pop, just you write it down. His memory is something terrible." He was buyer for a large chain of stores, and was interested in 'folk-weave, pottery, all that kind of peasant stuff' in Greece. By the time I had spotted the Ionian Islands for them, he was saying: "You know, I think you could be useful to me. Maybe, we could do some of this buying together. I'd like to have someone like you who knows the country, knows the language—and yet who's lived in a western city."

He was going to stay with friends in Kifissia—"they're very good friends of some good friends of ours in Knottsville"—and he gave me their address and telephone number on his card, telling me to call there that morning. Well, I thought, it was as easy as that: I'd fallen into a job, almost without trying.

That evening I went first to Zonar's and then to the Argentina: Greeks smell out money, as few Englishmen can, and since I had barely touched the fifty pounds given to me by Vrissoglou, I soon had all sorts of 'old friends' around me: patting me on the back, pinching my cheeks, hugging me in their arms. Of course I got drunk, and eventually ended up with one of the Argentina dancers in a maison-de-passe near to Omonoia Square. There were bugs in the bed, and through my drunken stupor I was aware of them crawling over my body.

The next morning when, with coated tongue and throbbing head, I went to telephone to the American, his card was not in my wallet. At first I thought that the girl must have robbed me: but my money was still all there, together with a lottery ticket, bought in my recklessly prodigal mood the previous evening. I could not even remember the American's name—'Homer' or 'Hamer' or 'Home': but was that the surname or Christian name? I telephoned to the American Embassy, to the American Mission, to American friends of Irvine: but no one could help me. Middle-aged American businessmen pass through Athens daily. Eventually someone suggested that I try the Aliens Police: I had not thought of that, myself. But by the time they had dug into their files, prodded out of their lethargy by my repeated visits, they could only announce that a Mr. Homer Drachman had left the day before. And was that the name?

Meanwhile I had seen in Teddy's one of the three American or, rather, Greek-American, 'investigators': the one whose cheeks were pitted with acne-scars. He was by himself, propped against the bar, with his long legs crossed and a beer-mug in one hand. There was a rim of froth along his upper-lip: I've always hated that —Christo always has one, when he's drinking beer.

"Hello," I said.

"Hiya."

"How are things?"

"Fine, oh, fine."

"Still here?"

"Yeah."

"Where are the others?"

"Which others?"

"Your two pals."

"Which pals?"

I left it at that: either he did not remember them, or he did not wish to remember them.

"What's yours?" I asked.

"Well, I must be off. Got a date. Nine o'clock."

"Oh, come on!"

"Another time."

"Come on. You can be five minutes late. Can't you?"

"O.K. Some more of this hog-wash." He held out his tankard, tipping it forward so that what was left in it slopped on to the floor. He seemed ill at ease, unamiable, perhaps guilty, certainly not pleased to see me.

"Well, what are you doing here? Thought you'd settled in England. That's what one of your buddies told me."

"I had. But now I'm back. Looking for a job." I drained my glass of 'ouzo'. "I suppose you don't know of anything, do you?"

"You shouldn't drink that stuff." He pointed to the 'ouzo'. "Rots the guts. . . . So you want a job, do you? Wa-a-l——" he drew the word out on a long yawn, without bothering to raise a hand to his mouth; then he yawned again. "God, I'm beat. I was at the Shay Noose with some Navy fellers until six this morning. . . . Jobs aren't easy, now."

"They never were. I was wondering if you knew of anything." I had begun to hate him now as much as when he had passed me twenty dollars for giving him the 'tip-off': that was when they had started to investigate poor Irvine. "I don't want your bloody dollars," I had shouted: it was in Teddy's then, too, and everyone had stared at us. "O.K., feller, O.K.," he had tried to calm me, carefully replacing the notes in his wallet. "That's O.K. Most of them expect the pay-off, that's all." 'Most of them . . .' That was the most humiliating thing of all: I was one of 'them'—the taxi-drivers, the bum-boys from Constitution or Omonoia Square, the hotel-porters, the professional spies, pimps, and informers. . . .

"Well, I'll see if I can fix anything. No promises. But maybe . . ." He walked out, the froth from his beer still making a ridge along his upper-lip, whistling softly to himself.

The next time I saw him, it was at Zonar's, and again he was alone. "You're the feller that wanted a job; that's right, isn't it?" He seemed to be more amiable; he even bought me a drink. I forced myself to match his amiability for the sake of the job: but I still loathed him, as I loathed myself whenever I thought of Irvine and what I had done to him. After Irvine's dismissal, there had followed a general 'clean-up': a marine was sent off to Naples for 'psychological treatment'; an army major disappeared, almost overnight; two or three Greek clerks were suddenly without their jobs at the Embassy. . . . And this was the sort of man who was employed as moral dish-washer.

With his second drink he suddenly and inexplicably seemed to get nervy: glancing either round him or out into the street, talking in even more staccato phrases than usual, fidgeting, scratching under the arm-pit or inside his thigh. "Must go along to the boys'-room," he said at last. "Won't be a moment." The lavatory is in the other half of Zonar's, with the café and restaurant. I waited.

But he never came back: and when I went along myself, I failed to find him. Presumably he had left by one of the other doors: but why? I haven't seen him again.

Did some other new, even harsher broom come to sweep him away? I should like to think it did: with his nylon wind-cheater in two shades of contrasting grey, his greasy quiff, his bitten nails, his acne-scarred cheeks, his jokes, his obscenities, his tales of women, his nosing, his buying of information from people too poor to resist his dollars, his stupidity, his callousness. . . . He used to call Irvine and people like him 'scum': it would be pleasant to imagine him drowning in that scum himself.

But this bitterness gets me nowhere: and am I really better? Cleaner perhaps, cleverer, better-mannered: but better? No. When I think what I have done to Helen and to Irvine and to Kiki, what right have I to pass judgment on someone like that? And the odd thing is that now, even as I think of them, I feel a pain, as though, somewhere inside me, a blow had been struck upwards from my stomach into my lungs. I never knew how much I loved them or how much I needed them, until I had lost them. It's like that address which the American gave me: I pushed it carelessly into my wallet and set no value on it, until I found it gone. Then I spent three frantic days trying to trace it.

So here I am, alone. On the rocks. Irvine I may see again. But who knows when? And can it ever be the same as it used to be? Oh, no. Kiki and Helen I shall never see: never, never, never. What a terrible word. Never.

There's nothing left to sell. The cuff-links given to me by Helen, the gold cigarette-case, the Brook Brothers overcoat, and last of all the ikon (I was superstitious about that): all of them are gone. And gone for what, for what? That liar Haralambides peered at the ikon, holding it under a lamp at the back of his shop, grunted and said: "Russian, early nineteenth century. No market for it." "But it's—it's . . . Everyone has agreed that it's . . ." "That's my opinion." He handed the ikon back. So I took the thousand drachmas.

. . . Well, it's no use moping here: I have a twenty-drachma note and a ten-drachma note and a fifty-lira note. And a twopenny-halfpenny stamp—mustn't forget that. The people are thickening in the street, which is already going dark. Sparks scatter downwards from the arms of the tram-cars; the neon signs are lit. From here, looking through that gigantic KOLYNOS, I can see the trees of the Zappeion. I suppose that that strange life—predatory, furtive, feverish—which quickens in all parks at twilight, has already started there.

I shall go down: once more to begin where I began. What else?